Schooled in Deception

A Michael Bishop Mystery

by

Anthony J. Pucci

This book is a work of fiction. Names, characters, places, and incidents are a product of the author's imagination or are used fictitiously. Any resemblance to actual events, locales, or persons, living or dead, is coincidental.

Epigraph

"The fault, dear Brutus, is not in our stars,

But in ourselves."

William Shakespeare, Julius Caesar, I, ii.

Chapter One

As soon as Michael Bishop drove into the faculty parking lot, he knew that Ed Cooper, the new night custodian at Holy Trinity High School, was about to set the school record for the shortest term of employment.

He pulled his Toyota Corolla along the edge of the driveway where five or six cars had already stopped. People were out of their cars and wandering in the parking lot. They were pointing at places on the pavement and laughing. A few had their phones out snapping photos. Bishop hopped out of his car to see for himself.

One of the boys shouted "Holy Shit!" He quickly got red in the face and managed to say "Sorry" when he realized that Mr. Bishop was standing right behind him. If that young man hadn't said it, Bishop might have said it himself. What had been a parking lot with faded stripes to indicate spaces was now full of bright yellow markings. Some lines were slanted; some were short; others were long. Some were jagged like a lightning bolt; others were wavy like a roller coaster. There was even something resembling a circle, no doubt to accommodate an alien spaceship. Near the middle of the lot was an enormous yellow splat like a Rorschach inkblot test. That must be the spot where Ed had kicked or dropped the paint can.

As other cars arrived, Bishop directed them to the student parking lot. To the group that was milling about he said, "Okay, folks, that's enough excitement for now. Let's get moving, please."

***

With the prospect of final exams just weeks away, the parking lot shenanigans provided a moment of relief. In fact, most of the school year had been a difficult one. Coach Zappala had been murdered, and Bishop reluctantly had become involved in the investigation. Ed Cooper's driveway fiasco seemed harmless in comparison. However, not everyone saw the humor in the situation.

As soon as Bishop entered the building, he began looking for someone to whom he could report the incident. None of the administrators or secretarial staff had arrived yet. He did find Jack Slater, the head custodian, with the morning paper spread out before him having coffee and a doughnut in the staff lounge.

"Hey there, Mr. Bishop, how're you doin' this fine morning?"

Jack, a short and slender man who had spent many years with the public works department, quickly found himself bored in retirement. He took the job at Holy Trinity more for the social interaction than the paycheck. He was wearing baggy jeans, an old checkered shirt, and a pair of unlaced work boots.

"I'm fine, thanks. Have you seen the faculty parking lot this morning?"

"No, I came in the back way as I normally do, but I imagine it's still there."

"It's there, all right, but it has a new look."

"Well, that new guy, Ed, must have gotten around to repainting the stripes like I asked him to do every day last week."

"I remember you telling a few of us at lunch that you were after him to do that."

"I tell ya, I don't know what the nuns were thinking when they hired that guy. Half the time he can't seem to remember to lock up before he leaves." He shook his head in disgust as if shaking his head could rid himself of the problem. Then he added, "He doesn't know how to do much of anything except disappear for hours at a time. How's the parking lot look?"

"Jack, you wouldn't believe me if I told you." He had to concentrate in order not to laugh. He was sure that Jack would find it anything but amusing. "I think that you need to take a look for yourself."

He polished off the rest of his doughnut, took another gulp of coffee, and went out to inspect Ed's work.

By the time Bishop made himself a cup of hot tea and went to check his mailbox, more people had begun to arrive for the day. Jack had seen Ed's handiwork and had reentered the building.

"What the hell was he thinking?" he shouted to no one in particular. "That guy's gotta go! It's gonna take me hours to undo that mess!" No one within earshot dare laugh or make any clever remarks. When Jack was upset, it was best to steer clear. He stormed right into the office of Sister Ann Cowie, the principal.

"Sister, you need to see this right away," he demanded, totally oblivious to the fact that Sister was talking to a student.

Sister Ann tried to explain that she would be with him in a few minutes, but Jack was too upset to be polite. "You need to come out here … now!"

Clearly annoyed but trying not to show it, Sister told the student that she would catch up with her later, and followed Jack into the main hall.

"Jack, what on earth is wrong with you?"

"Wait until you see Ed's handiwork. I think that you'll be upset too."

As if drawn by a magnet, Sister Patricia Meehan, one of two assistant principals at the school, stood beside her close friend, Sister Ann. She was about the same age as the principal but must have weighed at least a hundred pounds more. Her girth made even walking a chore, and she was already breathing heavily.

Sister Pat must have gotten out of the wrong side of the bed every morning as she was perpetually in a bad mood. She had earned the nickname, Sister Meany, among the students.

"I knew that that man was trouble from the moment I laid eyes on him." She turned to Sister Ann, "I told you not to hire that man." Then she turned to Jack, "It didn't take that moron long to screw up. What exactly did he do?"

"He striped the parking lot." Having regained his composure, he made this statement matter-of-factly.

"Well, isn't that what you wanted him to do once all the cars were out of there?" Sister Pat snapped, annoyed with Jack's response.

"It's the way he did it that's the problem. Come on. Let me show you."

Behind her rimless glasses, Sister Ann's eyes widened and her pale skin became even paler when she saw the yellow chaos on the pavement.

"Oh, my word!" said Sister Ann.

"Holy crap!" said Sister Pat. Her dark eyebrows, usually knit in a scowl, were lifted in disbelief. "He must have been drunk as a skunk, and he's probably still in the building." As the three of them walked back into the building, Pat said to Ann, "You've got to fire him this instant!"

"Jack, find that man and bring him to my office," ordered the principal.

"Yes, Sister. Will do."

Everyone in the immediate vicinity, including Bishop, pretended that they had not heard everything that had just transpired. Bishop headed upstairs to open his homeroom and prepare himself for the day ahead.

Apparently, Jack's initial attempts to locate the culprit were unsuccessful as the last morning announcement during homeroom included this terse request: "Mr. Ed Cooper, please report to the main office immediately. Mr. Cooper to the main office."

One of the boys in the back of the room gave voice to what many must have been wondering. "Mr. Bishop, do you think Mr. Cooper is going to get fired?" Several other students started laughing as they recalled the condition of the parking lot.

Although he was 99.99% certain that that would be the result, he simply replied, "That's not a question that I am in a position to answer, nor would I want to be." As the students gathered up their belongings and headed off to their first period class, Bishop thought of Shakespeare's Othello who dismissed Cassio for his drunken behavior, not knowing that his good friend, "honest" Iago, had gotten Cassio drunk assuming correctly that Othello would dismiss him. Bishop hoped that Sister Ann would at least give Cooper a chance to explain his behavior.

***

Ed Cooper did not report to the main office as requested. Terry Mortenson, one of the office secretaries, had perfected the art of multi-tasking. She could answer the phone, hand out student passes, check her Facebook page, and still be able to give a detailed account of any conversation that occurred within earshot. According to Terry, who later shared her observations in photographic detail with the crowd at lunch including Bishop, Sister Pat was beside herself when Ed did not present himself to give Sister Ann the satisfaction of firing him on the spot. Sister Pat beside herself would have made for a very crowded hallway, indeed, but Bishop kept that thought to himself.

Sister Ann directed Jack to check every room in the building, including the restrooms, convinced that Ed was surely somewhere sleeping it off. Half an hour later, Jack returned to report that Ed was nowhere to be found. Sister Pat burst out with an idea. "What about his car? Maybe he's asleep in his car. Did you bother to check there?"

Jack took some pleasure in shooting down her suggestion. "Well, Sister, I would have checked Ed's car, but the fact is that Ed didn't have a car. Don't you remember that he told us he took the bus to work, and we had to adjust his hours to fit the bus schedule?"

Sister Pat insisted that she had remembered that, and then asked Jack what he was doing just standing there. "You must have missed him. Go find him, and don't come back until you do!"

When Jack hadn't returned an hour later, Sister Ann was forced to interrupt class with another announcement: "Mr. Jack Slater, please report to the main office immediately. Mr. Slater to the main office." Now two janitors were missing. Sister Pat had goofed again, and Sister Ann was there to pick up the pieces.

Feeling that this situation might spiral out of control, Sister Ann asked the other assistant principal, Ron Jennings, to find Jack. Ron, in his mid-thirties, had a good rapport with just about everyone on campus. People trusted him. They knew that he listened and that he treated everyone with respect. He often found himself trying to undo damage caused by the other two administrators.

Ron later told Bishop that it hadn't taken him long to locate Jack. He was in a small room in the basement that doubled as his "office." When Ron walked in, Jack was whistling as he worked on a vacuum cleaner that one of the teachers had managed to jam. Ron knew that Jack only whistled when he was mad.

9

"Hey, Jack. Mind if I come in?"

"Not at all. What brings you down this way? Looking for Ed?"

"Well, no. I'm pretty sure that Ed must have left the building. I was actually looking for you."

"Me?" asked Jack in a tone of mock sarcasm. "Why would anyone be looking for me? I was told not to return unless I had Ed with me."

After reminding Jack that Sister Pat sometimes spoke without thinking, Ron offered to help Jack undo the damage to the parking lot after school. Although the janitor quickly declined the offer, he was, nonetheless, appreciative and agreed to scour the building and grounds in a third attempt to locate Ed.

With a massive key ring in hand, Jack opened doors to places that Ron had never seen. The places they checked included a dark room that had been abandoned years ago when students lost interest in black and white photography, and a small utility closet deep in the boiler room. They had even gone into an abandoned bomb shelter that had been a common feature of schools built in the 1950s. Once they had exhausted all possibilities, Ron informed Sisters Ann and Pat that this latest search had brought them no closer to finding Ed.

Sister Ann was prepared to wait until Ed came to work later that day to confront him with his inexcusable behavior; however, Sister Pat insisted that the showdown occur before the paint on that parking lot had a chance to dry. She added that there was a good chance that Ed wouldn't show up for work anyway. Ron had to admit that she was probably right for a change. Terry had been calling Ed's cell phone every half hour with no response. When Ron heard that, he decided to take a quick run out to Ed's home just to be sure that Ed had arrived there safely. Since Bishop was free the period after lunch, Ron asked him if he would mind tagging along.

***

Ron picked up Ed Cooper's address from Terry in the main office. As they left the building, they walked past the defaced parking lot. Several cones now blocked the entrance. When Ron started the engine of his Nissan Sentra, the radio blasted a country and western tune about love gone bad. It was a topic to which Jennings could relate. He had been in a couple of failed relationships including one earlier this year. After a few moments, Ron grabbed the dial and lowered the volume. Bishop, who preferred classical music, was relieved when Ron decided to turn the radio off. Bishop turned to Ron as they headed out. "I'm afraid that Ed isn't going to get a second chance."

"Probably not. Once Sister Pat puts a bull's eye on your back, you're as good as gone," observed Ron as he pulled out the piece of paper with Ed's address on it.

"It's too bad. Ed looked like he really needed that job." He knew that that wouldn't make any difference to Sister Pat who saw everything in black and white.

"Mike, have you ever heard of Canary Road?"

"*Cannery Row*? Sure, it's a novel by John Steinbeck. Good, but not one of my favorites."

Ron was concerned that his good friend, Michael Bishop, was starting to lose his hearing. Bishop was about seventy years old, and it was inevitable that he would start to slow down. The murder of their colleague, Al Zappala, earlier in the school year, had been difficult on everyone, but especially on Bishop who not only had found the body, but had also

11

determined the motive and the identity of the killer. Ron hoped that the veteran English teacher would stay at Holy Trinity for years to come.

Bishop smiled broadly as he said, "I believe that Canary Road is out past Hennigan's ice cream stand on the other side of town." Ron smiled as well. It wasn't the first time that he had been victimized by Michael's sense of humor.

Ten minutes later, Ron turned onto Canary Road which was nothing more than a narrow dirt road with houses separated by long stretches of emptiness. The car left a trail of dust as they looked for number 88. Most of the folks living out this way apparently didn't bother with posting their street number on their house or their mailbox.

"This is it!" announced Bishop as he noticed an 88 painted on a large stone at the edge of the driveway. Ron drove down the narrow path that resembled the surface of the moon with its dips and bumps until they reached a trailer. The Harley parked near the front door was the only evidence that suggested that anyone lived there. The trailer itself sat unevenly on cinderblocks. An old television antenna lay askew on the flat roof. A few pieces of the siding had started to peel away. Plywood had been nailed over one of the windows. There was a gaping hole where the screen for the front door should have been. A crate turned upside down served as a step to the door.

"If that bike is here, Ed must be here," Ron said hopefully.

"I didn't know that he rode a bike."

"Neither did I. I thought he took a bus to work."

Ron rapped hard on the door. Nothing. They looked at each not quite knowing what to do next. If Ed wasn't here, where was he?

Just as they were about to get back in the car, they heard the door make a grinding noise as it was opened.

"You lookin' for somebody?"

Jennings and Bishop looked to the source of that voice. She was young, probably in her twenties, and she was wearing a New York Yankee T-shirt and a pair of short shorts. She stood there barefoot, brushing her long dark hair from her face with one hand, while holding the door with the other. Her body language suggested that she had no intention of inviting them into her home.

Bishop spoke first. "We're very sorry to bother you. We're both from Holy Trinity High School. My name is Michael Bishop, and this is Ron Jennings, the assistant principal," as he gestured in Ron's direction. "We're looking for Ed Cooper."

"Yeah, well, join the club," she said sarcastically.

"Excuse me?"

"I'd like to know where he is, myself. He was supposed to work 1 to 9 yesterday, but he never came home last night."

Ron asked, "Have you received any calls or texts from him since he left for work yesterday?"

"Nope."

"Do you know any other place where he might go?

"Nope." Another one-word answer. Bishop thought it odd that this woman seemed more angry than concerned about Ed's disappearance. He also thought that she knew more than what she was telling them.

"Has he ever done this before?" asked Bishop, trying to coax some information out of her.

"Yeah. A couple times. He'll show up, eventually." As she said that, she began to close the door.

"Wait!" pleaded Ron. "Would you please have him call the school as soon as he shows up?"

"Yeah, sure," she replied as she began to close the door again.

Bishop stopped her by asking, "Ma'am, would you mind giving us your name and number so that we can call you if we happen to see Ed first?"

She hesitated for a moment, then rattled off her first name and her number.

Before either one could say, "Thanks, Amy," she shut the door with more force than necessary. When Bishop got in the car, he found a piece of paper in his pocket and jotted something down. He had learned that making mental notes didn't always work. He had to make some concessions as he got older.

As they made their way back to school, Ron pulled up to the drive thru window of a fast food joint. "Mike, want anything?"

"No thanks, Ron. I just had lunch not too long ago." That was true for Ron as well, but it didn't stop him from picking up a double cheeseburger and a soda. With his order in hand, he got back on the road, eating as he drove. Bishop wasn't sure if one could get a ticket for eating while driving, but he need not have worried. The burger and the soda disappeared in short order. As a bachelor, Ron ate out more often than not. Amazingly, he never seemed to gain weight.

Jennings and Bishop shared their impressions of the conversation that had just transpired. Neither man was too impressed with Amy. They both realized that there was a lot that they didn't know about Ed Cooper. How thoroughly had the school vetted him before hiring him? Ron knew that Sister Pat would be less than pleased when they reported that they had been unable to locate their wayward custodian. How could she have the pleasure of verbally ripping him to pieces if they couldn't locate him?

There was a slim chance that he had turned up at school, but if he had, someone would probably have alerted them to that fact.

Bishop mulled over some questions. Did that trailer belong to Amy or to Ed or to both? Why didn't she seem very upset by his disappearance? Did she know where he was? Did she stand by the door because Ed was actually inside? Was it possible that someone else was inside? Did that motorcycle belong to Ed? If so, why did he take a bus to work? If it didn't belong to him, did it belong to Amy or to someone else? Unfortunately, their drive across town had raised more questions than it answered. As Ron dropped Bishop off at the school's main entrance, Bishop had just enough time to pick up the key to the auditorium from Terry and meet his incoming class. Thoughts of Ed Cooper's whereabouts and his odd meeting with Amy would have to wait.

Chapter Two

As Bishop headed off to class, Jennings briefed the other two administrators on his drive out to Ed's trailer and his brief encounter with Amy. Neither sister was pleased with the lack of progress in locating their recently hired and soon-to-be fired maintenance man.

"Looks like you just wasted your time," said Sister Pat in her typically condescending manner. "Maybe it's time to call the cops." Sister Ann gave her a puzzled look. "Cops! What for? Cooper may have botched the striping job, but that's not much of a criminal offense. Think of the bad publicity we would get." She rolled her ideas heavenward.

It was obvious that Sister Pat had not given that consequence a thought. "Bad publicity! No way! That's the last thing we need!" She looked at Ron as if he was the one who had suggested calling the authorities. She flicked her wrist at him as if she were swatting a fly. As far as she was concerned, there was no reason for Ron to remain in the principal's office. He made no move to leave. Instead, he directed a few questions to Sister Ann.

"How much did you know about Ed when you hired him? Did you know that he had a problem with alcohol? Did you check any of his references?"

Sister Ann's eyes narrowed as she folded her hands tightly. She clearly did not appreciate having her judgment questioned by a subordinate. Rather than admitting that she had failed to do due diligence before hiring Ed, she began a vigorous defense of her actions.

"You know very well that when Duane Davenport quit without giving notice, I was in a tight spot. Jack made it clear that he wanted me to hire a replacement right away. When Debbie in the cafeteria told me that she knew a guy who was looking for a job, I knew my prayers had been answered. I had him come in the next day. He seemed okay, so I hired him on the spot." What Sister left out of her explanation was the fact that Ed was willing to work for minimum wage and no benefits.

Ron realized that there was no point in dwelling on the past. The more immediate issue was locating Ed. "Why don't we take a look at his job application? We might find some helpful information there."

Sister Pat glared at Ron. "Weren't you listening? Sister said she hired him on the spot. I entered his basic information in the computer, gave him an application, and told him to return it as soon as possible. It's not my fault that he never did."

Ron didn't respond to Sister Pat's feeble attempt to deflect criticism from herself and her cohort, Sister Ann. As he got up to leave, Sister Ann said, "By the way, Ron, there's something else I want you to investigate."

"Sure, what is it?" He had a feeling that this was payback for questioning her judgment.

"When Jack barged into my office this morning, I was in the middle of a meeting with a young lady, Alyssa Franklin. She came back while you were out. It seems that someone has taken $80 from her gym locker. I want you to find out who did it and get her money back."

Rather than promising more than he might be able to deliver, he simply said, "I'll look into it."

Feeling the need to add her perspective, Sister Pat shook her head in disbelief. "Stealing in a Catholic school? What's wrong with people these days?"

Ron waited until he got back to his own office to shake his head in disbelief as well. "What's wrong with those two?"

***

When Bishop arrived at the auditorium entrance, his Advanced Placement English class of sixteen students was waiting for him. With the grueling AP Literature and Composition test completed in early May, Bishop gave his students a chance to work on a group project. It was a chance to demonstrate their knowledge of the course material and to present their work in a fun yet meaningful way.

Bishop provided guidelines, but it was the responsibility of the group to design and implement the project under his supervision. In the years since he had started this tradition, most of his classes had done an outstanding job. Very infrequently, a group disappointed him. One year, a group of students could not agree on a project. They decided to split into two groups, each preparing a different project, neither one very successful. However, they learned some important lessons about working in groups, meeting deadlines, and the necessity of compromise.

This year's group had decided to present scenes from *Hamlet* but with a twist. They included a few characters from other works that they had read during the year. For example, Hamlet's famous soliloquy was to be delivered by Holden Caulfield from Salinger's *The Catcher in the Rye*. "To be a phony or not to be a phony/ That is the question." It was a wacky concept, but they loved it. After the group had written a script, they worked on casting, costumes, and props. With just a couple of weeks left, they had asked permission to do some rehearsals on the stage. They needed some practice with the curtains, lights, and sound system. That was the reason that Bishop met them at the auditorium.

Bishop sat in one of the front row seats, observing the feverish activity of the group, offering suggestions, and answering questions as needed. Since the class was only fifty minutes in length, the students understood that there was little time to be wasted. Everyone seemed to be on task until Bishop noticed Bill Delehanty grab the handle of a trap door near the back of the stage. The veteran teacher jumped to his feet as he shouted, "Bill, don't fool around with that door!" The last thing he needed was to have someone get hurt. His warning was too late. Bill had fully extended the door, and Andrea Wolinski, who had walked over to see what Bill was doing, started to scream hysterically. Everyone rushed to her side. As the girls sought to comfort Andrea, Bishop moved Bill away from the door. He looked down into the opening where a wooden ladder led to a storage room below. At the bottom of the ladder lay the lifeless body of Ed Cooper.

***

Although shaken by the discovery, Bishop took control in a firm voice. He directed all of the students to leave the stage and take seats in the auditorium. Some of the girls began to weep as Andrea told them what she had seen. Bishop closed the trap door as Bill remained frozen to the spot where he was standing when Andrea started screaming. Although the young man still didn't understand why, Bishop did.

"The handle was sticking up," Bill said, trying to explain what caused him to pull the door open.

"Everything's going to be all right, Bill. You didn't do anything wrong." He put his arm around the young man's shoulder and led him down the steps of the stage to join the others. Andrea's screams had turned to soft sobs as the girls tried to comfort each other. The guys huddled around Bill, speaking in muted tones. Surprisingly, no one had taken out a cell phone to call or text the news. As he watched over them, he took his own cell phone from his jacket pocket and punched in the school's number.

"Good afternoon. Holy Trinity High School. This is Terry. How may I help you?"

"Terry. This is Michael. I'm in the auditorium with my AP class. We found Ed Cooper. He's dead."

"What? Oh, my God! I don't believe this!"

"Listen, Terry! This is what I need you to do." He then gave her some specific instructions.

Within minutes, the school's crisis team was mobilized. Sister Ann, Ron Jennings, Sarah Humphries and Eric Redstone, the school's guidance counselors, and Margaret Foster, the school's nurse, arrived on the scene. Bishop's primary concern was the students. Sister Ann suggested that all of the students be taken up to the guidance office where they would have a chance to recover and receive any assistance that they might need. The students were still dazed as they left accompanied by the guidance counselors and the nurse.

Sister Ann sat quietly in one of the auditorium seats with her head in her hands. Perhaps she was praying for Ed. Bishop paced from one end of the stage to the other. He was lost in a flashback to another Monday earlier in the school year when he had found the dead body of a colleague.

Ron joined him as he paced. "Are you sure he's dead?"

Bishop looked at Ron but didn't reply. Of all the questions that had been running through his mind, that certainly wasn't one of them.

"I mean … well, you know, if he was intoxicated, and all indications are that he was, then he might have just passed out."

"No, Ron. He's dead. His arms and legs are at an odd angle, his eyes are still open, and there is blood on the floor near his head." As an afterthought, he asked Sister Ann, "When was Ed supposed to leave last night?"

She looked up at the two men. "It's funny, isn't it?" she said more to herself than to them. "Earlier this morning, I wanted to find that man so that I could fire him for his incompetence." She shook her head in disbelief at the sudden turn of events. "Now, he's dead, and everything else seems so pointless." It was an odd remark coming from a nun.

Bishop waited a moment to see if she was going to continue. She stared at the back of the stage where the trap door was located. Just as Bishop was about to repeat his question, she said, "He was supposed to leave at 9 p.m. We agreed on that time so that he could catch the last bus."

Just then, Jack Slater led several people into the auditorium. Sister Pat was having difficulty keeping up with Jack as they walked down the center aisle toward the stage, but that didn't mean that she couldn't say something critical. "Do you mean to tell me that you never even looked down there?"

"That's right," Jack shot back. "I walked through here this morning looking for him, but I never thought about that room beneath the stage."

Sister Pat gave him a condescending look of disapproval despite the fact that it was obvious that she had not thought of having someone check that area herself. She sat next to Sister Ann, although she met some resistance in squeezing her wide frame into the confines of the two armrests. As two EMTs and a police officer made their way onto the stage, the assistant principal gestured in their direction. "I suppose we'll have to stay here until they remove the body. This really will put a crimp in my day." Bishop looked at Jennings and rolled his eyes. Typical Sister Pat. No expression of sympathy. No concern for Ed or his family. No concern for the students who had discovered the body. She was one of two assistant principals, although no one had been able to determine exactly what her duties were. Having worked with the woman for many years, he shouldn't have been surprised by her lack of tact.

***

Bishop shook hands with the officer and introduced him to the administrators as well. Officer Hollins had short curly black hair, blue eyes, and a square jaw. Bishop guessed that he was in his mid-thirties. "Let's see what we've got here," he said to Jack. As the door was lifted open, the officer got down on his hands and knees to get a better look. He grabbed a flashlight from his belt and cast a beam of light down on the body. The EMTs stood at a distance awaiting direction.

"This ladder is unusable. Is there another way down there, or do you have another ladder that I can use?"

Jack seemed shaken by his glimpse of the body of his co-worker. "You can get in that room from a door at the back of the building. I can show you if you want."

"Please, lead the way." Looking at the others, he advised, "Stay clear of that opening."

When Bishop had first looked down into the storage area, he had noticed that the first rung of the old wooden ladder was intact, but the second and third rungs had given way. Something about that bothered him, but he couldn't quite put his finger on it.

In a moment, the voices of Jack and Hollins could be heard.

"And you say that that door is usually locked?" asked the officer.

"That's right, sir. It should be locked at all times, but as you saw for yourself, it was unlocked just now."

"Whose job is it to lock that door?"

Jack swallowed hard, and his Adam's apple bobbed up and down. "Mine, I guess, but he was supposed to have made sure that it was locked before he left last night."

"By 'he' I assume you mean the deceased?"

"Yes, that's right."

Hollins knelt next to the body. He touched his neck and his right hand, and then closed his eyelids. He looked around the room in all directions, gripped the ladder that wobbled when he shook it, and then looked up to the top where the door opened onto the stage.

Bishop and Jennings were still standing there when Hollins and Jack returned. Hollins walked over to Sister Ann who stood up as he approached. Sister Pat, with some difficulty, also stood. "Well, Sister, it definitely looks like an accident to me. There's a distinct smell of alcohol. If he were inebriated enough, negotiating that ladder would have been a challenge. A couple of rungs of that ladder just gave out, and his head must have hit that floor pretty hard. I think that he died instantly. I don't think that he suffered."

"Imagine getting drunk when he was supposed to be working! I guess he got what he was asking for!" No one responded to Sister Pat's insensitive comment. Bishop had long ago ceased to be surprised by her attitude, but he was, nevertheless, disappointed in the way she represented the Sisters of the Holy Rosary.

"Someone is on the way to take photos and so on, but this is fairly routine. The EMTs should be able to remove the body shortly. I do need to ask a few more questions for my report."

"Of course," replied the principal.

"Who found the body?"

"I can help with that," offered Bishop.

"My class was in the auditorium practicing for a presentation when one of the boys opened the trap door," explained the veteran teacher.

Hollins had a small notebook and pen in hand. "Name?"

"Bill Delehanty, but I can assure you that he opened that door out of idle curiosity. The entire class was visibly shaken by the discovery."

"What about next of kin?"

Sister Ann looked embarrassed as she admitted that she didn't know much about Ed at all. She explained that she had hired him on the spot two weeks earlier as she was in a rush to fill that position. Unfortunately, he hadn't returned the application that they had asked him to complete.

Ron told Hollins that he and the other school officials became concerned when they discovered Ed's erratic striping of the faculty parking lot.

"I noticed that on my way in," said Hollins. "I thought that maybe some of the students had pulled a prank." As soon as he said that, Bishop started to wonder whether or not that might indeed be the case. Had they all jumped to the conclusion they preferred in assuming that Ed was responsible? Then the image of Ed's lifeless body at the bottom of the ladder came back to him. There were splotches of yellow paint on Ed's pants and sweatshirt. No students were involved.

Ron went on to inform the officer that when they were unable to locate Ed, he and Bishop had gone out to his place on Canary Road hoping to find him there. He gave him the name and number of the woman who had answered the door. He wasn't sure if Amy was his wife or his girlfriend, but she was the one to contact first.

When some additional police personnel arrived, all of the Holy Trinity people except Jack left the auditorium to finish out the day, hoping

24

to shield the students as much as possible from the disturbing events of that morning, thinking that the worst was behind them. That turned out to be incorrect.

Chapter Three

Bishop was teaching his last class of the day. This English 9 group had been discussing George Orwell's *Animal Farm*. The students were quick to understand that the story could be read on different levels. On the surface, it was simply a beast fable in which animals acted like human beings. However, on an allegorical level, the story was so much more than that. It was the story of the Russian Revolution and in its aftermath, the rise of Joseph Stalin to power. It was a warning to the people of other nations to safeguard their freedoms or risk losing them.

Chad Evans, one of the more inquisitive young men in the class, raised his hand. "How come the other animals let Squealer get away with so much?"

"That's a good question, Chad." Squealer, one of the pigs who had taken the farm away from its owner, Mr. Jones, was a master of deception. "Give me an example of what you mean," Bishop said.

Chad didn't hesitate in his response. "Well, there are lots of examples. He changed all of the original commandments."

"That's right," Bishop said as he turned toward a girl who was looking out the window. "Ashley, which commandment should we use to illustrate Chad's point?"

"The one about alcohol." Ashley blushed as a few of the students reacted to her answer. Bishop wondered if a recent incident had triggered that reaction. They were 9th graders, after all, and some had undoubtedly experimented with alcohol if not worse. Bishop urged her to continue with her answer.

"The animals were not to drink alcohol because that's what Mr. Jones did, and they didn't want to be like him."

"Correct." Bishop then focused on Jerry, one of the giggling boys. "How did Squealer change that commandment?"

Still smiling, he said, "He changed it to say that it was all right to use alcohol as long as they didn't drink to excess."

"And that applied only to animals that were twenty-one or older," added Bishop without any change in his expression.

Jerry looked confused, but most of the others smiled knowingly at his facetious quip. "The key point here," Bishop said as he brought everyone back on task, " is that Squealer had the ability to manipulate words. He rewrote the commandments to the benefit of the pigs." As class was about to end, he left them with this thought: "This novel illustrates an important lesson: we can't just assume that someone is telling the truth."

***

When Bishop checked his email that afternoon, he found this message from Sister Ann:

> *We regret to inform you that our custodian, Ed Cooper,*
> *died in a tragic accident earlier today. Please pray for Ed*
> *and for his family.*

Bishop shook his head in disbelief. A co-worker dies in the school's auditorium, and all that merits is a two-sentence email from the principal. Bishop had worked with her for the last twenty years or so, but her lack of sensitivity continued to astonish him. Undoubtedly, the negative influence of Sister Pat was a factor. Was it possible that they were more annoyed by the need to hire a replacement than they were genuinely saddened by this young man's sudden death?

His own thoughts drifted back to the young woman that he and Ron Jennings had met at the trailer that morning. He wondered how Amy reacted when Officer Hollins gave her the bad news. Had she been Ed's wife or his girlfriend? Did he have other family in the area? He wondered about Debbie Bates, the cafeteria worker who had recommended Ed for the job. How well did she know him? Bishop hoped that she had left the building before that email arrived in her inbox. What a horrible way to learn of the death of a friend. He decided to stop by her place on his way home from school. Offering his assistance and support would be the least that he could do.

He packed up his papers for the night, closed the windows, and locked his classroom door. He went down to see if Ron was free. Not counting his glimpse of the body at the bottom of that ladder, something about what he had seen in the auditorium bothered him. He couldn't quite say what it was. He wanted to look around that area again.

On the way to Ron's office, he stopped by Terry's desk. Once the dismissal bell rang, the halls cleared out fairly quickly. Terry had to wait a half an hour after the bell before leaving the building.

"Rough day, huh?" she said, stating the obvious. Terry was in her mid-forties. A single mother of two, she had had her share of difficult times. When she was going through her divorce, Bishop was always there for her with a sympathetic ear. And when Bishop's wife, Grace, died suddenly of a burst appendix, Terry was there for him.

"That's for sure," he replied. "It brought back a lot of unhappy memories from earlier this year." As he answered, his mind drifted back to that September day when he had found the body of a colleague.

Sensing the need to prevent Bishop from dwelling on that sad chapter from the past, her eyes sparkled as she announced in a hushed voice, "I picked up a few tidbits about Ed this afternoon." Terry was a very efficient secretary. Her job often placed her in the middle of the action, and she just loved every minute of it. She also loved sharing her insider knowledge with those in her inner circle, and Bishop was one of them.

After taking a quick glance to her left and right to make sure that no one else was within listening distance, Terry spoke rapidly and in not much more than a whisper. "Debbie went home in tears after Sister Pat went into the kitchen and berated her for recommending Ed for the custodial job in the first place. Apparently, she referred to Ed as 'a big loser.'"

Bishop wondered whether making people feel bad made Sister Pat feel good. Did it ever occur to her to think before she spoke? He definitely wanted to stop by Debbie's place on his way home to see how she was doing.

The phone rang, and Terry held up one finger signaling that she had more to say and that Bishop just needed to wait a minute. After connecting the caller to the extension requested, she checked that the area was still all clear, and then continued the sharing of tidbits. "Ron went with Officer Hollins to give the bad news to that Amy person, the one you guys met earlier in the day."

"That poor woman. How did she handle it?"

"No hysterics or anything. She handed over a box of Ed's belongings. Apparently, that trailer is hers, and she just let him crash there for a while when he got out of prison."

"Prison?" Bishop said, louder than he should have.

Terry put her index finger to her lips. "Shush, for Pete's sake or you'll get me fired."

Bishop hadn't expected to learn that Ed Cooper had been in prison. That might have been the reason that Cooper had delayed filling out an application. It was unlikely that Sister Ann had known about that when she hired him. Then again, perhaps she had known. As long as he wasn't a sex offender, why shouldn't he be given a chance to start his life over after paying his debt to society? Officer Hollins would be able to check on Ed's prison record, but it probably didn't make any difference at this point.

"Now, don't go spreading this stuff all over the school," she teased because she knew that Bishop wasn't the type to do that. Besides, that would deny her the pleasure of doing that herself.

"Have a good evening," he said as he made his way to Ron's office.

***

Alyssa Franklin was just leaving the assistant principal's office. Clearly upset over something, she was dabbing at her reddened eyes with a tissue. She turned back to Ron and said in a shaky voice, "Thank you for your help."

"You're quite welcome," he replied, although he knew that he hadn't done anything to help her, at least not yet.

Bishop loosened his tie as he walked into Ron's office. He had already removed his lightweight sweater. Dressing for school could be tricky at this time of the year. The mornings were still cool enough that you needed that extra layer, but the afternoons could get quite warm. With all that had happened since he drove in that morning and noticed the striping of the parking lot, he hadn't had time to appreciate that it had turned out to be a picture-perfect, late-May day.

"Have a seat," Ron said as he took a tissue box from his desk and put it back on a low bookcase located behind him and to his left.

"Alyssa seemed upset. Did that have anything to do with Ed's death?" Ed had only been working at the school for a few weeks, but the

30

idea of someone accidentally falling and dying in the auditorium where graduation would soon take place had unsettled many.

"No, she never mentioned that. She had been in to see Sister Ann early this morning because she had had some money stolen, and Sister Ann told me to talk to her."

"That's the third incident in the last few weeks, isn't it?"

Ron looked at a piece of paper on his desk. "Actually, that's the fifth incident of late, all taking place in the gym locker room, and all for a sizable amount of money. There might be others that I don't know about."

One student had mentioned some recent thefts to Bishop. Donna Larson had lost $75. When he had asked her why she kept so much money in her locker, she explained that she was going to purchase a copy of the yearbook, the *Trinitarian*.

"How much did Alyssa lose?"

"Eighty bucks."

"Was she going to buy a yearbook?"

"Nah. Prom tickets." Ron began to vent his frustration. "Kids these days don't think twice about bringing a C note to school. Then, when someone clips it, they expect me to get it back. I'm afraid it's not that easy." He looked up at the ceiling as if the answers might be written there.

"Do you think that the thefts were committed by the same person?"

"Absolutely. I'd bet on it. Whoever is doing this is pretty clever."

"What makes you say that?"

He started counting with his fingers. "For starters, all the thefts have occurred in the girls' locker room. There's no camera in there for obvious reasons. Next, the only thing missing is money. An expensive watch, iPods, and iPads have all been there for the taking, but left untouched. Cash is a lot simpler to deal with. Plus, whoever it is has figured out a way to gain access to the lockers when no one is around. Finally, all the kids that I've talked to claim that the locks were locked and that they hadn't given anyone their combination."

Bishop reflected on the fact that those combination locks weren't the easiest to open even when you knew the combination. The same type of locks were used on lockers in the classroom wing, and he had been asked on many occasions over the years to help students get into their own lockers. Sometimes, he could open the lock on his first try which embarrassed the student to no end. On other occasions, he was as unsuccessful as the student had been.

"That's it!" announced Bishop in a eureka moment.

"What's it?"

"Anyone can open a lock if they have that little key that fits in the back!"

Ron shook his head. "I never thought of that," he admitted, "but only a few people have one of those keys."

"Who are they?"

"Well, Sister Pat has one, and Jack has one. There's also one in the main office that Terry uses if neither of them is available."

"It might be a good idea to see if one of them might have lost that key or loaned it out to someone else."

Ron agreed to look into that the next day. He also agreed to accompany Bishop down to the auditorium. The veteran English teacher couldn't explain exactly what he hoped to accomplish by going down there again other than to say, "I have a feeling that something's not right. Things happened so fast this morning that I didn't have a chance to process everything. I thought that if I went down there again, I'd remember what was bothering me."

Ron used his key to open the auditorium entrance. Once they were inside, he pulled the door closed behind him. He inserted another key in a small panel by the door, and the house lights slowly brightened. "I didn't even know that there was a storage room under the stage," said Ron as they walked down the main aisle.

"I imagine most people don't know that it's there. I remember seeing a few productions here in the old days in which the trap door was used. Mostly Shakespeare. That's how the ghost of King Hamlet made his entrances and exits. It was actually more trouble than it was worth, and they stopped using it years ago. The storage area still came in handy, however, because people had direct access to it from the back of the building."

As they walked up to the closed trap door, Ron remarked, "I'm surprised that people didn't trip on this handle."

Bishop tapped the handle with his right shoe, and the handle fell into place so that it was now flush with the floor. "There. That's the way it's supposed to be. I guess the officers didn't realize that the handle folded flat. Since the ladder is broken, let's go around the other way. I want to take a look around that storage area."

Ron didn't seem too keen on the idea. "Well, if you insist, but I don't know what you expect to find down there."

"Neither do I," replied Bishop with a slight smile. "That's why I want to look." As they left, Bishop spotted a safety cone off stage, pulled the door completely open, and placed the cone at the edge of the opening to prevent another accident.

The auditorium, with its seating capacity of one thousand, had a number of exits, including one on either side near stage front, and one from the balcony which opened to a hallway which eventually led to a service doorway. When they arrived at the entrance to the storage room, Bishop was looking up at the roof of the building.

"What are you looking at?" asked Ron, perplexed by his friend's behavior.

"Cameras."

"Excuse me?"

"Cameras," Bishop repeated.

"There aren't any cameras on this side of the building. Just a large wooded lot back here," added Ron, stating the obvious.

"That's just the point, my friend. Anyone coming out of that lot could approach this entrance without fear of detection."

Ron found that prospect a bit unsettling. "And this door was unlocked when Ed's body was discovered."

"Indeed, it was," replied Bishop as he waited for Ron to unlock the door.

It was quite dark as they walked into a corridor with the only illumination coming from the opened door. Ron noticed a bare light bulb in a socket suspended from the ceiling. He pulled the chain. "There, that's better." Pointing ahead, he added, "There's another light."

As they approached the area where the ladder led up to the trap door, the corridor led to a large open space. The walls were whitewashed cement, and the floor was composed of wide-width boards, not unlike those that had been used on the stage itself. They were dulled by years of neglect. There were boxes stacked against one wall, their contents unknown. Placed against the opposite wall was an old sofa, its cushions covered by some wrinkled sheets. Next to the sofa were a tall, skinny lamp and a small table with a stack of magazines and newspapers. Bishop was surprised to find that some of the magazines were only a few months old, and the newspapers were from within the last week. Had Ed Cooper made himself a man-cave out of this room? Is that why he seemed to disappear for hours at a time?

As Ron wandered around aimlessly, Bishop was lost in thought as he studied the ladder leading to the trap door. "We have to assume that Ed fell when those steps gave way, right?"

"Right," said Ron who was caught off guard by Bishop's sudden breaking of the silence.

"If that is so, would the door above be open or closed?"

Ron felt that he was in a class taught by Bishop and that he was in danger of failing. "Well, we know that the door was closed because it was Bill from your AP class who first opened it."

"That's right. My guess is that Ed stood on the top rung, grabbing the door by the inside handle. When the ladder gave, he let go of the handle, and the door simply slammed shut."

Ron's stomach was growling as it was past time for his afternoon snack. He tried to hurry Bishop along. "Well, that's it then. The combination of his inebriated state and the failure of those old wooden rungs did him in. It's a real shame."

"The wooden rungs!" Bishop shouted. "That's what was bothering me earlier."

"What do mean?"

"When I first looked down at the body, I noticed that there were pieces of the wooden ladder on the floor, but some were on the body itself. If Ed's weight had caused those two rungs to break, the pieces most likely would have fallen to the floor before his body. Those pieces should have been underneath his body, not on top of it."

"What are you saying?" said a confused Ron.

"I don't think that Ed fell because of the condition of the ladder. Those rungs were broken afterwards to make it look like an accident. Whoever did this made the mistake of leaving the handle on the stage side of the door in an upright position."

Ron stood there in disbelief as Bishop said, "I think we need to contact Lieutenant Hodge."

Chapter Four

Bishop made the call from Ron's office. The other administrators, the office staff, and most of the faculty had left for the day. Since Hodge was unavailable, he left a short message asking that he return his call as soon as possible.

Bishop began to feel that it was just as well that he hadn't connected with Hodge. Perhaps he was wrong. Bishop often had to caution his students from reading too much into a work of literature. There had to be textual support for an interpretation. He recalled one student's recent assertion in class that Iago's revenge against Othello was racially motivated. It was an interesting theory given what was happening in our world, but our world was not the world of Shakespeare. Iago himself offered a number of reasons for his own destructive actions. Ultimately, it was more likely that Iago sought to destroy Othello because he represented an innate goodness that Iago knew was lacking in himself.

What support did he have for his belief that Ed Cooper had been murdered? The way a few pieces of the broken rungs of the ladder had fallen to the ground? The fact that the handle of the trap door had been left in an upright position instead of flush with the stage floor? For Ed's death to have been murder, there would have to be a motive. Why would anyone have wanted to kill him? And since he had only worked at Holy Trinity for a few weeks, who would have wanted him dead? By the time that he left Ron's office, he had convinced himself that he, just as that student, had based his opinion on insufficient or flawed evidence.

***

Despite the fact that he very much wanted to get home, he felt an obligation to look in on Debbie Bates, especially after hearing of the way she was treated by Sister Pat. He had no trouble finding her place as he had given

37

her a ride on a few occasions. He pulled into the driveway and parked his Toyota Corolla behind her car, an old black Ford Bronco that had seen better days. The body panels were riddled with rust, and he imagined that the odometer would reveal that that vehicle had more miles on it than a one-way trip to the moon.

The house was quite small and in desperate need of a paint job. The roof had obviously been repaired as there were several patches of newer shingles that stood out among the rest. There was a pot of pansies on the porch landing that brightened an otherwise neglected front yard. As there was no doorbell or knocker, he rapped on the door a few times. A small dog began barking. At least it sounded like a small dog. When Debbie opened the door, an energetic Jack Russell terrier stopped barking and began sniffing at his shoes and dancing around him.

"Hi, Mike. I wasn't expecting you," she said as she opened the door wider and invited him in. "Don't mind Max. He won't bite." Turning to the dog, she said, "Be a good boy or I'll have to put you in the basement."

"He's not bothering me," Bishop said. "So this is Max," as he bent down to pat the inquisitive dog.

"After I picked him up at the shelter, I went to buy him some stuff at the pet store and found out that I'd maxed out my credit card, so that's how he got his name." Max kept launching himself in the air like a Mexican jumping bean. "Would you like a cup of coffee or something?"

"No, thanks. I can only stay for a few minutes."

"What brings you here?" she asked after she had invited him to sit on the sofa in the living room. The sofa, like everything else in that room, was well worn. An old television with rabbit ears sat on a small table opposite the sofa. There were a couple of oversized chairs on either side of the television. Everything seemed to have been a second-hand pickup.

38

Debbie was in her mid-twenties, Bishop guessed. Most of the time when Bishop saw her at school, she was wearing a long white apron. Now, she was wearing a sweatshirt, shorts, and flip-flops. She was of average height and slender build. Her dirty blonde hair was tucked behind her ears, both of which sported several small earrings. There was nothing particularly distinctive about her face except for a mole above her upper lip.

"I just dropped by to tell you how sorry I am about Ed. I knew that you and he were friends." At the mention of Ed's name, Debbie began to tear up. She grabbed a tissue from her pocket, and regained her composure quickly.

"Yeah, we were friends." She took a breath and exhaled deeply. "I'm going to miss him. It was nice of you to think of me."

"Not at all. Is there anything that I can do for you?"

She sat thoughtfully for a moment. Then she said, "Can you get that ogre, Sister Pat, off my back?"

Terry had told Bishop how thoughtless Sister Pat had been to blame Debbie for recommending Ed for the job, but he pretended not to know. "What has she done?" He was going to add "this time" but decided not to fan the flames.

Debbie then recounted Sister Pat's words and actions earlier that morning which closely resembled Terry's version. Bishop tried to console Debbie without defending the assistant principal. "Listen, I've known her for years, and that's just the way she is. She often says things without thinking. I wouldn't let her bother you."

"I work hard over there, and they treat me like dirt. Did you know that they called me in last week to inform me that I wouldn't be getting my measly ten-cent raise for next year?"

"Ten cents?" Bishop repeated in disbelief.

"That's right. A whole ten cents an hour. That's the raise I've had the last two years, and next year, I'll get zilch."

There wasn't any way that Bishop could defend that decision. Was their commitment to the Christian value of a decent living wage merely lip service? It was clear that Debbie was just scraping by on her current wages. "Did they offer any explanation?" he asked.

"They said something about the school having some financial difficulties. Yeah, right. Didn't they just come into a big bundle of money?"

The veteran teacher told her that it was true that the school had been named one of the beneficiaries of a large estate, but apparently, that had evaporated quickly along with most of their cash reserves when the price tag for a new roof went, well, through the roof. The teachers had heard rumors of a salary freeze which had prompted several of them to quietly examine other options. Bishop wanted to turn the conversation back to Ed even though that might be difficult for Debbie.

"How long had you known Ed?"

"Oh, jeez" she said, "I've known him since high school." Thinking back to those days brought a smile to her face. "We dated off and on, and then he up and enlisted."

Bishop didn't say anything. He hoped that his look of interest would encourage her to continue talking. It did.

"Ed was smart as a tack, but he hated school. He skipped so often they were going to kick him out, but he managed to graduate. I told him I wasn't gonna wait for him, and he was okay with that. He was back in less than six months, and we started dating again."

"Why was he back so soon?"

"He got kicked out for insubordination. He never was one to be bossed around." She stopped for a moment, perhaps recalling something that she didn't want to share with Bishop.

"Then what?" he asked, hoping to glean as much information about this man's past as he could. In the back of his mind, he harbored the notion that Ed Cooper had been murdered although it would be irresponsible to share that speculation with Debbie at this point. If it was murder, the more he knew about Ed's life, the more likely he might figure out who had killed him. The amateur sleuth in him that had emerged earlier in the school year at the age of seventy was back.

"He lived here for a while." She stopped to gauge Bishop's reaction to that news. The information registered, but there was no outward sign that it mattered. She continued, "He picked up a few odd jobs here and there but nothing that amounted to much." Suddenly, she started to cry. "That's what so ironic about that accident," she said as she wiped her eyes with a tissue. "Just the other day he told me that he was coming into some big money."

"Really?"

As if anticipating his next question, she added, "He didn't tell me nuthin' more than that. He was coming into some money, and he was happy and now he's dead." Max, sensing that something was wrong, started jumping up at her, trying to give her a kiss. That made her smile through her tears. "Sorry," she said to Bishop. "I didn't mean to lose it."

"Nonsense. It's perfectly understandable. Well, I really must be going." As he stood up to leave, Max began darting around his feet. "Debbie, if there's anything I can do, please don't hesitate to ask."

"Thanks for stopping by, Mike. It means a lot to me. It really does."

He gave her a quick hug, and walked back to his car. This might have been the warmest day of the season so far. The interior of his car felt like a furnace. He lowered all the windows and headed home.

He usually listened to NPR radio on his drive to and from his place on Pleasant Hill Road, but not this time. He was thinking about his conversation with Debbie. He was certainly sorry for her loss. Ed was not just a high school friend or a co-worker. They obviously had some sort of a relationship. What she said about him was interesting. He was a bright guy, but he couldn't keep a steady job. He had been in the military, but that hadn't work out too well. He wasn't very good at taking orders. And then there was that business about the money. He was coming into some big money. Bishop wondered what that was all about. Ed might have made the whole thing up to please Debbie. Otherwise, how would he come into big money working for minimum wage as a janitor at Holy Trinity?

Yes, what she said about him was interesting, but what she didn't say was even more interesting. She hadn't mentioned the fact that Ed had been in prison. She must have known about that, mustn't she? And what about Amy? Ed was using her trailer as his address. Amy certainly gave Ron and him the impression that Ed was living there. Did Debbie know about Amy?

As he pulled into his own driveway after a very tiring day, he had the feeling that there was more to the story of Ed Cooper, much more.

Chapter Five

Even though his home was only about fifteen miles from the school, it always seemed to Bishop that the two places were worlds apart. He thought of Wemmick, a character in *Great Expectations* by Charles Dickens, explaining to Pip the separation between his home and his place of work: "When I go into the office, I leave the Castle behind me, and when I come into the Castle, I leave the office behind me." Just as Jaggers, the mercenary lawyer who is Wemmick's boss, had never seen his Castle, so too, Sister Ann and Sister Pat, who were more mercenary than missionary, had never been invited to Bishop's home.

His "Castle" on the hill had been discovered by his late wife, Grace, who was a very successful real estate agent. As soon as she had noticed the listing, she drove out to take a look. She was immediately taken by the beauty of the countryside and by its old-farmhouse charm. She knew that her husband would love it too, and she insisted that he accompany her on an inspection of the place the next day. They put an offer in, and to their delight, it was accepted. It was a decision that neither of them regretted.

Pulling into his driveway, he was struck by the day-to-day changes in the flower gardens. At this time of the year, there was an explosion of roses, daffodils, tulips, peonies, and foxglove. Grace loved to garden, and the areas devoted to flowers expanded each year. Michael thought of these gardens as a gift from Grace that he continued to enjoy years after her passing. The hours that he could devote to the proper care of the gardens were limited, and nothing looked quite the same after her death, but that was true of everything in his life, not just the gardens.

After changing into a seersucker short sleeve shirt and a pair of lightweight chinos, he opened some windows and turned on a few ceiling fans to bring in some fresh air. He put on a CD of Vladimir Horowitz playing Rachmaninov's Piano Concerto No. 3, made himself a cup of Earl Grey tea, flopped into his favorite chair in the sunroom, and put his feet up on the ottoman. Even though this was his "Castle," he could never truly leave his "office" behind him. He figured that for every hour of teaching, he spent another hour at home in preparation and grading. Some of his non-teaching friends teased him about working only one hundred and eighty days a year. Those in the profession knew better. Even summers were a time for reading and professional development. At his age, most teachers were well into their retirement. As long as he continued to enjoy good health and continued to enjoy the classroom experience, there was no reason for him to retire. Bishop thought that he might try his hand at writing a murder mystery some day, but fiction could wait. When Bill Delehanty had opened that trap door earlier that morning, Bishop faced the challenge of another real-life murder mystery.

After going through his mail, he planned out his work for the evening. Since his AP class was working on a presentation, he focused on the other classes. He had a few sets of papers that he hadn't managed to look at during the past weekend. He definitely wanted to complete at least one set this evening.

Twenty graded essays later, he decided to take a break. As the day's warmth faded, he closed the windows and headed for the kitchen. As he had never been much of a cook, he ate out quite often. The day before, he had had a spaghetti and meatball dinner at Consentino's Family Restaurant, and the leftovers were in a Styrofoam box in the fridge. That would do nicely for tonight's dinner. Just as he was about to reheat his meal, his cell phone began to vibrate. He didn't recognize the number, but

44

since he hadn't started his dinner yet, he decided to take the call. Luckily, he did. It was Lieutenant Hodge returning his call.

***

"Thanks for getting back to me, Lieutenant."

"It's been a while since our paths have crossed." Bishop had helped Hodge bring a killer to justice earlier in the school year. "How have you been?"

"Fine, just fine. Thank you. How are you and your family?"

"Can't complain. Wendy had another baby, a girl. Her name is Emily."

"Congratulations!" Hodge's daughter, Wendy, had attended Holy Trinity back in the '80s.

After a bit more small talk, Hodge got down to business. "I understand from your message that you wanted to talk to me. What's up?"

"I'm sure that you are aware of the tragic accident that occurred at Trinity this morning."

"Yes, I am. Hollins mentioned it to me."

Bishop hesitated a moment before sharing his theory that Ed Cooper had been murdered. He admitted to Hodge that he had little evidence to back up such a claim. Some fragments of the wooden ladder had landed on top of the body and not underneath it. The stage-side handle of the trap door had been left in an upright position instead of flush with the stage floor. The outside door that led into the storage area beneath the stage had been unlocked, and there was no security camera on that side of the building. Someone could have crossed through the wooded lot behind the school, and entered and exited the building without being seen. He was prepared for Hodge to dismiss his speculation as complete nonsense.

"Mr. Bishop, I wish that Officer Hollins had been as observant as you. Don't misunderstand me. Hollins is a good man, but he assumed that Cooper had fallen to his death as a result of his inebriation and the poor condition of that wooden ladder."

"What are you saying?"

"I'm saying that the medical examiner found that Cooper had suffered a blow to the forehead, and several bones in one hand had been broken. The awkward fall itself resulted in his death. However, Cooper didn't fall accidentally. Someone wanted it to look like an accident."

Bishop said nothing as he reflected on the enormity of the situation. The school community had recovered from one murder investigation. Now, they faced a second, and even more baffling case. Who would want to kill Ed Cooper, a man who had only recently been hired at Trinity? And why?

"Are you still there?"

"Yes, Lieutenant. I'm here."

"I'd like to get a look at the stage area for myself. I've already spoken with Sister Ann. She promised to cooperate in any way that she could. I'd like you to meet me there tomorrow morning if you don't mind."

Bishop agreed. Whoever was responsible for Ed's death had to be apprehended, and with graduation on that stage only weeks away, the sooner the better.

***

While he was talking with Hodge, Bishop had received a call from Ron Jennings who left a brief message. *Please call as soon as you can.* What could be so urgent? Had he heard something about the school's financial condition? Had he figured out who was stealing money from the girls' locker room?

Jennings answered on the first ring. "Thanks for calling back."

"Sure. What's up?"

"Sister Ann called me a few minutes ago. She told me that Lieutenant Hodge had called her to let her know that Ed Cooper's death is now considered a homicide." He put special emphasis on that last word. "I must admit I was skeptical of your theory earlier this afternoon, but you were right."

"Well, I take no pleasure in being right. I just got off the phone with Hodge. He asked me to meet him in the auditorium tomorrow morning. Why don't you join us?"

"Sister Ann and Sister Pat might not approve, but I will if I can. Any idea who might have done it?"

Bishop pondered the irony. In the murder investigation that had taken place earlier in the school year, there were a number of suspects, and that made the case difficult. In the current situation, there didn't appear to be any suspects. What case could be more difficult than that? "Not really," was Bishop's reply.

After concluding that call, Bishop went into the kitchen. While the leftovers were heating up in the microwave, he reconsidered his answer to Ron regarding suspects. Was it really true that there were no suspects? What about Jack Slater, the head custodian? He had certainly made it clear that he had no use for the recently hired Ed Cooper. Might those two have been in an argument that had gotten out of hand? Jack was something of a snoop. What if Jack had learned something about Ed's past? What if he had discovered that Ed had been in prison and threatened to tell the administration? In Ed's drunken state, Jack would have had a better chance of overpowering the younger man. And Jack did have a temper. When he was searching the building looking for Ed, why had Jack not checked the

47

storage room under the stage? He obviously knew of that room and of the trap door. Perhaps, he also knew that the body was there.

As he ate the spaghetti and meatballs and drank a glass of red wine, Bishop thought of two additional suspects. What about Amy Davis, the woman living in that trailer on Canary Road? She didn't seem very concerned when he and Ron had informed her that Ed was missing. From what Terry told him, she didn't seem too upset when Hollins informed her of Ed's accidental death either. What exactly was her relationship with that man? Might she have confronted Ed at school? The door at the back of the building was unlocked. Anyone could have entered unnoticed.

And then there was Debbie Bates. She seemed quite upset with the news of Ed's death. Could that have been an act? As she described it, her relationship with Ed was rather complicated. They had dated off and on for some time. Did she know that Ed was spending time with Amy? Could she have been jealous enough to kill? She works in the cafeteria which means that she arrives at school long before the faculty and the students. She could have entered the auditorium by way of the kitchen entrance without drawing suspicion.

To complicate matters even further, according to Amy, Ed had been in prison. That opened other possibilities. What if someone didn't like the fact that he had been released from prison, and decided to exact his own brand of justice? What if he had made an enemy while in prison? Once released, that person might have sought to confront him.

After dinner, he found himself unable to work efficiently on his papers. He was more tired than usual, so he decided to get to bed early. He had a feeling that tomorrow would prove to be a long day.

48

Chapter Six

Weather-wise, Tuesday promised to be another picture perfect late-May day. Yet, so much had changed in the twenty-four hours since Bishop first observed the bizarre striping of the faculty parking lot. The administrators, in their typical knee-jerk reaction, had been poised to dismiss Ed Cooper, the perpetrator of that fiasco, as soon as he could be located. Now, they were intent on conducting business as usual despite the fact that Ed had been murdered on school grounds.

That much was made clear to all at a special faculty meeting held before the beginning of homeroom period. As the teachers, some still bleary-eyed and in desperate need of a caffeine jolt, filed into the library, Sister Pat concentrated on marking her attendance sheet. Anyone who missed a meeting could expect a not-very-subtle reprimand. A few of the teachers cast hopeful glances in the direction of a table where doughnuts occasionally appeared. This was not one of those occasions. At precisely 8:10 a.m., Sister Ann began the meeting with a prayer. Bishop thought it strange that she made no mention of Ed in her prayer. The repose of his soul was not, apparently, her concern. She introduced Dan Morehouse, a member of the school's board of directors.

Dressed in a finely tailored charcoal suit, Dan flashed the same smile that had helped him sell so many cars at his dealership, Morehouse Motors. "Good morning, everyone. Thanks for giving me a few minutes of your time."

Frank Wilson, who was seated next to Bishop, leaned toward him and whispered, "As if we had a choice." Without any change in expression, Bishop nodded slightly in agreement.

"As you may have heard, the school is experiencing some serious financial challenges. Consequently, I am sad to say, the board has recommended a freeze on all salaries for the next academic year."

There was absolute silence in the room. Sister Pat looked menacingly around the room, hoping to deter anyone from making a comment. If she was expecting people to say, "Thank you," she was soon disappointed.

Frank didn't bother to raise his hand. "What gives, Dan? How bad can it be?"

Dan maintained his smile and his cool demeanor. It was the same approach he used on a customer who balked at a low-ball trade-in offer on a vehicle. "Well, I'm afraid that I can't discuss all the particulars, but suffice it to say that these problems are substantial, and it would be irresponsible of the board to ignore them."

Sister Ann was nervously looking at the clock and at Sister Pat, hoping that Dan would not take any further questions. Before she could send the teachers off to their homerooms, Diane Ramos raised her hand, and Dan acknowledged her.

"I don't understand how this could happen so suddenly. Isn't it rather late in the year to inform us of this decision?" She looked around the room, expecting support, but found little. Most of the faculty were willing to forego their hard-earned increase in salary rather than speak out and incur the wrath of the administration in which case they might be looking at losing their job, not just the increase.

Dan stumbled in his attempt to answer Diane's question. His look of self-confidence had faded noticeably. "Well, part of the problem was converting our entire financial system to a new program. That caused quite a few glitches, let me tell you. Another factor was that the cost of replacing

50

the roof came in much higher than we anticipated." If he was looking for sympathy from this group, he was mistaken.

Bishop directed his comment to Sister Ann. "I think that this illustrates the importance of having a faculty member on the board or at least on the finance committee so that we would be better informed, and also so that the faculty would have some input in how such crises are handled." Several teachers dared to verbalize their agreement.

Sister Ann stood up. "This is neither the time nor place to have that discussion, Mr. Bishop," she said sharply. The homeroom bell rang. The meeting was over. Dan seemed visibly relieved as everyone filed out.

Out of the corner of his eye, Bishop caught a glimpse of Charlie Mitchell, one of his colleagues in the English department, approaching Sister Ann.

***

When he arrived at his homeroom, all of his students were congregated near the door. As he greeted them, they stepped aside so that he could unlock the door. Some began a frantic effort to complete an assignment from the previous day. The rest talked quietly as they waited for morning announcements.

Sister Ann made no mention of Ed Cooper in her announcements. Perhaps she didn't want the students dwelling on the death of a second staff member within the school year. A good number of them might not have known who Ed was since he had only recently been hired and his work hours were primarily after school. Regardless, Bishop was disappointed in the principal's failure to model the Christian values to which she, as a Sister of the Holy Rosary, had dedicated her life.

She directed the last announcement to the faculty: "Mr. Mitchell has misplaced an important manila folder. All teachers are asked to check their belongings in the event that someone picked up this folder by mistake." That would explain why Mitchell had approached Sister Ann at the end of the faculty meeting. Bishop had hoped that he might have voiced his support for faculty representation on the board. Having worked closely with Charlie for the last dozen years or so, he knew that the chances of him opposing the tandem of Sister Ann and Sister Pat were between slim and none. It would be far more likely that he would commend the administration for having the courage to make such a difficult decision as instituting a salary freeze. He would save ripping them to shreds for the safety of a private conversation.

No sooner had that thought crossed Bishop's mind than Charlie materialized at his door. "Can you believe the nerve of those people? They're like the soup Nazis. 'No raise for you!'" As he spoke those words, his voice became harsh, and he gave a salute with his right arm extended. Bishop decided to let that pass without comment. He simply said, "I hope that your folder turns up," and began to greet the students coming into his first period class.

***

Bishop took attendance as the students took their places, opened their books and notebooks, and readied themselves for class. This group had made great strides since September, and not just in terms of academics. He remembered thinking back then that this class was going to present its share of challenges. Some, not all, were immature and unmotivated. The veteran teacher laid out his rules and expectations as he did for each class. He subscribed to the theory that "before the students care what you know, they need to know that you care." He learned their names quickly, and always tried to treat them fairly but firmly, and with respect.

As the year progressed, this class that he thought of as his least favorite had become one of his most favorite in the last few years, not that he would ever tell them that. They were able to accomplish good work together, and have some fun at the same time. They might not all become English majors, but they allowed him to share his passion for good literature with them. Hopefully, something from that class would stay with them long after they left the halls of Holy Trinity.

The class period went by quickly, and as soon as the students left, he locked up and headed down to Ron's office. It was time for Lieutenant Hodge to see the auditorium for himself.

***

Hodge had called to say that he would be a few minutes late. Frank Wilson was just leaving Ron's office as Bishop arrived. Frank always looked as if he had just gotten out of bed. His clothes were rumpled, and his hair disheveled. For a man in his thirties, he carried most of his excess weight around his middle. He greeted Bishop with a nod, looked at the clock, and said, "Jeez, I've got to run."

Gesturing for Bishop to have a seat, Ron remarked, "Frank's not a very happy camper."

"This morning's meeting?"

"Yup. I get so frustrated myself," he said as he took a sip of coffee from the mug on his desk. "I've had three or four people in here already this morning. If they only could see what they are doing to faculty morale."

"Ron, don't tell me that you're surprised by that announcement. We've both been around that dynamic duo long enough to know that they not only make some really poor decisions, they also have a knack for communicating them in a way that makes the situation even worse."

"Sad but true," said Ron, shaking his head as if he could wake himself from a bad dream.

Just then, Terry buzzed Ron to tell him that Lieutenant Hodge had arrived. Both men went out to the main office to greet him. "Would you like a cup of coffee, Lieutenant," asked Ron.

"No thanks. I'd like to take a look at the auditorium." He didn't appear to be in a particularly good mood. Homicides in Groveland were, thankfully, infrequent, but when a murder occurs, the focus is on evidence, motives, and suspects, all of which were in short supply in this case.

As the three men walked down the hall towards the auditorium, Hodge's shoes squeaked on the highly waxed floor tiles. "We located his next of kin. His mother moved out to Ohio some years ago. The body will be shipped out there for burial," said Hodge. He indicated that he had given Sister Ann Ed's ring of school keys, and that his personal effects had also been sent to the mother. That included the box that Amy had given to Hollins. "The guy sure didn't leave much behind. There was one item that I couldn't figure out," he added. "There was a piece of paper with something written on it in his wallet."

"Do you still have it?" asked a curious Bishop.

"No, but I wrote it down just in case. He kept walking as he pulled a small notebook from his pocket and found the page he was looking for. *Avignon 1868*. Any idea what that means?"

Ron thought for a second, and said, "Nope."

Bishop, on the other hand, knew the reference immediately. "Avignon is the city in France where Genevieve Devereux lived. She founded the order of the Sisters of the Holy Rosary in 1868."

Ron and the lieutenant both gave Bishop a quizzical look. "How did you know that?" asked Ron.

54

"You must remember that I've taught here for over forty years. I've heard that story many times." After a short pause, he added, "Why would Ed have that piece of paper in his wallet?" Bishop explained to his students on numerous occasions that it was often more important to know the right questions than it was to have all the right answers. In this case, the question was easy; it was the answer that was elusive.

The three men spent the next thirty minutes examining the crime scene. At one point, Hodge asked, "Who knew about this trap door?"

Ron didn't think that many people other than Jack Slater and Sister Ann knew about its existence. "I didn't even know about it myself," he admitted.

"My guess," offered Bishop, "is that more people knew about it than you might think. A lot of students are very inquisitive. Just like Bill Delehanty from my AP class. Once he saw that handle, he was compelled to open that door."

"And the back door entrance to the storage area was unlocked?" asked Hodge.

Both Ron and Bishop answered in the affirmative. Bishop added, "Jack told me that he had found that door, and other doors in the building for that matter, unlocked several other times since Ed had started working here."

"That means that anybody could have entered the building, confronted Cooper, killed him, and left unseen." He sounded somewhat exasperated by the endless possibilities.

"I think that Ed knew the person who killed him," Bishop said with conviction. "Amy Davis told Ron and me that Ed sometimes disappeared for a day or two. He might have been with another woman, but I think he spent some nights here for whatever reason. He could sleep on that old sofa and use the facilities in the locker room."

"Any idea who this other woman might be? Maybe there was some sort of love triangle," said Hodge.

Bishop felt obligated to share what he knew with the lieutenant even if it meant that a friend might be considered a suspect. "I know that he had dated Debbie Bates off and on in the past. Debbie works in the school's kitchen."

Ron interjected, "I don't think that a woman could have overpowered Ed. He looked to be in pretty good shape."

"Well, he wasn't in pretty good shape that morning. Remember, he had been drinking. Plus, the wounds on his body could just as easily have been inflicted by a woman as a man."

"I'm afraid I have to agree with the lieutenant on that one, Ron. It seems to me that Ed must have met with his assailant in the storage area. For whatever reason, the assailant must have climbed the ladder towards the trap door with Ed following. As Ed reached the top, the killer must have kicked Ed in the head and stomped on his hands so that he lost his balance and his grip on the ladder and fell backwards to his death."

"I totally missed the bruises on Cooper's body," admitted Bishop. He had thought of himself as a fairly observant individual. Perhaps, it was time to reassess his abilities.

"Hollins missed them, too," replied Hodge with a bit of irritation in his voice, "and he's been trained to be observant." He added that the injury to his forehead was obscured by his hair that hung down to his eyebrows.

"And then 'whoever' did it must have smashed the rungs of the ladder to make it look as if the rickety condition of the ladder had caused his fall. Quick thinking on the part of 'whoever.'" Each time he said "whoever" he gestured quotation marks with his fingers raised in the air. What next occurred to Bishop, he kept to himself. If Jack had done it, he wouldn't necessarily have thought of a way to make it look like an accident so quickly. Since he would have been the only who knew where the body was, he could have returned to the scene when he was ostensibly searching for the missing janitor, and broken the rungs of the ladder then.

"One thing is for sure," concluded Bishop. "Sister Pat couldn't be responsible. If she had attempted to go through that trap door entrance, she'd still be stuck in there right now!" Jennings and Hodge looked at each other and then at Bishop, and then all three burst out in laughter. It was a moment of relief in an otherwise bleak situation.

The lieutenant was just about finished with his examination of the area. The end of the second period was rapidly approaching, and Bishop excused himself so that he could get back upstairs for his next class. He definitely wanted to talk with Jack, Amy, and Debbie. He had a feeling that one of them knew more than what had been said so far. Not just one of them, he decided. Most likely, all three were holding something back.

Chapter Seven

After class, Bishop grabbed his lunch bag and headed down to the faculty lunchroom. He expected a lively half an hour if Sister Ann and Sister Pat were not there.

Several people were already seated when he walked in. He made himself a cup of green tea and sat down next to Sarah Humphries, one of the guidance counselors who had assisted his students after the discovery of Ed's body.

"Those AP kids were pretty upset yesterday. Andrea called her mother so that she could go home early," said Sarah.

"I know. That incident was upsetting for all of us."

"Are you planning on meeting them in the auditorium today?"

"No. I got word out that I wanted to meet them in my room today. I'll let them decide if they want to return to the stage for practice. They could adapt their presentation for the classroom if necessary."

"I'd like to be there for the finished product."

Bishop wasn't sure if she invited herself out of her interest in supporting these young people. Given her propensity to chatter, she might just be looking for something that she could later share with others. He knew that if his class messed up in any way, Sarah would have a field day recounting the events blow by blow. For that reason, he wasn't wildly enthusiastic in inviting her. "The door is always open," he responded noncommittally.

A few minutes later, Charlie Mitchell walked in carrying a tray. He was about fifty years old and single. Occasionally, rumors about his personal lifestyle circulated, but for the most part, people who knew him didn't care. "I can't believe this!" Without waiting for anyone to ask him what he meant, he continued. "I can't believe that they started charging us for *this*." As he spoke, he plunked the tray on the table and sat down. The more he thought about it, the more upset he became. "That free lunch was one of the few perks teachers had around here, and now they've taken that away."

Russ Chandler, one of the gym teachers, took a big swig from his milk carton, and said, "I don't mind paying a few bucks for lunch, but that salary freeze is friggin' bogus, man." Everyone agreed with the sentiment, although others might have phrased it differently.

Ron came in carrying a tray with two chili dogs, two orders of fries, a small salad swimming in dressing, and two milks. As someone who liked to eat but didn't like to cook, lunch was an important part of his day. "How much did that set you back?" asked Charlie.

"Five dollars! I guess I'm going to have to start brown-bagging it," he said as he took a big bite out of one of the chili dogs. In between bites, Ron switched topics. "Hey, Mitch, did that folder turn up?"

"Nope." Bringing up the missing folder caused him temporarily to suspend his filibuster on the unfairness of taking away free lunches. "My June final exam for Modern Novels was in that folder. Sister Ann told me that if it didn't turn up by the end of the day, I would have to write another one! Does that woman have any idea how long that would take? Of course not, she's an administrator." Realizing what he had just said, he pointed to Ron. "No offense, my good man."

Bishop certainly hoped that the folder had simply been misplaced, but he realized that it was possible that a student had clipped it. As chairman of the English department, he knew that Mitchell recycled tests from year to year, sometimes changing a question or two, but other times just changing the date at the top. Writing a new exam might be a good idea.

"When I told Sister Ann about the missing folder this morning, Sister Meany ... I mean, Sister Pat, just stood there laughing. She was laughing so hard I thought she was going to have an asthma attack. If that folder doesn't materialize, I am going to be screwed big time." If he was expecting any sympathy from his colleagues in the lunchroom, he was destined to be sorely disappointed. His "woe is me" act had worn quite thin over time.

***

Bishop met with his AP class after lunch. Despite the sugar rush that their junk food diet usually provided them at that time of the day, they were rather subdued as they entered his room.

Tim Kelleher, a young man who had already parlayed his academic achievements into a hefty scholarship to Villanova, had obviously been chosen as spokesman for the class. Given that he was student council president, it was a role with which he was comfortable. "Mr. Bishop, is there any chance that we will be able to get back on the stage? I think that the quality of our presentation would really suffer if we were confined to the classroom." Several others murmured their agreement.

"Well, I'm not opposed to using the stage, but I want to be sure that everyone is on board with that decision." He took note of Andrea's reaction in particular. She was the one who had unfortunately first noticed the body on the storage room floor. She seemed as excited as the others. Bishop had witnessed another example of the resiliency of youth. His students were always teenagers, and each year the gap between him and them widened. When would that gap become a gulf that he could no longer bridge? "All right. That's settled. Back to the stage tomorrow, but that doesn't mean that you should waste time today. I want you to break into smaller groups, and see if there are places where you can punch up that script."

As they tossed around ideas, including bringing in Randall Patrick McMurphy from Ken Kesey's *One Flew Over the Cuckoo's Nest*. One suggestion was for McMurphy to deliver the lines of Polonius regarding Hamlet with a twist: "That he is mad, 'tis true/ 'Tis true, 'tis pity./ And pity 'tis 'tis true,/ And that goes for Nurse Ratched too." After the initial laughter, they debated the merits of actually adding that to the script. The class was doing just what he had hoped. They were having fun, being creative, and using critical thinking skills. He thought back to the first day of class when he read the poem, "The Bridge Builder," by Will Allen Dromgoole. It was the perfect way for him to explain why he was still teaching after all these years. His intent was to build a bridge for them into their futures. At least for this group, he felt confident that the gulf was not too great; they had allowed him to build that bridge.

***

Once the dismissal bell rang, Bishop headed down to Ron's office. He wanted to know if Ron had checked with Jack, Sister Pat and Terry regarding their keys to the combination locks. Knowing how much was going on, he doubted that Ron had remembered, and was surprised to learn that he had not forgotten.

"Sister Pat was somewhat taken aback by the question, but she told me that she couldn't remember the last time a student had asked to use her key to get a locker open."

"That's not too surprising," replied Bishop.

"That she couldn't remember?"

"That no student would ask her," he said with a smile. "What about Terry and Jack?"

"Terry said that she almost always accompanies the student to the locker so that accounts for that key."

"And Jack?"

"I didn't have a chance to talk with him. He's been super busy trying to keep up with everything. They'll need to hire another janitor, but I hope they do a better job of vetting the applicants this time."

Bishop cleared his throat. After a full day of teaching, he sometimes had trouble with his voice. "I was wondering about the set of keys that Hodge returned this morning. Did Ed have one of those keys?"

"Those would have been Duane Davenport's keys. I doubt that he had one, but let's check right now." Ron asked Terry if she knew where Ed's keys were, and she opened her desk drawer, pulled out the ring, and plopped it in Ron's hand. "Service with a smile," she said as she forced a smile.

Ron flipped through the keys twice and said, "Nope. He didn't have one."

"He might have removed it from the ring, you know," offered Bishop.

"Yeah, that's true." He thought for a moment, then added, "I haven't had a locker theft reported in the last two days."

"You better knock on wood," Bishop advised as Ron sought out a nearby bookcase on which to rap his knuckles.

Could Ed Cooper have had that key? Could he have been the one responsible for that string of locker thefts? He certainly would have had access to the girls' locker room after school. The cash might have been quite a temptation for someone just scraping by. And he did tell Debbie that he was coming into some big money. For him, several hundred dollars, and the possibility of more, might seem like big money.

"Let's go back to my office," Ron said to Bishop.

"What's going on that's so hush-hush?" said Terry, only half teasing.

"Nothing's going on, and besides, if there was, you'd probably know before me," he said, only half joking.

When they arrived back at his office, Ron picked up a couple of memos that were on his desk. He quickly scanned each one as he sat down and loosened his tie. Bishop sat in a chair used over the years by hundreds of students who had broken some school rule. Having finished reading the messages, he got up, closed his office door, and sat down again. He had a worried look on his face. "I had a visit from Dan Morehouse this afternoon."

Bishop thought it unusual for Dan to meet with Ron. Why would a board member want to talk with an assistant principal? The veteran teacher didn't know Dan very well. He did know that Morehouse Motors was one of the more successful car dealerships in the area. He poured a good sum of money into local advertising using television, radio, billboards, and frequent mailings. He had heard the slogan, *Get more car at Morehouse Motors*, so many times that it didn't even register with him any more. Dan had become a member of Trinity's governing body a few months after he had donated a brand new Toyota Prius to the school. That was the way it worked around here. Flash some money in front of Sister Ann, and you became her life-long friend.

"Did his visit have anything to do with the salary freeze announced this morning?"

"I wish it were that simple," said Ron as he shifted around in his chair to get more comfortable. "He told me that he and a couple of other board members had spent most of the day going over the budget with

Sister Ann and Sister Pat. They've decided that they need to cut some teachers in order to deal with their financial problems."

"You've got to be kidding me!" was all a stunned Bishop could manage to say.

"It gets worse, I'm afraid," said Ron reluctantly.

"Worse? How could it get any worse? This will be devastating for the faculty and for the students as well."

"They want you to support their decision and smooth things over with the faculty."

Bishop looked directly at Ron. His voice was suddenly stronger. "No way! I can tell you right now that that will never happen." Bishop felt that Sister Ann and Sister Pat had reached a new low. With graduation just a few weeks away, how could they even consider giving any teachers notice? And the surest sign of their delusional thought process was assuming that the teacher with whom they had deep philosophical differences over the years would actually help them dismiss teachers, increase class sizes, and destroy the quality of a Trinity education.

"I told Dan that you would never agree," said Ron apologetically. He had been backed into a corner by Dan and the nuns. He had to at least broach the topic with Bishop or risk unleashing their wrath on himself.

"Don't worry about it, Ron. I know that you're just following orders. It's just another terrible decision on their part compounded by a glaring lack of communication."

"You'll get no argument from me."

"How many teachers are they planning to cut, and when are they planning on telling them?

"They didn't say exactly. I got the impression that they want to cut one teacher from each department. I don't think they plan on making that public until after exams."

"Did they mention anything about cutting an administrator?"

Ron looked as if the idea had not occurred to him. "Well ... no," he said haltingly.

"Listen, I don't want you to get fired, but don't you think that that's a logical question to ask?"

"Absolutely. It makes sense. I guess I just wasn't thinking."

"Don't worry about it. Listen, I thought that you and I should go back out to Canary Road and offer our condolences to Amy. Why don't I meet you back here in fifteen minutes? I want to see if Sister Ann is available."

"I would have thought that would be the last place you'd want to be."

"Normally, that would be true, but I have an idea." He didn't bother to elaborate, and Ron didn't ask. "Why don't you see if you can locate Jack before he leaves for the day and ask him about his locker key?"

"Man, you don't let go, do you?" He admired the relentless determination of his friend.

"No. I guess you're right about that," he said as he opened the door to Ron's office and headed directly for the office of the principal.

***

Bishop knocked at the open door. Sister Ann looked up from the stacks of financial reports on her desk. "Michael, what can I do for you?"

He wasn't always greeted so cordially, but then again, he wasn't often asked to assist the administration in dealing with the faculty. "Ron just explained to me that, in addition to the salary freeze, you and the board plan to cut faculty."

"Sit down for a minute," she said as she gestured to the uncomfortable wooden chair on the opposite side of her desk. Bishop did as she requested, knowing that it would emphasize her position of authority over him. "Michael, these cuts can't be avoided. Our finances are a mess right now."

"I don't understand how that can happen over night."

"Actually, neither do I, but facts are facts," as she gestured to the papers on her desk, and we will have to act decisively."

"There has to be another way. If you let teachers go, you will destroy morale for those who remain. If you increase class size, you will destroy an effective learning environment which, I don't need to remind you, is one of the major selling points of this institution." Hoping to take advantage of the absence of Sister Pat, he spoke calmly but firmly to convince the principal to do what was best for the students.

"I hear what you're saying, but that doesn't help me close a $1.2 million gap in our finances," she replied as she slammed her pen on the desk.

"$1.2 million?" It was inconceivable to Bishop that the finances could be that out of kilter given the infusion of cash from a bequest earlier in the year.

"That's right. $1.2 million. And I am going to need your help in dealing with the teachers when this news comes out. You've been here forever. They'll listen to you."

Bishop ignored the 'been here forever' comment. She probably hadn't meant it as a dig since she was asking him to do her a favor. A big favor. "Sister, I'll help you on one condition."

Suddenly, she looked hopeful but also cautious. "What condition?"

"I'll support the decision to cut faculty if you agree to cut one administrator, and that one has to be Sister Pat." He sat back in his uncomfortable chair, feeling very relaxed.

"How dare you suggest such a thing!" she exclaimed with indignation. Her hands were visibly shaking as she picked up her pen. "Sister Pat was right. She urged me not to ask for your help. I should have listened to her. Please close the door on your way out." She adjusted the glasses on her nose, grabbed a piece of paper from the stack, and waited for Bishop to leave.

***

When Bishop returned to Ron's office, Ron was leaning against his desk with his sport coat slung over his shoulder. "How'd it go?"

"Don't ask. Let's just say I won't be on her Christmas list this year as if I was ever on it in the first place. Did you find Jack?"

"Yup. I must have caught him at a bad time. I didn't realize that he had such a temper. Oh, well. Let's head out to Amy's. I'll tell you about it on the way."

Chapter Eight

As the two men climbed into Ron's Nissan, Ron was reminded of something. "Did I tell you that when Dan was leaving my office this morning, he asked me what I was driving. When I told him that I was driving a Sentra, he laughed and promised that he'd give me a great deal on a brand new Prius."

"I hate to sound like a cynic, but I would be leery of any car salesman offering me a deal."

"I hear ya. Dan seems like a good guy. Too bad the administration set him up to be the fall guy this morning."

"I don't think anyone is really blaming him. They know who calls all the shots around here. I think that if you went through the entire roster of board members, you would find that they have all been carefully selected, either because they have a big bank account or because Sister Ann knows that she can manipulate them to do what she wants when necessary."

"Maybe she should have gone into politics," Ron said with a smirk on his face.

"Dictator of a small country would be more like it," Bishop countered.

Suddenly, Ron pulled into the drive-thru lane of a fast food place. "Mike, what can I get you?"

"Nothing for me. Thanks."

In a couple of minutes, they were back on the road. After making quick work of a burger and a shake, Ron told Bishop about his earlier conversation with Jack Slater.

"Jack insisted that he hadn't loaned his keys out to anyone in the last few months. He said that if a student asks him to open a locker, he usually sends them to Terry in the main office because he's too busy to deal with that stuff."

"That makes sense."

"He seemed very defensive when I asked him."

"How so?"

"He felt that I was implying that he had something to do with the recent string of locker room thefts. He seemed to get madder the more he thought about it. He even threatened to quit if people felt that he couldn't be trusted."

"Sorry I put you on the receiving end of that."

"No problem. It comes with the territory," he said as he shrugged his shoulders.

Bishop thought about Jack's response. Perhaps he was a bit on edge considering all that had happened in the last couple of days. He might feel guilty that he had not thought to check the storage area beneath the stage when everyone was looking for Ed. Jack had worked for Holy Trinity for years after retiring from his job with the city. He had never been untrustworthy, and there was no reason to believe that he would start stealing money now. Clearly, his good name was important to him.

Jack's response reminded Bishop of the response of Iago in Shakespeare's *Othello* when Cassio laments the loss of his reputation in the eyes of the noble Moor:

"Reputation is an idle and/most false imposition, oft got without merit and/ lost without deserving." Over the years, he had had many good discussions about that insightful comment. Cassio had lost his reputation "without deserving" as Iago had manipulated him into the drinking episode that had resulted in his dismissal. More importantly, Iago had enjoyed a reputation as honest and trustworthy "without deserving." It was an important lesson for his students to understand. The insight applied not only in literature, but also in life itself. Too often students with a good reputation among the faculty were given a break when guilty of some infraction while students with a poor reputation were assumed guilty and treated more harshly.

***

A spring storm had been brewing, and just as they reached Canary Road, the wind kicked up and heavy drops of rain pelted the car. The ruts and potholes in the road quickly filled with water, and the car lurched along as Ron drove cautiously. When Bishop spotted the number 88 on the stone, he alerted Ron who pulled into the driveway, and they waited a few moments for the deluge to subside. That gave Bishop a moment to consider what he would say to Amy, assuming that she was home and that she would open the door even if she was.

Just as quickly as the storm had arrived, the torrents of rain became little more than a sprinkle. Both men got out of the car, and approached the trailer door, walking carefully so as to avoid the puddles. After firmly knocking on the door, they stood on the crate that served as a step, and waited. Just as Ron was about to knock again, Amy opened the door leaving the broken screen door between them. Today, she sported a Mets T-shirt and khaki walking shorts. She held a wet mop in one hand. Had she been cleaning, or was she thinking of it as a weapon should she need one?

She glanced from the younger man who looked as if he had played some college football to the older man with a thick salt and pepper mustache who was slight in stature and less intimidating. "Whadaya want?" She gave no indication that she would be inviting them in for coffee and cake.

70

Undeterred by her abrupt greeting, Bishop gave her a warm smile and re-introduced himself and Ron. They had dropped by to offer their condolences and to offer their help if needed.

"Well, thanks for coming, but I'm fine. I don't need anything. Look, I've got a minor flood in the bedroom. Damn roof leaks every time we get a hard rain from the north."

Under normal circumstances, Bishop might simply have apologized for the intrusion, reiterated his sorrow for her loss, thanked her for her time, and left. However, these were not normal circumstances. A man had been murdered on the campus of Holy Trinity High School. He didn't know much about that man and even less about who would want to kill him and why. What he did know was that he wanted answers and that meant asking questions. Before she had a chance to close the door, Bishop pressed on. "It must have been difficult to find out that he had been murdered."

Amy's face registered the shock. "Murdered?"

"Yes, that's what the authorities believe. I'm sorry. I thought that you already knew."

She leaned the mop against the wall and folded her arms across her chest as if she suddenly felt a chill. "The cops told me it was an accident."

"That's what they thought at first."

Ron merely observed as Bishop continued probing for information. "Do you have any idea who might have done it?"

She hesitated before answering. "He wasn't exactly an angel, ya know what I mean?"

"Well, I know that he spent some time in prison," trying to give the impression that he knew more than he did.

"Yeah, there's that, and the fact that he pretty much messed up his whole life." She grabbed the mop again and seemed to be ready to end this conversation.

"Was he in trouble again?"

"Who knows? More'n likely. Listen, I shouldn't be talking bad about the dead."

"No, of course not," he said. He had probably gotten as much from her as he was going to get. He hoped that Lieutenant Hodge would be more successful when he questioned her. He thanked her again for her time and turned to leave. Ron had taken a couple of steps away from the trailer when he looked back to Amy and said in all sincerity, "I'm sorry about your boyfriend."

"Boyfriend?" she smirked. "He wasn't my boyfriend. I just let him crash here for a while when he got out of jail. He was gonna give me fifty bucks a week for expenses. What a joke! I never saw a stinkin' dime!" With that, she slammed the door on them since she wouldn't have a chance to slam the door on Ed.

Ron started the engine, made a u-turn, and drove slowly out of the driveway. The storm clouds had been replaced by large, puffy clouds driven by the wind amidst patches of blue sky. "Tough cookie," Ron said in reference to Amy.

"Tough life," Bishop responded. He reflected on how little he had actually learned. Life had taught her to be leery of strangers. About the only thing he knew for sure was that the next time it rained hard from the north, her trailer roof would leak. And she wouldn't let him try to fix that either.

***

72

Ron dropped him off at school where his car was one of the few remaining in the lot. Steam was rising from the pavement as the sun beat down on the recently soaked surface. On his way home, Bishop stopped at the supermarket to pick up a few items. He had always relied on his wife to do that unpleasant chore. Since Grace's passing eight years ago, he had learned to do enough to keep body and soul together. He was never going to enjoy shopping. When he arrived at the store, he usually forgot half of the items that he had intended to buy and walked out with others that he had not.

He carried a hand basket as he wandered up and down the aisles, hoping that when he saw the items on the shelves, he would remember what it was that he needed. He worried that he might be starting to lose his memory. However, the problem only seemed to surface in connection with activities in which he had little interest such as shopping and cooking. He didn't have any trouble remembering the names of his students although at the end of a class before a long weekend or a vacation, he would often say, "I hope that you enjoy your days off, and I hope that I remember your names when we return." Many of the students understood that he was kidding, but there were probably a few that worried about the old man losing his memory. The reality was that he often could recall the names of former students, even ones that had graduated many years earlier. As long as memory lapses didn't extend to his teaching, he felt reassured.

Walking by a display case filled with rows of barbequed chickens slowly rotating under the lights, he was lured in by the familiar aroma. That was certainly the intent of store management. The dilemma of what to have for dinner was at once resolved as he placed the box containing a whole freshly cooked chicken into his basket. This would even solve the dinner question for the next day as there were bound to be leftovers.

Satisfied with that decision, he headed straight for the checkout, forgetting that there were other items that he had intended to buy.

He stood in line at what was supposed to be an express lane. In his experience, however, that lane never seemed to live up to its name. Somebody ahead of him was always writing a check or trying to use an expired coupon or both. His mind drifted to other issues as he waited. He was vexed by the possibility that somewhere in Amy's knowledge of Ed's past was a detail that might lead to the identity of his killer. How could he acquire that detail if he didn't know what he was looking for, and she definitely wasn't inclined to share much of anything on her own? He wanted to talk with Debbie Bates again as well. He still wasn't clear if Debbie knew about Amy or if Amy knew about Debbie. Could either one, as a jilted lover, have lashed out at Ed? Might Debbie provide a clue that would lead to an understanding of who might have wanted to kill her friend? He also couldn't let go of the possibility that Jack might have had an argument with Ed. It was obvious that Jack felt that Ed was fairly useless as a worker. Why was Jack so defensive when Ron questioned him about the key to the combination locks in the gym?

"It's your turn," said the customer behind him as she gently nudged him on the shoulder.

Flustered and embarrassed, Bishop glanced back, and said, "Sorry!" He paid for his purchase as quickly as possible, pocketed his change, grabbed the bag containing his dinner, and headed for the exit. As he did, he looked back at the woman who was next in line. The cashier was scanning and bagging her items as she waited with her charge card in hand. She definitely looked familiar. Walking out to his car, he tried to remember who she was.

Even though he had been teaching at Trinity for many, many years, he didn't think that she was a former student. He had run into this situation on numerous occasions, and it invariably bothered him until he figured it out. Sometimes, he would run through the alphabet trying to come up with a name. Other times, he would be able to recall random details about the individual, and eventually the name would come to him. Occasionally, he just had to apologize and admit that he didn't remember the person's name. Some people changed quite dramatically over the years so that his failure to recognize them was more understandable. Others aged so gracefully that they looked just about the same as they did in their yearbook photo.

This woman wasn't a former student. Was she a neighbor? He didn't have too many neighbors out where he lived. Had she been a friend of his late wife? That was a possibility. Grace belonged to several book clubs and movie groups that sometimes met at their home. This woman was not only older; she was not well. Her illness undoubtedly made her appear older than she was. Although he had only glanced at her, he could still visualize her pale, gaunt face and the bony hands and wrists that extended from the sweater that seemed too big for her frame. Just as he started the engine, the name came to him. It was Mabel Slater, the wife of the school's custodian. Although he only saw her a few times a year, he was sure that's who it was. He should have said something, but it was too late for that now. He knew that Jack's wife had been ill, but he hadn't realized just how serious her illness was. Jack always steered the conversation in another direction when he was asked about his wife. Having to deal with such a stressful situation would certainly explain Jack's occasional flashes of temper at work. How ironic it was that he was thinking of Jack's strange behavior just as his wife had nudged him out of his reverie. Was that enough to cause him to eliminate Jack from his list of suspects? No, not really.

Chapter Nine

As soon as Bishop got in the house, he removed the chicken from its packaging and put it on a platter. The aroma alone made him hungry. He turned the oven on, and popped his dinner in there to keep warm. Looking in the fridge for something to accompany his main course, he found a container with some leftover carrots. He poured himself a glass of Two-Buck Chuck merlot, carved up the chicken, microwaved the carrots, and turned on the television to catch the evening news. Since he hated eating alone about as much as he hated cooking and shopping, he finished his meal in under five minutes. The leftovers would provide another quick meal.

After cleaning up in the kitchen, he changed into a sweatshirt, sweatpants, and sneakers. Since the skies had cleared up nicely, he decided to go for a walk. He often did his best thinking while walking. Spring had been slow to arrive in Groveland this year as was usually the case. Grace would never plant the vegetable garden until Memorial Day when the likelihood of a frost had diminished significantly. Now, trees, fully leafed-out swayed in the breeze, dandelions blanketed the fields, and chickadees squawked as he walked by. He remembered lines from a poem by William Wordsworth in which he explained the powerful effect that nature had on him: "And then my heart with pleasure fills,/ And dances with the daffodils."

He headed up the road toward the house where a colleague had been murdered earlier in the school year. A young couple had bought the place and had already made some much-needed improvements. The cream-colored vinyl siding accented with light green shutters and a maroon front door transformed what had been something of an eyesore into a showplace. That was just one small example of the good that had emerged from that dark chapter in the school's history. He wondered if the same would one day be said of the school's current troubles. Could either Jack, or Amy, or Debbie provide a clue that would lead to the perpetrator of the trap door murder of Ed Cooper? Had he not taken the janitorial position at Trinity only a few weeks earlier might he still be alive? Or had he sealed his fate by some previous act? How had the school's financial condition deteriorated so rapidly? Would the administration implement its plan to cut teachers after exams? How would the rest of the faculty respond? As he turned around and headed back down the hill, Bishop had to believe that no problem was impossible to solve.

***

After he settled in at his desk with a cup of Earl Grey tea and Vivaldi's *Four Seasons* playing in the background, he pulled out several sets of spelling and vocabulary quizzes from his English 9 classes that had to be marked. He had long ago come to terms with the fact that grading papers was the least appealing aspect of teaching although quizzes did not require the same level of concentration as essays or research papers. With June exams rapidly approaching, the steady barrage of essays was easing up. While his Advanced Placement class was working on its group presentation, his freshmen and juniors were primarily in review mode.

Spelling and vocabulary lists were not the ideal way to improve in those areas. Obviously, the best way to develop those skills was through reading. And for many of his students, that was the problem. They simply didn't read more than what was assigned, and sometimes, didn't read what was assigned either. He recalled one class in which a number of students had unfortunately resorted to online summaries of Mark Twain's *The Adventures of Huckleberry Finn*. As their rather tortured discussion of the novel came to a close, he looked at the class and said as he suppressed a smile, "You know, this really is a wonderful novel. You ought to consider reading it someday." He waited for a reaction, and slowly, he saw the grins on their faces as they glanced at each other and then looked at him, now smiling broadly. He had made his point without making a scene.

As he worked his way through the second set of spelling quizzes, he took note of the few students who still misspelled "business" by writing "buisness" despite the mnemonic device he had given them that the word "bus" was in the word "business." Over the past forty-five years, he had probably graded over a million spelling words, but these errors still made him cringe. There were times when he saw the same word misspelled so often that he was almost convinced that it was correct. That's when he knew he needed to take a break from grading.

Just as he was about to raid the kitchen in search of a snack, his cell phone rang. It was Frank Wilson who taught history at Trinity. "Sorry to bother you at home, Mike. Are you busy?"

"No. I should thank you for rescuing me from some quizzes. What's up?"

"Listen, far be it from me to keep you from those quizzes, so I'll make this brief. There are rumors going around that the administration is planning to give some of us a pink slip at the end of the year. Do you know anything about this?" His voice clearly reflected a mixture of anger and anxiety.

Sister Ann had put Bishop in a difficult situation. From his conversation with her at the end of the school day, he did know that cuts were in the offing. However, he had definitively refused to assist her in carrying out that plan unless the departure of Sister Pat was part of the deal. Since he knew that hell would freeze over before the principal would agree to that, he had effectively eliminated himself from any role in the planned cuts. He couldn't share that exchange with Frank, so he decided to answer his question with one of his own. "Who's spreading these rumors?"

"Sarah Humphries, for one. She's already planning next year's master schedule. Apparently, Sister Pat told her to wait a few more weeks before starting that process because, to use Pat's words, 'We're going to be dropping some of the dead weight around here.'"

Bishop wanted to say that if anyone fit the description of "dead weight" at Holy Trinity it was Sister Pat herself. Instead, he replied, "Frank, you know as well as I do that Sister Pat sometimes speaks before she thinks."

"Yeah, I know that. But in this case, she might be right. It would be typical of Sister Ann to wait until after exams to fire some people. We don't have a union, but we ought to do something."

"What do you have in mind?" He hoped that Frank wasn't going to suggest that he talk to the principal. He had already done that, without success.

"A few of us were discussing this after school today. We were thinking of refusing to grade final exams unless we had assurances that no faculty members would be let go."

Bishop immediately thought that this was a bad idea. Based on his many years of observing the principal, he knew that she didn't respond well to threats. In fact, if anything, any hint of a rebellion would more firmly entrench her in her decision. He had to make Frank see his proposal as a tactical failure.

"I understand your frustration, but I don't think that you would achieve the desired result. If only a few teachers felt strongly enough about this to make such a threat, they would risk making themselves targets.

Refusing to grade the exams would give the administration reason for dismissal."

"What if we got most, if not all, of the teachers to join us?" asked Frank in desperation.

"That just wouldn't happen. Some members of the faculty would likely refuse out of fear of retaliation. In addition, you have to consider the students. They are the reason that we're here in the first place. How would such a work stoppage affect them? Refusing to grade the finals would be extremely detrimental to them, especially to the seniors whose college plans might be put in jeopardy."

"I hadn't thought of that," admitted a dejected Frank. "Well, maybe someone will come up with a better idea."

"Exams are still a couple of weeks away. Who knows? A lot could change between now and then." Bishop didn't express that view with much conviction. It was more wishful thinking than anything else, but it was all that he could offer Frank at the moment.

He finished the stack of quizzes on his desk and entered the grades in his laptop. He went into the sunroom and spent a few moments watching the rising moon as a CD of Claude Debussy's *Clair de Lune* played in the background. In a few days, it would be a full moon. Many believed that there was a connection between the full moon and human behavior. Law enforcement officials often reported a spike in criminal activity during that time. As a teacher, Bishop could attest to a definite increase in the decibel level in the cafeteria. Holy Trinity had already had its share of strange occurrences, large and small, in the last couple of days. He had an uneasy feeling that there was more to come.

As if a light switch had been turned on, he almost jumped out of his comfortable chair and headed straight for his clothes hamper. Tossing aside some dirty shirts and socks, he found the light grey trousers that he had worn to school on Monday. He reached into the pocket on the right side and found what he was looking for. As a concession to his advancing age, he had begun to rely less on mental notes in favor of making notes on little slips of paper. That new approach also had its limitations. He had to remember where he put the piece of paper, and he had to remember what the notation meant. When he left Amy's trailer yesterday, he had jotted down something and then forgot about it. Until now. On the crumpled sheet, he had written, SL8996. He knew exactly what that was and decided to call Lieutenant Hodge before he forgot. He would worry about the increasing memory lapses later. If he remembered.

***

Hodge didn't mind taking a call at home. In fact, he had planned on calling Bishop the next day. He had checked into Ed Cooper's prison record.

"Cooper had just been released from state prison in Madison about three weeks ago." Bishop could hear the shuffling of papers as Hodge consulted his notes. "He was sentenced to a year in jail for an aggravated DWI but was released after ten months for good behavior."

"I suppose his driver's license had been revoked."

"Yeah, that's automatic in a case like his."

"Anything else interesting?" asked Bishop, hoping some detail might provide a clue as to who killed him or why.

"Not really. Somebody did make a note that the inmates called him "Warren Buffett" because he was always reading the financial section of all the newspapers."

"Doesn't sound as though he made any enemies while he was locked up," Bishop concluded. He had thought it possible that someone that Ed had crossed while in jail might have been responsible for his death.

That seemed less likely now. He asked the lieutenant about another potential source of information. "What about his cell phone? Were you able to pull any leads from that?"

"What cell phone?" asked the puzzled detective.

"He must have had a cell phone. Terry in the main office called his number repeatedly before we discovered the body."

"I thought it a bit odd myself, but we didn't find a phone on the body or in the box of his personal effects that Amy gave us."

"I wonder if Amy forgot to include his phone, or if she held onto it for some reason." He paused for a moment, then added, "And I wonder whose number Terry was dialing."

Hodge laughed. "You sure do think like a detective. Well, good night, Mr. Bishop."

"Wait! I almost forgot. There's one more thing." He grabbed that wrinkled piece of paper. That was the reason that he had called Hodge in the first place. "When Ron and I were at Amy's trailer looking for Ed yesterday morning, there was a motorcycle parked near the front door. We thought it might belong to Ed, but that doesn't seem likely given what we know now. Of course, it might belong to Amy, but it wasn't there when Ron and Officer Hollins went back yesterday afternoon, and it wasn't there when Ron and I went there after school today. I did manage to get the plate number. Do you think you could run it?"

Hodge started laughing again. "I've heard lots of people, including my own daughter, say you're a good teacher, but you seem a natural in my line of work. What's the number?"

"SL8996."

***

Before it got too late, he wanted to give Duane Davenport a call. Ed Cooper had been given Duane's keys when he was hired, and Lieutenant Hodge had returned those keys to the school earlier in the day. Ron looked through all the keys on that ring and verified that the small key used to open the combination locks was not among them. If Ed didn't have that key, he couldn't have been the one stealing the cash from the girls' gym lockers. That would certainly put the focus on Jack once again since Sister Pat and Terry were unlikely to be involved. Even though the thought of Sister Pat being arrested for theft in front of the entire school brought a smile to his face, there was little reason for her to steal since all of her needs were provided for by the Sisters of the Holy Rosary. As for Terry, although she had access to a key, she wouldn't have had the opportunity to enter the locker room when no one else was around. It had to be either Ed or Jack.

He wasn't quite sure why this bothered him so much. It was nothing compared to finding Ed's killer or even to preventing the administration from sacking some good teachers. He did, however, want to help Ron solve those petty thefts if he could, and one call to Duane was a step in that direction.

Duane answered on the second ring. His nasally voice was unmistakable.

"Duane, this is Michael Bishop. I hope I didn't get you at a bad time."

"Not really. I was just watching the Yankees game. They're getting crushed by the Red Sox at the moment. What can I do for ya?"

Duane had worked at Trinity for the last three years. Unfortunately, he was quite self-conscious about his lack of education. He had been overheard many times telling some student, "You better study hard, boy. You don't wanna end up like me." As far as Bishop could tell, he was a hard worker. He often helped teachers without being asked. Since no one seemed to know why he had abruptly resigned a few weeks earlier, he wanted to tread carefully. "A lot of folks at school miss seeing you around. I hope that you're doing well."

"Ya, I miss them too, at least some of 'em," he said with a laugh. "I want to thank you for sending me that card when I left. That was real thoughtful."

"You are more than welcome."

"I didn't get no card from Sister Pat, that's for sure."

Bishop didn't respond right away, hoping that Duane would have more to say. That approach worked.

"Ya know, she's the reason I quit."

"No, I didn't know that." Clearly, Duane wanted to share his story, and Bishop was not going to get in the way.

"Not too long ago she started giving me this long list of stuff to do, and if I didn't get it all done, she'd get after me the next day. And she never said nothin' to Jack even though he spends half of his day doin' diddlysquat."

"She can be a bit difficult at times," he said sympathetically. The veteran teacher surmised that the lists and the harassment were part of a campaign hatched by Sister Pat and approved by Sister Ann to force Duane to quit. If they let him go, they would have to pay his unemployment claim; however, if they made him miserable enough, he would quit, and they wouldn't owe him a dime. He had observed this practice succeed on several occasions in the past.

"The last straw was when Sister Pat told me that they were cutting me from full-time to part-time. I'd be losing my insurance, too." The

85

words spilled out as he became more agitated. "I grabbed my ring of keys, slammed them to the floor, and walked out."

"I'm sorry that you were treated that way," he said. He was more than sorry. He was saddened to think that those two religious women in leadership positions were such poor role models of the Christian values of which they so often spoke.

"They actually did me a favor. I got a job over at Groveland High, and I'm working days and making more money."

"Is that so? Good for you! I'm glad to hear it!" Fortunately, before he ended the call, Bishop remembered why he had called him in the first place. "You mentioned your keys a moment ago. Do you mind if I ask you if you had a key that opened the combination locks used in the locker room?"

"Yeah, that tiny one? I know the one you mean. We had to put it on a small ring and attach that ring to the larger ring. Yeah, I had one. Can't say I ever used it. Why do you ask?"

It was clear to Bishop that Duane had not yet heard about what had happened to the man who replaced him at Trinity, so he filled him in on the essential facts of the case.

"I'm sorry to hear it. Poor guy. Ya know, in all the time I worked there, I never used that trap door. That storage room was Jack's place. That's where he'd go when he wanted to get away for a while."

Bishop thanked him for his time and wished him well in his new job. He wondered how likely it was that when Duane slammed his keys to the floor, that small key popped free from the rest.

***

He decided to shed himself of all of his worries before bed by immersing himself in a book. He picked up his copy of *Death and Restoration*, a

86

mystery novel by Iain Pears, and settled in on the living room sofa. The book would be due soon, and he had already used the library's allotted two renewals. Having read several other books by Pears, Bishop enjoyed the way in which main characters, Flavia di Stefano and Jonathan Argyll, used a combination of hard work, intelligence, attention to detail, and a bit of luck to solve the crime. An added plus was that the action mostly took place in Rome. Bishop and Grace had planned on traveling upon retirement, and Italy was high on their list of places to visit. His wife's unexpected death from a ruptured appendix eight years ago had ended those plans. He would have to be content with books that could take him there.

Once he started reading the same paragraph over and over again, he knew that he was sleepy enough for bed. He went into the bathroom to brush his teeth. Looking in the mirror reminded him of his age. Occasionally, a curious student would look up his picture in an old *Trinitarian*, the school's yearbook. Even though he still felt the same inwardly, those photos were powerful evidence of the changes that had slowly crept up on him over the years. His moustache had turned quite grey, and what remained of his hair was cut short. Some age spots had developed on his face, but he had avoided the jowls and wrinkles that might have been expected. At seventy, how much longer would he be able to teach? He was starting to worry about losing his memory. What would he do without the stimulation of the classroom? Perhaps he would write a mystery novel of his own.

As he lay in bed in those moments before sleep, it was as if Flavia di Stefano had whispered in his ear, *Avignon 1868*. It had been written on the sheet of paper found in Ed Cooper's wallet. How could he have forgotten that? It might not mean anything, but then again, it might turn out to be a crucial detail in solving Ed's murder.

Chapter Ten

His arrival at school on Wednesday morning lacked the drama of an unannounced faculty meeting in which a salary freeze had been imposed, but it made up for it in other ways.

Sister Pat, all three-hundred-plus pounds of Sister Meany, had parked herself at the front entrance. She directed a venomous glare at him as she triumphantly announced, "I'm still here, Bishop! I'm still here!"

He smiled as he walked up to her. He was well aware of the fact that Sister Ann would have shared his suggestion that Sister Pat's dismissal was the price for his help in selling the salary freeze to the faculty. "I accept my status as *persona non grata* in your eyes," he said in a very genial tone. Knowing that she was baffled by Latin, he took pleasure in weaving some phrase in whenever he could. She made a clucking noise with her tongue to indicate her disdain.

He walked down to the faculty lounge to make himself a cup of tea. The place was usually empty this early in the morning except for Jack who was reading the sports section of the newspaper while sipping a cup of coffee. When he glanced up from the paper to see who had come in, he said, "Morning, Mike." That wasn't the typical upbeat greeting that he received from Jack. Was it possible that he was still upset by Ron's questioning him about the key to the combination locks?

"Good morning, Jack. Looks like another nice day." When that failed to get a response, he added, "That parking lot looks great. Nice job!"

"They hired somebody to stripe it. I've got too many other things to do," he said somewhat defensively. Changing topics, he asked, "Are you planning to take your class to the auditorium today?"

"Yes. Why do you ask? Is there a problem?"

"No problem. I just wanted to let you know that I removed the broken ladder and nailed the trap door shut. Those were Sister's orders."

"That's probably for the best. We don't need another incident to take place down there. By the way, I hear that Duane Davenport got a maintenance job with the public school district."

"That so?" He didn't appear to be very interested in pursuing that topic as he turned his attention back to the newspaper.

Bishop decided to push the issue. "Looks as if the master key to the locks was removed from Ed's key ring since Duane said that it was there when he turned his keys in."

Jack slammed the paper to the table. "I didn't have a good feeling about Ed right from the start. Those nuns always think they're so smart. I bet they're sorry now that they ever hired him. If that key is missing, Ed either took it for himself, lost it, or gave it to someone else because I sure as hell didn't steal any money from those lockers." Needing some outlet for his frustration, he picked up the paper and slammed it down again.

"Of course not," Bishop replied with as much conviction as he could muster. He knew that Jack tended to explode occasionally, but his bursts of anger seemed to be more frequent of late. Could his wife's illness be the cause? Could he be upset that his private escape to the storage room had been taken away from him? What else could it be?

"And did you notice that the thefts stopped once Ed was out of the picture?" Jack asked as he regained his composure.

"Well, that's a good thing," he said, wondering how Jack knew that. Perhaps it had been Ed. Perhaps the guilty individual had stopped stealing for now in order to shift the focus to Ed. If that was the case, the strategy seemed to be working.

***

90

As he walked down the hall, he kept thinking about that key. The theft of some cash from the girls' locker room was a relatively minor event. What if Ed wasn't guilty? What if Ed had caught the thief in the act? Could that be the reason that Ed was killed?

When he arrived at the copy room, several teachers were discussing the handwritten sign taped to the wall directly above the copy machine.

Due to financial considerations, the school will not
provide copy paper for the remainer of the school year.
Thank you for your cooperation.

The misspelling of "remainder" was as good an indication of who had written the note as Sister Pat's signature.

"They've got to be kidding!" exclaimed Mary Nickerson, one of the math teachers, in exasperation. "I have tons of review sheets that I need to copy. What do they expect me to do?"

Roger Willis, a theology teacher, answered. "I think it's clear they expect us to buy our own supplies from here on out. First, they take away our free lunches, then they freeze our salaries, now this." His frustration was evident in his tone. "Just how bad are the school's finances?" he asked of no one in particular. Apparently, he hadn't heard the rumor of impending teacher cuts, and Bishop was certainly not about to mention it now. Teacher morale was bad enough as it was.

"Let's not make a big deal out of this paper business. I have a free period later this morning. I'd be happy to pick up a couple of cases of copy paper. If anyone wants to chip in a couple of bucks, just leave it with Terry."

The few teachers who were in the room at the time thanked Bishop for making that offer. They promised to spread the word to the other teachers. Bishop stopped at Terry's desk on his way up to his room. The sweet scent from a large bunch of lilacs in a vase was hard to ignore. "Who brought those in?" he asked as he gestured toward the purple blossoms.

"Charlie did. At least somebody in the English department thinks of me," she said teasing him. "He gave some to Sister Ann and to Sister Pat, too."

"How thoughtful of him!" He hoped that he sounded sincere when he said that. He then told her about the collection to purchase copy paper. "I hope you don't mind that I dumped that on you."

"No problem," she said dismissively. "And you don't even have to bring me flowers. I can't believe they put that sign up."

"Terry, you've been around here long enough to know that nothing they do should surprise you."

"You're right about that!" she said with a smile. "Do you want me to keep track of who gives?"

"No. That won't be necessary. I know that some will give and some won't. We're not all in similar financial circumstances. I'm more fortunate than most, and I don't have a family to support. The paper will be for anyone who needs it."

"Aren't you worried about what our fearless leaders will say?" She spoke in a hushed, conspiratorial tone.

He smiled broadly as he replied, "Nope!"

After walking out of the main office, he stopped, turned around, and walked right back in. Terry had gone back to her typing, but no one else was at her desk. "I'm sorry to bother you again, but I just remembered something that I was going to ask you." Perhaps it really was time to start worrying about the early stages of memory loss. On the other hand, he reasoned, he did actually remember what he wanted to ask without the help

92

of a written note. "Do you remember when we were desperately looking for Ed on Monday morning?"

"How could I forget? To think that he was lying there all that time!" Her entire body shook as if she had just felt a cold wind.

"I remember that you kept calling his number and getting no answer."

"That's right."

"Well, Lieutenant Hodge tells me that Ed didn't appear to have a cell phone, so I was wondering whose number you were calling."

"I don't know." When she was confused, she usually scrunched her face as she did now. "I used the number that he gave us. All we had was his address and phone number."

"I've got to get to homeroom. Do you think you could look up that number and get it to me later?"

"It won't take a sec. I've got it right here." She shuffled some papers around on her desk and found an index card with a number on it. "Here," she said as she handed him the card, "I won't be needing this any more."

***

During homeroom period, Charlie Mitchell popped in to Bishop's room and approached his desk. He leaned in toward him so that the students wouldn't pick up on the conversation. "I heard about your offer to buy some copy paper. That's good of you. I'd like to contribute, but I find myself a bit strapped for funds right now."

Bishop raised his hand as if to signal a stop. "There's no need to explain." He glanced at the students in his homeroom. Some of them were talking quietly while others were scrambling to finish an assignment in the few minutes before first period began. He wondered what the students in

Charlie's homeroom were doing without any supervision. Perhaps they hadn't noticed that he had left the room. He relied on their good behavior as he was often out and about during homeroom chatting it up with one faculty member or another.

"Did that folder with the exam in it turn up?"

"No, damn it! And that troll of an assistant principal is insisting that I come up with an entirely new one." Bishop was certain that the lilacs were an attempt to curry favor with the troll.

"Everyone have a good day!" Bishop said to his homeroom as the period ended. As his colleague headed back toward his own room, Bishop said, "Good luck with that exam, Charlie!"

As his first period class came in, he pulled the index card that Terry had given him out of his pants pocket. He looked at the number and recognized it instantly. It was the same number that Amy Davis had given Ron and him the other day.

***

After his first two classes passed uneventfully, Bishop grabbed his car keys and headed out to buy the copy paper at the closest big box store. He checked his mailbox before he left and found a message from Lieutenant Hodge asking him to return his call when he had a free moment. As he passed the main office, he made eye contact with Terry and gestured that he would be out of the building for a while. She grabbed an envelope and waved it in the air. He signaled a thumbs up, but didn't stop to pick up whatever money the envelope contained. He made a mental note to see Terry at the end of the day. It would also serve as a test to determine whether or not he could still function with mental notes.

He was curious to know why Hodge had called, so he decided to touch base with him while he drove to the store. Luckily, Hodge was at his desk.

"Thanks for calling back so quickly."

"Sure. What's up?"

"I just wanted to let you know that I ran that license plate number that you gave me."

"And?"

"It sounds like you're driving. You could get a ticket for using your phone while driving, you know."

"Don't worry. I have you on speakerphone," he said with a laugh. "Now, what about that plate?"

"It belongs to a Ryan Baxter, 28. He lives out on Railroad Avenue."

"Anything else?" Bishop asked hopefully.

"Arrested twice for simple assault. Bar room fights. Charges dropped in both cases. Arrested once for disorderly conduct. Paid a $100 fine."

"Sounds like a man with some issues. I know that Amy was upset with Ed for not giving her any money for expenses. Maybe she asked Ryan to use a little muscle on Ed to get some cash. Maybe Ryan was jealous of Ed living in Amy's trailer even though, according to Amy, nothing was going on between those two. Maybe ..."

Hodge cut him off right there. "That's a lot of maybes," he said with laugh. "Maybe I'll pay Amy a little visit this afternoon."

"Do you mind if I tag along?"

"Not at all. It might actually be helpful if you're there. What if I pick you up at school at 4:00 p.m.?"

"Perfect! I'll see you then."

There weren't many people shopping for copy paper at this time in the morning. When he realized that there were only eight reams in a case and that a case cost twenty dollars, he decided to buy four cases. He had no idea how fast the faculty would run through 16,000 sheets of paper. Making copies of final exams would take up a good portion of that. If needed, he could always come back for more. He put the purchase on his credit card, and one of the stock boys helped him load the paper in his trunk.

As he drove back to Trinity, he tried to understand the decision of Sister Ann and Sister Pat to cut off the teachers' paper supply. Saving a few dollars here and there wouldn't make a dent in the school's deficit, but it would affect teacher morale at a time when it was already about as low as he had ever seen it. It crossed his mind that he could solve the school's financial crisis if only printing money weren't illegal.

He parked his car close to the entrance, popped the trunk, and walked into the building with a case of paper in his hands. The halls were empty except for one young man who was headed upstairs. When he saw Bishop, he walked up to him and asked, "Do you need some help with that, Mr. Bishop?"

The student obviously knew who he was, but he didn't know who the young man was. All of the boys wore the same uniform consisting of khaki trousers, a white dress shirt with the "HT" monogram on the pocket, and a navy blue tie with a similar logo. His red hair was parted down the middle, and he wore dark-rimmed glasses. This fellow was taller than Bishop. Many of the students, even some of the 9th graders, towered over him. Students these days were taller than students from the past, but it was also true that he had lost an inch or two over the years.

Just as he was about to answer the young man's question, he heard Sister Pat bellowing at him from a distance. "What are you doing out in the hall? You better get somewhere fast before I put you on detention!" Bishop hadn't been in her line of vision. Maybe she would have threatened him with detention as well. He stepped forward so that Sister Pat could see him. Her next directive was aimed at him. "I want that boy out of the hall this instant!"

"This young gentlemen is helping me, Sister Pat." He was pleased to rescue the student from her senseless overreaction. He had long ago concluded that Sister Pat's aggressive and bullying behavior was her way of coping with her own insecurities. Sister simply grunted at Bishop's explanation and returned to her office.

He turned back to the student. "What's your name?"

"John Fisher."

"Nice to meet you, John. Are you supposed to be in a class right now?"

"No, sir."

"Good. I could use your help. I've got some more boxes in my car that are needed in the teachers' copy room." Since he was still holding the box, he gestured with his head toward the open trunk. Within a few minutes, all four boxes were stacked neatly in a corner. Bishop thanked John who replied, "No problem." As he took off down the hall, he glanced in the direction of Sister Pat's office, obviously hoping that he could avoid another skirmish with her.

There weren't any teachers in the room at the time he made the delivery. Just as he was about to leave, Sister Pat confronted him. Her presence in the doorway effectively precluded his exit. "You like playing the big hero?"

In most cases, it was best to simply ignore her comments, but on this occasion, she left him little choice. The fact that no one else was in the room created the perfect opportunity for him to respond. He tended to speak with his hands, and this occasion was no different. He tapped the fingers on his left hand with his right index finger as he tallied his points. "First of all, you may be playing games by cutting off the paper supply, but I'm not playing." Sister Pat took a step backward as if she had gotten too close to a hornets' nest and was about to get stung.

"Secondly," as he tapped again, "if anyone is big around here, it certainly isn't me." He decided to leave his meaning ambiguous so that she could interpret it any way she wanted. "And thirdly, buying some copy paper doesn't make me a hero. Just trying to help out my colleagues. Isn't that what Christianity is all about?" Without giving her a chance to respond, he took out his red pen, walked up to the sign posted above the copy machine that she had made, inserted a caret between the "n" and the "e," and added a big red "d." "By the way," he added as he walked past her, "you misspelled 'remainder.'"

Chapter Eleven

Lunch turned out not to be as relaxing as he had hoped. The best lunch periods were the ones in which people talked and laughed at just about anything other than school. Bishop much preferred a discussion about sports or some news event to rants about what a student or a class did or didn't do. He was certain that Sister Pat would be in Sister Ann's office recounting and dramatizing his exchange with her in the copy room. That meant that the faculty could speak openly at lunch, and that they did.

People were still grousing about the fact that their lunches were no longer free. Frank Wilson was the most vocal. His concerns, however, extended beyond the salary freeze to the rumors of staff cuts. He directed his anger towards Dan Morehouse, the board member who had announced the freeze the previous day. "It just doesn't seem fair to make cuts this late in the school year. What chance would any of us have to find another job for September?"

Dan had been meeting with the principal earlier and had decided to grab a quick lunch here before he went back to his car dealership. It was a decision that he was undoubtedly regretting at this point. "Listen, Frank. I hear what you're saying, and I agree with you. We're working on a lot of things to solve this financial mess that we're in."

Frank was so focused on this issue that his grilled cheese sandwich and cup of tomato soup sat untouched on his tray. "What kinds of things, if I may ask?"

Dan looked around the room to be sure that Sister Ann and Sister Pat were not there. "You didn't hear this from me, but they are looking at a significant tuition increase."

Bishop, who had been content to eat his peanut butter and jelly sandwich, injected himself into the conversation. "That would be a disaster in my opinion. Again, the timing is part of the problem. It doesn't seem right to hit parents with a big increase without advance notice. Many families are on a tight budget, and I'm afraid that some of them might be forced to pull their kids out of Trinity. That, in turn, would cause an additional loss of revenue and further damage the school's financial situation."

"Believe me, Mike, I know exactly what you mean. The board was against the salary freeze and against a large tuition increase also. You know, as well as I do, that the board doesn't really have any power. It's an advisory group." He made a quotation marks sign in the air as he said "advisory." "That doesn't mean they take our advice. Sister Ann pretty much does what she wants."

Frank addressed his next comment to Bishop. "That's why I think we should go on strike."

Bishop shook his head in disagreement. "That would only end up hurting the students, Frank, and it would only cause Sister Ann to dig her heels in even more firmly. I think that it's the wrong thing to do."

Diane Ramos, who had been following the discussion, threw her hands up in frustration. "There must be something we can do!"

Eric Redstone, one of the guidance counselors, spoke up. "What if we all refused to do all the extra things we always do?"

"Like what?" asked Frank.

Eric had obviously given this some thought. "We could refuse to chaperone the senior prom. That's not part of our job."

That hit Bishop like a small jolt of electricity. It wasn't that Eric's idea was a good one. It wasn't. It was that he had completely forgotten that the prom was this Friday. He had promised the kids a couple of months ago that he would chaperone. "I agree with you," as he made eye contact with Eric, "that it's not part of our job, but I personally still think that it's a bad idea. If we all refuse to chaperone, the seniors will lose their prom. Without at least some teachers as chaperones, Sister Ann will cancel that dance without a second thought."

"I guess you're right, Mike. I hadn't thought of that. It wouldn't be right to take that away from the kids."

As the lunch period ended, everyone left the room with the frustrating realization that certain events were out of their control.

***

His afternoon classes went quickly. Other than the AP students who were working on their presentation, everyone else was preparing for their final exams. It wasn't unusual for students, especially the younger ones, to spend more time worrying about exams than actually studying for them. One group of freshmen seemed to be more stressed than the rest.

Tiffany Hanson raised her hand. Taller than most girls her age, she was already playing on the varsity basketball team. Her straight dark hair fell to her shoulders. "There's so much stuff to study," she said as she exhaled her frustration. "I don't know where to begin." A few other students nodded in agreement.

"I understand what you're saying, Tiff," Bishop began, "we have read a substantial amount of good literature." Dylan, seated near the front of the room, began flipping through the pages of his notebook as if to emphasize the futility of trying to master all of that material.

"You have to remember what I said previously when I outlined the exam for you. You aren't expected to know every single detail for every single work. Much of the exam is geared toward applying what you have learned over the course of the year. For example, instead of asking questions about a specific short story that we discussed months ago, one

101

section of the exam contains a story that we didn't read during the year, one that isn't even in our text. Your task will be to analyze that story using the strategies that you've learned. That's why I say that this exam is going to be fun." That last statement was met with facial expressions of disbelief and confusion.

"What's so fun about taking exams?" asked Tom Miller, a rather chunky, red-faced young man. "I tend to draw a blank when I take a major exam."

Bishop took his comments as an opportunity to make an important point. "There's no question that exams can be stressful. It's quite normal to feel some anxiety. I'd be more worried if you didn't. It shows that you care enough to want to do well." As he spoke, he moved away from the cardboard box that served as his podium and stood between two rows of desks. "This class has been all about developing skills in reading, writing, and critical thinking. When you look at it that way, all of you have been preparing for this exam since the first day of classes. Now you have a chance to demonstrate those skills. You should be looking forward to that opportunity. That's why I say that this exam should be fun!"

One of the young men seated in the back of the room quickly reacted. "I can think of a lot better ways to have fun!" When he smiled, he revealed a mouthful of braces. Everyone, including Bishop, had a good laugh as various possibilities came to mind.

"You're absolutely right, Kevin," as he recaptured their attention. "However, you are going to come out of this exam knowing more than when you went in. If you've put in the work all year long, and I know that most of you have done that, then you don't have to panic over this test. You'll do just fine." The class period was just about over. He knew that he hadn't convinced many that taking his exam could be fun, but he hoped, at least, that he had lessened some of their fears.

***

When the dismissal bell rang, Bishop remained in his room in case any of his students came in with a question. He straightened up his desk and packed his briefcase for the evening. The stack of papers that needed grading was getting smaller as exams approached. As he sat in his green leather swivel rocker, all of the worries that he was able to suppress while teaching returned. Foremost among them were the questions of who killed Ed Cooper and why. Ed clearly didn't have much money so that eliminated greed as a motive. If not money, perhaps he knew something that someone perceived as a threat that had to be eliminated. Could he have been killed in a jealous rage? Amy, Ryan, and Debbie each might have wanted to lash out at him. What if there was no motive? He might simply have been in the wrong place at the wrong time. Such musings always led him back to Jack. His dislike of Ed was obvious. Equally obvious was Jack's knowledge of the trap door to the storage area. Jack's temper had flared more than once in the last couple of weeks. Could he have killed Ed in a fit of rage? If he hadn't done it, was it possible that he knew who did? There were so many questions, and at this point, still no answers.

Lieutenant Hodge was picking him up in thirty minutes. He locked his room, grabbed his belongings, and headed downstairs. As he approached the main office, he saw that Sarah Humphries, sometimes referred to as Sarah the Gabber, and Terry were engaged in a private conversation. Although both were in their mid-forties, Sarah could pass for a college student with her Taylor Swift haircut and her trendy wardrobe. From the looks on their faces, the topic of conversation was something other than the lilacs that Terry had received that morning. Sarah's job as a counselor was a tough one. She listened as others unburdened themselves of their problems, and offered encouragement and advice. Her most noticeable flaw, however, was her penchant for sharing bits of gossip with her friends, one of whom was Terry. Bishop wondered which one of the guidance counselors the administration was planning to cut. Could it be Sarah?

Bishop greeted them both with a warm smile. "Hope I'm not interrupting anything. I just stopped by to pick up that envelope. I'm lucky that I remember much of anything at my age!" A little self-deprecating humor wasn't a bad thing.

"Mike, you've got the memory of ten elephants!" Sarah teased. "Anyway, I was just on my way out. I've got an appointment with my hairdresser." Maybe the Taylor Swift look was on the way out as well.

Terry handed over the envelope. "There's over a hundred bucks in there!" she said excitedly.

"That's more than I spent!"

"When Dan Morehouse heard about it, he threw in a twenty. That was awfully nice of him. I think he feels bad about the way you-know-who is handling the situation."

"He definitely seems to be stuck in the middle." He thought for a moment and came up with an idea. "I think I'll use the rest of the money to have some pizzas delivered for the faculty tomorrow."

"Maybe you should wait to see if you're going to have to buy more paper. That copier has been humming all day," she said with a grin.

"You're right, I guess, but I still like the pizza idea. The faculty could certainly use a bit of a morale boost."

Just as Bishop was about to leave, Terry said, "Aren't you going to ask me what Sarah and I were talking about?" Her tone of voice, and even her body language, suggested that she was dying to share her newly acquired information with someone.

"No," he said simply. Even though he was mildly curious, he didn't have to admit that to her. He knew that she would tell him anyway. He was reminded of something Benjamin Franklin once said: "Three can keep a secret, if two of them are dead." That was especially true in a small school such as Trinity.

Terry went on to share what she had heard from Sarah because she thought he ought to know. Although there were teachers who didn't know of the trap door in the stage floor or of the storage area below, some students did. According to Sarah, one of the senior girls had used the trap door to get to the storage room on several occasions. She was quite upset to think that Ed Cooper had been murdered in that same place.

The secretary's account left a number of unanswered questions. "I wonder why that girl would have gone down there?" Bishop's only interest in what he had just been told was in terms of how it might provide some clue to solving the mystery surrounding Ed's murder.

"Well," replied Terry with a mischievous laugh, "she didn't go down there alone."

The look on his face indicated that Bishop was still confused. "I believe that there is a sofa in that storage room." Terry was clearly enjoying parceling out the information bit by bit.

"I don't understand," admitted Bishop. "What does the sofa have to do with anything?"

Like a card player finally revealing a winning hand, Terry added, "She met her boyfriend down there!"

"Oh, my!" was all that Bishop could say.

Chapter Twelve

As he waited near the main entrance for Lieutenant Hodge to pick him up, he reflected on what Terry had told him. He shouldn't have been so surprised. He had taught *Romeo and Juliet* enough times to understand the risks that young lovers would take to be together. These two would not have been the first couple in the school's history to seek privacy in some out-of-the-way place. Putting aside the poor decisions that they made, Bishop wondered if these two young people had been discovered by Ed. Might one of them have lashed out at Ed to prevent him from reporting them to the administration? Was it possible that they had seen or heard something or someone in that area? How could he question them if he didn't even know who they were? Would Sarah give him the names of the students? Even if he had the names, there was no guarantee that they would talk to him.

His reverie was interrupted by the sound of a car's horn. When he looked in that direction, he saw Hodge waving to get his attention. Instead of a patrol car, he was driving a black Chrysler 300. Bishop tossed his briefcase in the backseat, and hopped in.

"I didn't expect you in a car like this," Bishop admitted.

"I just thought it would be less intimidating than pulling up in a marked vehicle."

"I hope that we can convince her to open up a bit more. I'm convinced she knows more than what she's said so far."

"If we're really lucky, Baxter will be there, too. I'd like to know how he fits in to all of this."

They engaged in small talk until Hodge turned onto Canary Road. As Hodge maneuvered his car around the potholes, he said, "I've been down this way a couple of times in the past. Not the best part of town."

"I hope she's home," said Bishop.

The music emanating from her trailer eliminated that concern. A couple of windows were open, and the sounds of Kenny Chesney's "Wild Child" blasted the air. Bishop preferred classical music, but he had picked up some knowledge of country music from his friend, Ron Jennings. He wondered if Amy Davis identified with the girl in the song.

Hodge had to pound on the door to get her attention. The music was cut off mid-beat as Amy opened the door for the two men standing on the crate. She was wearing skinny jeans and a lightweight hoodie. Hodge held his identification in front of her as he introduced himself. Before Bishop had a chance to say anything, she looked in his direction. "I know who you are. This is the third time you've been here in three days." It was obvious that that was a fact that annoyed her. Turning back to Hodge, she asked, "Whatdya want?"

"I have a few questions I'd like to ask. Do you mind if we come in?" His tone was intentionally non-confrontational.

"Well, somebody's picking me up pretty soon so this will have to be quick." With that, she stepped aside and let the men enter the trailer. The interior looked as dingy as the exterior. The carpet was worn and frayed in several places, and the walls were yellowed from smoke. A sofa and two large upholstered chairs made the living room seem smaller than it actually was. A glance into the kitchen area revealed a stack of dishes in the sink. Amy sat on the sofa and lit a cigarette, and Hodge and Bishop each sat in one of the chairs. Hodge wasted no time in getting down to business. "We're trying to figure out who killed Ed, and we need all the help we can get."

"What makes you think I know who killed him?" She took a deep drag from her cigarette and grabbed an empty beer can from the coffee table to use as an ashtray.

"You might know more than you realize," Hodge suggested. "How did he seem to you when he left for work on Sunday?"

"Okay."

"Did he seem upset or nervous?"

"Nope."

Bishop instantly recognized her trademark pattern of one-word answers and sought to change that. "When Mr. Jennings and I were here the other day, you didn't seem very concerned that Ed hadn't come home from work that night. Amy, if you don't mind my asking, why not?"

She got more comfortable by pulling her feet up beneath her on the sofa. "I told you he'd done it before. If he missed the last bus, he just stayed there over night and came back in the morning. It didn't make any difference to me."

"Didn't it bother you that he wasn't giving you the money for expenses that he promised?"

"In a way, yeah. But that was Ed. I'm sure he meant it when he said it, but he usually spent money as fast as he got it."

"Did he mention recently that he was expecting to come into some big money?"

"Yeah, he said that more than once, but it never happened and probably never would. He knew all this stuff about the stock market, but you can't make money if you don't have any to begin with." She covered her mouth as she yawned. These questions were clearly boring her. She glanced at the clock on the kitchen wall.

Bishop decided to ask the obvious question despite the fact that it was awkward. "If he wasn't your boyfriend, and he wasn't helping with expenses, why did you let him stay here?"

She took one last drag from her cigarette, tapped it out on the top of the can, and pushed the butt through the opening. She seemed upset with Bishop for asking the question. "Because he was my half brother, that's why."

"Oh! I'm so sorry, Amy," he said contritely. "I had no idea." Hodge offered his condolences as well. Amy opened up a bit more after that.

"Yeah, well, how were you guys supposed to know? Both our fathers are dead. I never got along with my mom. She's out in Ohio now. When Eddie got out of prison, he didn't have anywhere to go, so I let him stay here. It wasn't going to be permanent or anything." She was about to light up another cigarette when she heard a car pull into her driveway. "That's my girlfriend. I'm gonna have to get going," she said as she stood up. Hodge and Bishop stood up as well.

"One more question, Amy, if you don't mind," said Hodge. "What can you tell us about Ryan Baxter?"

The question was clearly unexpected. The driver of the car in the driveway tooted the horn several times. Amy went to the door and gestured to her friend to wait a minute. She turned back to face Hodge. There was an edge to her voice as she asked, "How do you know about Ryan?"

"His motorcycle was parked outside your trailer on the morning that Ed was killed."

"So what?" she snapped back. "He's my boyfriend. Is there any law against that?" She didn't wait for an answer as she got ready to leave the trailer by slamming a couple of windows shut and grabbing her purse from the kitchen counter.

"Of course not," said Hodge who was determined not to let Amy conclude this interview without answering a few more questions. "Did Ryan get along with your half brother?"

"You don't think he had anything to do with Eddie's death, do you?" Her resentment at the implication was evident in the tone of her voice and the scowl on her face.

"Amy, we're investigating a murder. We have to look at everything." Hodge was matter-of-fact in his response as he tried to diffuse her anger. "Did Ryan and Ed ever argue?"

Amy dismissed that question with a little laugh. "They hardly ever saw each other if you want to know the truth. Eddie worked mostly evenings and weekends. Ryan works early mornings, and he doesn't live here anyways. Listen, I don't want to keep my friend waiting any longer. It's rude." She walked to the open door, hoping that her uninvited guests would follow.

Bishop realized that Amy's remark about rudeness was really directed at them. As they stepped out onto the crate, he and Hodge thanked her for her time. Pretending that he had forgotten, Bishop asked, "Where did you say Ryan worked?"

She smiled as she said, "I didn't," without a moment's hesitation. Bishop smiled at Amy. She was good; he had to give her that. Realizing that they would get the information one way or another, as she walked past them on her way to her friend's car, she said, "Ryan works at the UPS. You can check it out if you like." Her friend had spiked blonde hair with streaks of purple. She was listening to some country music as she waited, but Bishop didn't recognize the song or the artist. She shut the car door

110

with more force than necessary. Her friend's car left a trail of dust as it pulled out of the driveway.

***

Once they were back in the car, Hodge and Bishop checked their phones for messages. Ron had left a message for Bishop asking him to return his call when he had a chance. He decided to wait until later that evening.

They were each silent for a few moments as they gathered their thoughts on the interview that had just taken place. Bishop spoke first. "Lieutenant, I don't envy you your job. That wasn't a very pleasant ten minutes."

"It wasn't that bad. In fact, I thought that it went fairly well. We now know that Ed was Amy's half brother. I think that eliminates her as a suspect. She might have wanted him to pay his share of the expenses, but I doubt that she would kill him for it."

"She could be lying about her relationship," countered Bishop as he played devil's advocate.

"One phone call to Ohio will settle that, but my gut feeling is that she's telling the truth."

"What about Ryan Baxter?"

"I'll have him checked out, but again, I don't think that she lying about him working for UPS. She knows that if that turned out not to be true, we'd be after both of them. He doesn't appear to have a motive to kill Ed. And if what Amy told us about his work schedule is true, he wouldn't have been anywhere near the school at the time of death established by the medical examiner."

"You're probably right. If he had been at Holy Trinity early that morning, someone would have heard that motorcycle." That reminded Bishop of a thought that he had had earlier. "It's possible that the assailant

111

parked on Newbury Street which is on the other side of the wooded lot behind the school and approached the building on foot."

"I'll have Hollins and a few of the boys canvas the neighborhood."

That was exactly what Bishop was hoping Hodge would say. They didn't talk much for the remainder of the ride back to school. The mild weather drew people outside. They passed a park where little kids were riding the swings, making the arc as high as possible while older kids practiced their skateboard acrobatics. They drove through a residential area where the smell of freshly cut grass momentarily filled the air. A cluster of cars lined the side of the road near a field where a softball game was underway. Bishop appreciated the fact that Groveland was in many respects a sleepy little town. It reminded him of Thornton Wilder's fictional town of Grover's Corners in the classic American drama, *Our Town*. Wilder used that town to illustrate the enduring truths about life in any town in any time period. Nevertheless, there was one disturbing fact that Bishop could not forget. One of the inhabitants of his sleepy little town was a murderer.

***

As soon as Bishop arrived at home, he stripped out of all of his clothes that reeked of smoke and jumped in the shower. He couldn't understand the fascination of smoking. It especially bothered him that a young woman such as Amy had picked up that habit since it was a difficult one to break. Whenever he visited someone at the hospital, he was always struck by the number of nurses standing the required number of feet away from the building with a cigarette in their hands. Smoking was one way to relieve the stress, but a very destructive way at that. Fortunately, the number of smokers at Holy Trinity had decreased over the years, following a national trend. What they might have substituted for cigarettes was another matter on which he preferred not to dwell.

After his shower, he decided to start a wash so that the clothes that smelled of smoke wouldn't sit in the hamper until the weekend. He placed a CD in the player of Vladimir Horowitz playing sonatas by Lizst. Then he sat down at his desk with a cup of green tea to look through the day's mail. There was the usual assortment of junk mail, bills, banking statements, and magazines. He put the important envelopes in a tray on his desk. The magazines including the latest issue of *Mental Floss* went into a nearly full bin next to his desk. He knew that he subscribed to too many magazines, but selling subscriptions was a good fundraiser for the school. He promised himself that he would begin to tackle the accumulation of magazines as soon as his final exams were graded.

One piece of junk mail caught his attention because it had been addressed to Grace. Out of idle curiosity, he opened the envelope and read that since her birthday was approaching, she was being offered a chance to buy life insurance before the rates increased. He considered calling the toll free number to inform this company that Grace had died eight years ago. He took a sip of tea and decided not to call. Let them continue to think that she was alive. Sometimes in his dreams, he could do that himself.

Her birthday, June 8th, was only days away. This year, she would have been sixty-six, her full retirement age. They had occasionally discussed their post-retirement plans. He was going to give up teaching since they both wanted to travel. Hawaii and Italy were high on their list of destinations. Had Grace lived, he realized, these last few weeks would have marked the end of his teaching career. Without her, what was the point of retiring? He had no interest in traveling the world alone.

The vibration of his cell phone brought him out of his reverie. It was Ron Jennings.

"I'm headed out to dinner. Do you want to join me?" Ron was a bachelor who hated cooking for one as much as Bishop did.

"Thanks for the invite, but I have leftovers in the fridge for tonight." He would have invited Ron over, but there weren't enough leftovers for two.

"If I had leftovers, I'd be doing the same thing," admitted Ron. Switching gears, he asked, "Did you know that Debbie Bates hasn't been at work since Monday?"

"No, I didn't. I meant to stop in the kitchen to see how she was doing, but lunch period was rather unsettling today, and I forgot all about it." He tried to convince himself that this latest example of forgetfulness was quite normal. "She didn't quit, did she?" he asked, suddenly quite worried about Debbie.

"Well, if she did, she hasn't told anyone yet. According to Terry, she hasn't called in sick, either."

"I'll have to give her a call and see if I can find out what's going on." Several possibilities occurred to him. Debbie might simply have had enough of Sister Pat's verbal abuse. She might have been more distraught over Ed's death than she let on. The last possibility was the most worrisome. Perhaps she was responsible for Ed's death and decided to skip town.

"Lee has called her several times, but Debbie doesn't pick up." Lee Davidson had been the kitchen manager for years. She was a short, heavyset woman who rarely smiled. She was one of the reasons that Bishop had stopped going through the line even when lunches were free. He simply didn't care for the nasty way she treated the kids. Bishop knew

114

of several workers over the years who had quit because of her. She ran the kitchen with military precision, and anyone that didn't pass muster either quit or was fired. Needless to say, Lee and Sister Pat were the best of friends; therefore, complaints about her, and there were many, were ignored.

"By the way," said Bishop, "don't plan on buying a lunch tomorrow. I'm treating the faculty to some pizza and wings."

"That's awfully nice of you. What's the occasion?"

"I had money left over after I bought the copy paper so I thought this would be a good way to spend it." He did not need to remind Ron that the faculty could use a bit of a boost, and free pizza and wings usually put people in a good mood even if beer wasn't included.

"Frank filled me in on some of the lunch room conversation that I missed today. All these rumors of faculty cuts really seem to have him rattled," Ron observed.

"I don't agree with his ideas, but I can't blame the guy for wanting to do something." He was reminded of a scene in Ken Kesey's *One Flew Over the Cuckoo's Nest* in which McMurphy bets with the other patients on the ward that he can lift a control panel, smash it through the window, and break out of the mental hospital. McMurphy knows that he will be unable to succeed, but he gives it his best effort before admitting defeat. Although he lost the bet, he proved to the patients that they needed to stand up to Nurse Ratched in order to maintain their human dignity.

"Speaking of doing something, after that lunch, Dan Morehouse came up with an idea to save those jobs. Apparently, he went into Sister Ann's office and told her that he was going to contact the other board members and some other heavy hitters in the community for special

115

donations to prevent any staffing cuts." It was obvious that Ron was heartened by the gesture. "And he's making the first donation of $25,000."

"That's awfully nice of him, but don't you think that it's too little too late?" Bishop didn't want the faculty riding an emotional roller coaster. What was the likelihood that Dan's initiative would raise the $1.2 million needed within the next few weeks? And what guarantee did they have that whatever money raised would actually be used for the purpose for which it was intended? Sister Ann had a tendency to direct funds where she wanted them to go.

"You're probably right," Ron conceded as he munched on a handful of chips, "but I'm glad that we have a guy like Dan on the board."

"You should head out to dinner before you lose your appetite."

"Me? Lose my appetite on a few chips?" he laughed. "I could polish off the whole bag and still be hungry by the time I sat down to eat." His friend didn't disagree. "Listen, there's one more thing I wanted to tell you before I go."

"What's that?"

"I've been pulling in some kids, trying to get a lead on those locker room thefts." He stopped again as he took a drink of something to wash down the chips. Bishop knew that Jennings had a good rapport with the students. He was the one administrator in the building that they knew they could trust. "I didn't come up with any suspects, but I did find out that the problem was worse than I thought. Some of the girls who lost money didn't report it because they were afraid their parents would find out. In the last few weeks, more than five hundred dollars has been taken."

"Ouch! I hope you're telling these kids not to keep valuables in their lockers."

"Not that it does much good."

116

"I know what you mean. Well, enjoy your dinner, and I'll see you tomorrow."

"Enjoy your leftovers," Ron laughed before ending the call.

***

The Sonata in B Minor had just begun as he turned up the volume. Bishop propped himself up on the sofa and closed his eyes as Maestro Horowitz delivered a dazzling display of virtuosity. A couple of years of piano lessons as a child had convinced him that he would never become a concert pianist. He sometimes thought that he would be one of the world's best performers; the only problem was that the instrument with which he would achieve that stardom hadn't been invented yet. His lack of musical talent, however, did not prevent him from an appreciation of the work of others, and he had the CD collection to prove it.

When that piece ended, he lowered the CD player's volume so that he could make a call. He hoped that he might catch Debbie at home, but he reached her voice mail instead. He left a brief message expressing his hope that everything was okay, left his number, and urged her to call him when she had a chance. Next, he called Christy's Pizza and ordered enough pizza and wings for forty people. What did it say about his eating habits that Christy's phone number was in his list of contacts? Fortunately, his penchant for fast food had not led to an increase in his waistline. He knew from experience most of the faculty and staff would partake, especially since the school had started charging for lunch. He told the owner, Luigi Catania, that he would settle the bill on delivery. This surprise treat for the teachers was going to cost him much more than what was left of the donations for the copy paper, but he didn't mind. The end of the school year was always a stressful time, this year more than most, and a little pizza party might lift everyone's spirits, if only temporarily.

117

He poured himself a small glass of red wine and ate the leftover chicken while seated on a stool at the kitchen counter. With his laptop next to his plate, he checked his email and caught up on the day's news, weather, and sports online. Over the years, he had noticed the decline in the quality of television network news. They provided little depth to important stories, and instead played up human-interest stories in the hopes of winning the ratings game. In addition, it seemed that the pharmaceutical industry dominated the commercials as they peddled the latest drugs. When it took longer to list the possible harmful side effects of a medication than it did to explain the drug's benefits, he decided that the fewer pills people took the better off they were.

After cleaning up in the kitchen, he turned on a reading lamp in the darkened sunroom and sat in his favorite chair. Using a lap desk, he started grading a set of vocabulary quizzes. There were many ways to test vocabulary including matching, fill in the blanks, and word banks. He had always insisted that in addition to the meaning, students know the part of speech and how to use the word in a sentence. Evaluating sentences took more time, but he was convinced that his students were more likely to remember the word and its meaning if they felt comfortable using it in a sentence. He was moving through a stack of papers at a satisfactory clip until he read this sentence from the paper of Nancy Dunwoody: "I feel apathy for the starving children of Africa when I see pictures of their tear-filled eyes and distended bellies." Good context clues, Nance, but shouldn't that be "empathy" that you feel? Was it possible that she really did feel apathetic? Was it possible that Nancy had used the word incorrectly as a test for the teacher? Did he really read all of those sentences thoughtfully, or he did just skim them and place a grade at the top? Whatever the case, she was unlikely to confuse "empathy" and "apathy" in the future.

He had a hard time concentrating on his work after Nancy's paper and decided to put the rest of them aside for the moment. He picked up the remote and flipped through the channels looking for a good ball game. He settled on the Mets game against the Cubs for at least this half inning as he noticed that the Dark Knight, Matt Harvey, was on the mound. He watched as three straight Cubbies flailed at Harvey's high heat and lunged at his devastating hook. He felt that he was striking out as well in his attempts to find Ed Cooper's killer. At first, Jack Slater appeared to be a good possibility. He had a temper, he didn't like Ed, he knew about the trap door, and he was unusually defensive of late. But did that make him guilty? Amy Davis was another candidate when Bishop thought that she might be a jealous lover. But she turned out to be his half sister who gave the guy a place to crash when he had no place else to go. Then there was Ryan Baxter, Amy's boyfriend, who might have been jealous of Ed. But Amy's revelation had squelched that theory, and if his alibi checked out, he was nowhere near Trinity when the crime took place. Strike three.

Bishop decided that he would have to alter the baseball analogy. Instead of using the rules of a regular season game, he preferred to think of his quest for the killer as the Homerun Derby. In that case, a batter was allowed ten strikes for each turn at the plate. He hoped that he wouldn't need all ten.

Chapter Thirteen

Strangely, he could hear no noise in the halls as he sat in the straight-backed wooden chair in Sister Ann's office. She kept waving a paper in the air. Bishop wasn't sure if she was trying to fan herself or swat at a fly. Sister Pat, a.k.a. Sister Meany, who was in the office as well, was eating a large slice of pizza with pepperoni. "This stuff always gives me heartburn," she said as she took another bite.

"Tell me again," the principal demanded. "What does 'Avignon 1868' mean?" There was a real sense of urgency in her voice. He had the impression that this meeting wouldn't end until he told them what they wanted to hear.

All he could do was tell them the truth as he had done previously. "Avignon is the city in France where Genevieve Devereux founded the order of the Sisters of the Holy Rosary in 1868." He couldn't understand why they kept asking the question since both of them undoubtedly knew that that was true. Sister Pat laughed hysterically as she picked up a chicken wing from a plate on the principal's desk and started gnawing at it. With her mouth still half full, she managed to ask her friend, "Got any beer?"

The principal opened a small fridge in the corner of the room and pulled out a bottle of Heineken, twisted off the cap, and handed it to the assistant principal who proceeded to chug about half of the contents. Bishop didn't have a problem with a nun having a beer, but drinking during the school day was a different matter. A teacher doing the same thing would have been fired on the spot. Bishop wanted out of that room. "If you don't have further questions, I'd like to go now." He glanced at his watch. It seemed as though he had been in the office for hours, but not even a minute had passed. Maybe his watch battery had died. He checked the wall clock. It read the same time as his watch.

Sister Ann was waving the paper again as if she were waving a checkered flag at the Indy 500. "You're not going anywhere until you sign this!" she screamed as she slammed the paper down in front of him. Bishop picked it up and read it. What were they up to now? It was a letter addressed to the principal containing only one sentence. It was his letter of resignation.

"I didn't write this!" protested the veteran teacher.

"Doesn't matter," snapped Sister Pat as she took another swig from the bottle. She was chewing noisily on another piece of pizza. "Just sign it!" Both nuns were laughing diabolically as the principal placed her pen on top of the letter. Although every fiber of his being told him not to relent, he reached for the pen. As he did so, the pen turned into a snake, and he awoke.

***

While in the shower, the memory of his nightmare faded. He could still visualize that pen turning into a snake. Earlier in the week, he had reviewed some Hawthorne short stories with his freshmen. In "Young Goodman Brown," the main character believes that the old man's walking stick had turned into a snake. Of course, Goodman Brown had been dreaming as well, or had he? One part of the dream that seemed plausible involved the nuns trying to force his resignation. He had thought about it seriously after his wife died. The years since then had proven that he had made the right decision. As long as he enjoyed the classroom, he had no intention of retiring in the near future. And when he did decide to leave, it was going to be on his terms, not theirs.

He was so wrapped up in his thoughts that the hot water was beginning to run out. Grace, who could take a shower in just a couple of minutes, often teased him about the length of his showers. She suggested that they purchase a tankless water heater that supplied hot water on demand. Fearing that he would take even longer in the shower, he resisted the idea. He used that time to think about the upcoming day or to work through a problem. Once the hot water started to run out, he knew that he had to finish up quickly. He dressed and had a quick breakfast of cereal, tea and toast. He grabbed his briefcase and headed out at the usual time although he sensed that the day ahead would be far from usual.

***

On his drive in, he stopped at a convenience store a few blocks from the school to pick up some paper plates, cups, napkins, and soda for the faculty lunch. The place was fairly busy with people buying coffee, cigarettes, morning papers, and lottery tickets. There was only one clerk on duty, but the checkout seemed to be moving right along. There was a young woman behind him holding a baby in one arm and a large package of disposable diapers in the other.

"Why don't you get ahead of me in line?" he said to her as he moved his cart out of the way.

Her face brightened. "Thanks!" she said as she slipped past him.

Despite the floppy sun hat that she was wearing, he thought he recognized her. "Aren't you Amy Davis's friend?"

The question caught her off guard. "Yeah, I am," she said as she took a closer look at this elderly gentleman, trying to figure out how he would have known that.

"I was at Amy's place yesterday when you stopped by to pick her up."

122

She moved up to next in line at the checkout. "Oh, you must be one of the cops that was questioning her. I only saw you for like two seconds. I don't know how you recognized me."

"I guess I have a good memory for faces." He didn't say that it would have been even easier to recognize her if that hat wasn't covering her blonde spiked hair with the purple streaks. "And I'm not a cop, by the way. My name is Michael Bishop. I teach at the school where Ed worked, and the detective thought I might be of some help."

"I'm Lori," she said. "Nice to meet ya." She gave the cashier a twenty, got her change, and as she headed out, she looked back and smiled. After Bishop paid for his items, he loaded everything back into his cart. He always managed to pick a cart that had squeaky wheels, and this time was no different. As he approached his Toyota Corolla, he realized that Lori had parked her Dodge minivan next to him. With the hatch wide open, she was almost finished changing the baby.

Hearing the approach of the squeaky cart, she looked in that direction. "Am I in your way?" she asked politely.

"Not at all," said Bishop as he popped the lid of the trunk and began transferring bags. "What a cute baby! What's her name?" Content with a fresh diaper, the baby was kicking her feet in the air.

"Thanks. Her name is Ivy," she answered as she smiled at the baby who smiled back. She picked up the baby, and closed the hatch with one hand. She must have received a text message as she pulled her phone out of her purse and studied the screen for a moment. Bishop was about to return his empty cart to the designated location when Lori tapped in a quick response, and tossed the phone back in her purse. With a sigh of exasperation, she simply said to no one in particular, "Men!"

"Is something the matter?" he asked although he realized that it was none of his business.

"Not really. My girlfriend, the one we were just talking about, broke up with her boyfriend. Just like Ivy's dad. Lies, lies, and more lies." As she spoke, she placed the baby in her car seat and snapped the buckle in place. She closed the rear passenger door and walked around to the driver's side.

"Sorry to hear that," he responded, realizing that that would be of little comfort to either Lori or Amy. As she backed out of her parking spot, Lori waved at Bishop who stood there with the empty cart, lost in thought. He realized that the lives of these young people were so much more difficult than his own. Nancy Dunwoody's quiz paper came to mind. What he felt was "empathy" for Lori, a single mom, and Amy who had lost her half brother and her boyfriend within a week.

As he drove to school, he wondered what lies had caused Amy to breakup with Ryan. Just yesterday, she had been so adamant in defending Ryan from any involvement in her half brother's death. What lies had he told her? Could she have found out that Ryan wasn't at work at the time of the murder? Amy had said that the two men had never argued. Might she have been lying as well?

***

He pulled into the faculty parking lot later than usual. A couple of boys were walking by at that moment. Neither one was carrying any books or bags. Normally, it irritated Bishop that some students never seemed to need to bring books home. Didn't they have homework? Was it possible that they could complete it all during a study hall? Even more troubling to him was the reality that some teachers arrived and left school on a regular basis with nothing more than their car keys in hand. In this case, however, he was happy to find these boys empty-handed as he enlisted them to help him bring all of the items that he had just purchased into the building.

Sister Pat had taken up her usual position near the main entrance. The antithesis of a Walmart greeter, her frequent response to a "Good morning!" from any unsuspecting student or teacher was a grouchy, "What's so good about it?" Most had learned not to greet her or even make eye contact. Similar to running a gauntlet, the goal was simply to walk past her without incurring a nasty comment or disapproving glare. The two young men helping Bishop were not so fortunate. "Stop right there!" she barked. "What are you doing with all that stuff?"

"They're helping me, Sister," Bishop said in as much of a non-confrontational tone as he could muster. He directed the boys to drop the bags off in the kitchen and thanked them for their help. They seemed relieved to escape Sister Meany.

With her hands on her hips in disbelief, she spoke slowly. "You're not having a party, are you? You know that classroom parties are strictly prohibited!" She made it sound as if having a party was the equivalent of dumping toxic waste in the town's supply of drinking water. Bishop noticed some students and a few teachers silently move by, grateful that they were not her current target.

"Actually," he said with a slight smile, "I am having a party." He hated to admit it, but he rather enjoyed provoking her outrage.

"Well, we'll just see about that!" She practically spit out the words as she turned, undoubtedly to report him to the principal.

Before she had taken a step, Bishop clarified. "It's a party for faculty. We're having pizza and wings, and of course, you're invited." What he didn't say was that her presence would put somewhat of a damper on the festivities, but that was an unavoidable consequence. The prospect of good eats had a remarkable effect on her demeanor. Without a word of apology or of thanks, she stepped aside. As he walked past her, he had a vague flashback to his nightmare vision of her laughing diabolically over a plate full of chicken bones.

***

After that skirmish, he realized that he was running late. He brought the remaining items for the faculty lunch to the kitchen. The ladies were well into their morning routine preparing lunch for the students. He looked around for Debbie, but she was nowhere in sight. Lee Davidson, the kitchen manager, was at her desk going over some paperwork. Bishop told her to expect a delivery of pizza and wings from Christy's before noon and that he and a few others would take care of setting up and cleaning up afterwards. Lee mumbled an acknowledgement, and Bishop turned to leave as she spoke. "It's a good thing that you didn't expect us to help. We've been shorthanded all week."

"Are you referring to Debbie?"

"Of course, I am. Not that she did such a good job even when she was here. Nobody seems to know where she is. I asked Sister Pat to find a replacement if Debbie doesn't show up by the end of the week."

"I'm sure that there is a reasonable explanation for her absence," Bishop replied despite the fact that he couldn't imagine what that excuse might be. He had wanted to talk with Debbie again in the hope that she might remember something that would lead to solving Ed's murder. Now he had another reason to find her. She was about to lose her job.

He briefly stopped by the main office to enlist Terry's help with the setup for the pizza party, checked his mailbox, and headed upstairs. There were more students than usual waiting for him to unlock the door.

During homeroom period, he sent a message to the entire faculty and staff inviting them to a lunch of pizza and wings and "good conversation among friends." Had he known what would happen at that gathering, he would not have included that last phrase.

Charlie Mitchell wandered into Bishop's homeroom, once again leaving his own homeroom unattended. He was wearing a yellow long-sleeved shirt with a navy blue cravat tucked in the open collar, charcoal dress pants, and black wingtip shoes. As he entered the room, he took a long look at the wall phone near the door.

"I just read your email. The way things have been going around here of late, a pizza party sounds awfully good. Thanks for doing that."

"No problem," said Bishop as he looked at the open plan book on his desk. He didn't want to be rude, but he did have other things to do.

"I hate to ask, but do you have a spare telephone cord?" He spoke softly so that the students wouldn't hear him.

Bishop thought it a strange question. Each classroom had a telephone mounted on the wall near the door. The receiver was connected to the base of the phone by a short length of coiled cable. "Sorry. I don't. Isn't yours working?"

"Working?" he replied with a hint of irritation in his voice. "I wish it wasn't working. It's missing! And if it doesn't turn up soon, Meany is going to nail me to the wall."

Snatching the cord took only a few seconds. Bishop knew that students occasionally pulled this prank. The missing cord usually reappeared in a day or two. He couldn't help but think that Charlie's frequent forays, which left his room unattended, accounted for the disappearance of the cord as well as of the folder containing the final exam. He wondered if the same person was responsible for both. "I hope that it turns up soon," he said with as much sincerity as he could muster.

***

As soon as his first period class ended, Bishop walked down to the office of Sarah Humphries, hoping that she would not be in a conference with a student. Fortunately, that was the case. He knocked on the open door as she had shifted her chair sideways to look at her computer screen. "Got a minute?" he asked with a smile.

"Sure. Come on in," she said without hesitation as she swiveled her chair back into position behind her desk. She gestured for him to sit down. "What's up?"

"Do you mind if I close the door?"

Her face lit up, and she rubbed her hands together as he took a seat. "This must be good. Have you heard anything about who's getting cut?" Even if he had, it wasn't his place to deliver the bad news. Apparently, it hadn't occurred to Sarah that she might be on such a list herself.

"No. No. It's nothing like that." He had thought about how he was going to approach her on his request for information, but whatever strategy he had devised, escaped him at the moment. Perhaps he should have written it down. He decided just to be direct. "It's come to my attention that a young lady was in your office recently to discuss her feelings regarding the death of Ed Cooper."

Sarah gave him a quizzical look. "Might that information have come to you by way of Terry by any chance?"

Bishop hesitated. If he said "yes," he would be jeopardizing his friendship with Terry and perhaps hers with Sarah; if he said "no," he would be lying. As he often advised his students, it was ultimately best to tell the truth. "Well, yes, but I don't want you to blame Terry. She knew that I would be interested in talking to anyone who might have seen or heard something while in that area where the murder took place. And she didn't give me any names," he added quickly, "which is why I'm here." Bishop waited for her response. She was either going to give him a lecture about student confidentiality, or she was going to help.

"Terry didn't give you any names because I didn't tell her who was involved. Actually, I was hoping that Terry would tell you. If she hadn't, I was going to tell you myself. These kids might have information pertinent to a homicide investigation. I think that they will be more comfortable talking to you rather than to Lieutenant Hodge."

"I won't bring him into this unless absolutely necessary, and I won't bring your name into this either. They don't need to know how I know."

"I trust you on both counts," she said firmly. "The young lady who was sitting here yesterday is Hannah Ward, and the young man she met in the storage room is Tim Kelleher."

Bishop didn't react when he heard the names other than to say, "Thank you." During his forty-five years in secondary education, he had just about seen or heard it all, so nothing much surprised him. "Well, I won't take up any more of your time." He stood up, opened the door, and thanked her again. "Your hair looks very nice by the way."

She smiled at his compliment, and as he walked out of her office, she called out, "Good luck!" Bishop knew that he would need a lot of that in order to solve the mystery of Ed's murder before graduation.

Chapter Fourteen

As he walked from the guidance office to the library, he mulled over how he would approach Hannah and Tim. He knew that it would be best to talk with each of them separately. He decided that he would start with Hannah. She had been a student in his English 9 Honors class a few years ago. He remembered her as quiet and shy. Since she didn't always make the required effort in her academics, she wasn't recommended to continue in the Honors program. Tim, on the other hand, excelled in academics, had earned a full scholarship to Villanova, and was currently in Bishop's AP English class. Would either one of them be willing to talk with him? Did they know anything that might be relevant to solving Ed's murder?

When he walked into the library, he found it deserted except for a couple of students seated together at one of the tables near an open window. With the arrival of the Internet, traditional libraries all over the country had seen a decline in activity. Who needed a library when you could find just about anything by using a computer, tablet, or even your phone? Libraries needed to adapt to the changing times. Merle Howard, the librarian, was perched on a stool behind the semi-circular main desk flipping through a magazine. Merle, who was about sixty years old, had a full head of almost white hair. He kept the place in good order, but he was slow to incorporate new technology. If the administration did have a list of faculty and staff cuts, Bishop wondered whether or not Merle's name was on it.

Bishop asked Merle for permission to send his AP class to the library to continue work on the script for their project. He needed that time to get everything ready for the faculty lunch. Merle readily agreed, and Bishop thanked him as he left the library and headed back to his classroom. He wanted to make a couple of phone calls before the end of the period.

Back in his room, he closed the door for privacy and kept the lights off. His first call was to Debbie. He was both surprised and relieved when she answered. "It's good to hear your voice. I've been trying to reach you for a couple of days."

"Sorry if I made you worry. I just had to get away from Trinity for a few days."

"I understand," he replied even though he didn't fully understand. Yes, she had lost a friend in Ed Cooper. Yes, she had been verbally abused in front of her co-workers by Sister Pat. Yes, she was upset to learn that she wasn't getting a much-needed raise. Yes, she found it difficult to work for the irascible Lee Davidson. Despite all of that, did she really want to lose her job?

"Listen, I don't have much time before my next class comes in, but I wanted to let you know that if you don't show up for work tomorrow, they are going to replace you."

"Thanks for the heads-up. It's nice to know that somebody cares."

The sounds of laughter and the clanging of locker doors meant that the class period had ended. "I've got to go. Can I tell them that you'll be in to work tomorrow?" He disliked having to be so abrupt, but he didn't have much of a choice. If she failed to show up for work on Friday, she would be unemployed, and without a favorable recommendation, she might have a difficult time finding another job.

"I guess so," she answered without much enthusiasm.

"Great! Would you mind if I stop by your place after school today?"

"I'd like that. There's something I need to tell you."

He wondered what that something might be. Was it something that related to Ed? Was it something related to work? He had to let the speculation go. There wasn't even time to make another call. He put his cell phone on airplane mode, turned on the lights, and opened the door to about two dozen students who would become his sole focus for the next fifty minutes.

***

The rest of the morning passed quickly. Bishop could never quite understand teachers who complained about how slowly their days dragged. He often wished that he could slow the pace down a bit. Perhaps that was a result of getting older. The entire school year seemed to him to move more quickly than the previous one.

Once he had given instructions to his AP class and sent them off to the library, he headed for the teachers' lunchroom. In the few minutes that he spent with his seniors, he resisted his desire to say something to Tim Kelleher. He planned on arranging to have a chat with that young man in the very near future.

Much to his surprise, when he arrived at the lunchroom, preparations were already well underway. He learned that Charlie Mitchell, who always was on the best of terms with the ladies on the staff including Lee Davidson, had borrowed some tablecloths from her to make the occasion more festive. He had placed a small vase of flowers at each table. Bishop had no idea where he had come up with those. Terry Mortenson had flagged a parent volunteer to cover her desk in the main office so that she could help with the preparations. She had placed pitchers of ice water at each of the tables. The paper plates, napkins, and cups were stacked on a table and ready for use. Soda bottles were cooling in a tub of ice. A few teachers had started to gather in anticipation.

A somewhat embarrassed young student knocked at the door. The teachers' lunchroom was clearly not a place where she felt comfortable.

132

Terry asked the girl if she could help her. "Is Mr. Bishop in here? He's wanted in the kitchen." Bishop thanked her and asked her name. "Follow me, Lynn." The student queue for lunch was already more than halfway down the hall. "There's no reason that you should go to the end of the line just because you were kind enough to deliver that message to me."

"I'm fine, really," she pleaded. Bishop realized that bringing her to the front of the line and budging would cause her even more embarrassment.

He thanked Lynn again and walked into the kitchen that was in a state of controlled chaos as the staff prepared to serve hundreds of meals in a limited amount of time. Luigi, the owner of Christy's Pizza, had delivered boxes of pizza and wings, assisted by his son, Luca. Bishop shook hands with both of them. "Luigi, it's good to see you again!" Since the death of his wife, Bishop made regular visits to Christy's for a quick and easy meal.

"It's a good to see you too!" he replied. Despite having arrived in America about five decades earlier, he still spoke broken English. He explained that some of the food had been placed on serving carts, and the rest was being kept warm in one of the large kitchen ovens.

"Everything is perfect, Luigi. How much do I owe you?" he asked as he pulled his checkbook from his back pocket.

"Don't worry about that now. Just enjoy your party. I send you a bill. Okay?"

"Sure. That's fine. Thank you."

Terry came into the kitchen, and she and Luca began wheeling the carts into the lunchroom. "You've got a hungry crowd over there. We better get some food to them before they get ornery," she said with a wink.

Bishop was about to join them when Luigi asked him a question. "Is Jack okay?"

"Jack Slater? As far as I know, he's fine. Why do you ask?"

Luigi explained that about a month earlier Jack had won $500 on a scratch off ticket that he had purchased at a vending machine in his store. Hoping to duplicate his success, Jack came in every day after that to buy more tickets, every day, that is, until this week.

Bishop hadn't thought of Jack as much of a gambler. He also knew that one large win was enough to hook some people into playing more often and for higher stakes. Once the spiral of losing began, they often convinced themselves the next big winner was just one bet away. Once they won their money back, the theory was that they would be able to stop gambling. If Jack wanted to gamble with his own money, that was his own business. He did find it troublesome, however, that Jack had suddenly broken his pattern around the same time that Ed's body had been found. Could the two events be somehow connected?

When Bishop walked into the lunchroom, there was a smattering of applause as those with their hands free expressed their appreciation for his generosity. "There's more in the kitchen," he announced for all to hear, "so enjoy!"

Just about everyone was there who had the first lunch period. There was much more food warming in the kitchen for those who had the second lunch. Some of the teachers were seated while a few others remained standing. Everyone appeared to be in a good mood. Sounds of laughter, which had been in short supply recently, filled the room. At least for a half an hour, people could forget all of their worries.

Bishop grabbed a Pepsi and a slice of pizza with black olives and green peppers. He sat down next to Ron Jennings whose paper plate already had a pile of chicken bones on one side. "This was a great idea, Mike. Christy's pizza is the best," Ron said as he got back to the serious business of eating.

Bishop leaned toward Ron and whispered, "I talked with Debbie this morning, and she told me that she's coming back to work tomorrow." Ron signaled his approval with a thumbs-up.

As Terry walked by, she put her hand on Bishop's shoulder to get his attention. "I invited Dan Morehouse. I hope you don't mind. He's been here all morning working on next year's budget." Bishop told her that he didn't mind at all and thanked her for her help in getting everything set up.

After finishing his pizza, instead of going for seconds, he approached Sister Ann and Sister Pat who were seated at a table by themselves. The principal spoke first. "It's a very nice party, Michael. Thank you." The monotone of her voice and her lack of facial expression suggested that the sentiment might have been expressed grudgingly. Sister Pat said disapprovingly, "Where's the salad?" as she folded over a piece of pizza so that she could eat more efficiently.

Bishop laughed although he was certain that the question was intended to be taken seriously. "Salads are available in the kitchen. I said that we were having pizza and wings. *Ipso facto*, we have pizza and wings."

Sister Pat dropped the pizza that was in her hands back to her plate. She turned to her best friend, and asked in disbelief, "Did he just call me fat?" Sister Ann shook her head slightly from left to right. "I'll explain later," putting the emphasis on the last word. Bishop knew that Latin phrases befuddled Sister Pat, so he tried to work one in to the conversation whenever he had a chance.

Before walking away, he added, "By the way, Debbie will be back to work tomorrow so there's no need to look for a replacement. Isn't that good news?"

"I'm not so sure that it is," replied the principal. "Lee tells me that Debbie has been late to work several times recently and that she's not always working even when she's here." She wiped her mouth with her napkin and tossed it on her empty plate. The finality of the gesture suggested that she planned on ridding herself of Debbie just as easily.

Bishop realized that the administrators most likely still blamed Debbie for having recommended that they hire Ed Cooper. That would absolve them of any responsibility for their own failures to properly vet him as a candidate for employment before hiring him. "I know that Debbie has been under a great deal of stress lately. I'm sure that Lee and Debbie can work out their …"

He was interrupted mid-sentence by someone shouting, "It's all your fault! You son of a bitch!" and the sounds of a scuffle as chairs were knocked over. He looked across the room where Frank Wilson had launched himself toward Dan Morehouse, overturning the table where they had been seated, sending unfinished plates of food and cups of soda in every direction. Dan had unsuccessfully avoided contact as Frank landed a couple of punches to his face. Everyone stood in disbelief as to what was happening. Someone shouted, "Stop it!" Ron Jennings pushed a few bystanders to the side and pulled Frank away from Dan who was bleeding from the nose. Several people went to help Dan to his feet. Others righted the table and chairs and started cleaning up the mess of broken glass and litter from the floor.

Ron still held Frank in a bear hug from behind. "What got into you, man?"

136

"That son of a bitch! Some of us are gonna lose our jobs because of him!" He cast a venomous look in Dan's direction.

"That's enough out of you!" he shouted as he shoved Frank towards the door. "Let's go to my office."

After an initial moment of shock at what had just taken place, people went on with their day. Terry and Charlie helped Bishop put the room back in order again. The second lunch was not likely to be as eventful, but he certainly knew that the pizza and wings would not be the number one topic of conversation.

"Nice party, Bishop," said Sister Pat sarcastically as she waddled out of the room.

"Don't listen to her," Terry said in an attempt to lift his spirits.

"Other than Sister Ann, who does?" he asked with a broad grin on his face.

***

As he headed off to class, he stopped in the kitchen to thank Lee for her cooperation and to tell her that he had some people lined up to make sure that the second lunch went smoothly.

"I heard that ruckus over here," she announced in a tone of disapproval. "You don't expect that kind of behavior from the teachers."

She was right, of course. If students were involved in a fight, there were consequences. How could teachers not face consequences for similar behavior? He knew that Frank had been quite upset over the prospect of losing his job with his talk of a teachers' strike. Now, he had given the administration more ammunition to silence one of their most vocal critics. In addition to losing his job, Bishop feared that Frank might be facing an assault charge.

As if Frank's behavior wasn't troubling enough, he also wondered why he hadn't seen Jack in the lunchroom. Ordinarily, the lure of pizza and wings would have been too much for him to resist. Perhaps he was busy in another part of the building. Then he remembered what Luigi had said about Jack and his purchase of lottery tickets. Why had he suddenly stopped playing around the time of Ed's death? And what about Debbie? Would Lee and the administrators allow her to come back to work tomorrow? And why had she missed work without calling in the first place?

After school, he had an important phone call to make. He had also arranged for Hannah Ward to come to his room at the end of the day. And he had promised Debbie that he would stop by her place on his way home. He definitely wanted to know whatever it was that she had decided to tell him. For now, however, he would put all of that aside and concentrate on what really mattered, the students in his afternoon classes.

Chapter Fifteen

A couple of productive afternoon classes fortified him for what he knew would follow. As the last of his students left his classroom, Ron Jennings walked in. Bishop immediately sensed that the news would not be good.

"How is Frank doing?"

"That's what I came up to tell you," said Ron, somewhat breathless from walking up the stairs. "They suspended him without pay for the rest of the school year." His disappointment was evident as he looked down at his shoes.

Just then, there was a knock at his open door. It was Hannah Ward. She had the note that he had sent to her in her hand. "Hannah, would you give us just a minute, please?" asked Bishop.

"Is it all right if I go to my locker and pack up my stuff?"

"That would be fine. I'll see you in a few minutes."

"What's that about?" Ron inquired after Hannah left.

"Nothing really. I just need to ask her a few questions." There was little point in informing him of her trysts with Tim just yet.

"Who's going to sub for him for the next few weeks? It's not that easy to find a qualified history teacher at this time of the year."

"They've asked Sister Annunciata to cover for him." She had retired a few years earlier after a long career at Holy Trinity. In Bishop's view she was a shining example of what a Sister of the Holy Rosary should be. She was a dedicated and excellent teacher as well as a kind and compassionate person.

"How did Frank take his suspension?"

"I think he realized that if he didn't accept their terms, he would have been fired on the spot. As you know, the way our contracts are written, the administration can fire anyone at any time for any reason and for no reason. He also has to apologize to Dan."

"How's Dan doing?" Bishop kept an eye on the door in anticipation of Hannah's return.

"He's shaken up, and he's going have a shiner, but his nose isn't broken. He's basically he's fine. Frank really clocked him," said Ron as he made a fist with his right hand and hit his open left hand several times.

"I'm glad you were there to grab him before he could do more harm. Did Frank tell you why he did it?" asked a curious Bishop.

"Apparently, Dan was talking about job cuts as if they were inevitable since he hadn't been able to convince any of the other board members to add to his own donation of 25K. Dan's been working hard to help us get out of this mess. I guess Frank needed someone to blame."

At that point, Hannah knocked on the door once again. Bishop asked her to come in. As Ron left, he greeted the senior girl. "Hey, Hannah Banana, how are you doing?"

"I'm fine, thanks," she said with a smile on her face. It must not have been the first time that Ron had greeted her that way. Bishop got up from behind his desk and arranged two student desks so that they faced each other. As he sat at one of the desks, he invited Hannah to sit at the other. She dropped her backpack and her purse next to her seat. The big smile that she had given Ron had been replaced with a look of nervous tension.

Bishop suddenly realized that this was more awkward than he had anticipated. He should have asked Sarah to talk with her again, but it was too late for that now. "The last time you were in this room, you were a freshman," he said with a laugh. She looked around the room as that reality sank in. Although the room hadn't changed much in those few years, she

140

certainly had. The frightened and shy little girl who traveled in a pack with other frightened and shy little girls had become a mature and self-confident young woman with the exception of the present moment as the reason for her summons to this room remained unclear. She looked back at him and waited.

"What are your plans for next year?"

"I've been accepted in the pre-med program at Northwestern," she said proudly.

"Congratulations! I'm sure that you will do well."

"Mr. Bishop, you didn't send for me just to ask about my college plans, did you?" So much for his attempt to ease into the heart of the matter. He cleared his throat, folded his hands, rested them on the edge of the desk, and leaned forward.

"You are quite right, of course. There is something very important that I want to discuss with you." He could see the muscles in her jaw clench as he spoke. "First, let me assure you that you are not in any trouble whatsoever." That did little to abate the look of concern on her face. "It has come to my attention, and I am not at liberty to say how, that you frequented the storage area beneath the stage where Mr. Cooper was found dead, and...."

Before he could continue, she burst out in disbelief, "You don't think that I had anything to do with that, do you?"

Since he had left the door open intentionally, he gestured for her to lower her voice. "No, no. Of course not!" How could he explain to her that he had taken it upon himself to unravel the mystery of the murder of a man whom he barely knew? He wasn't sure that he could fully explain that even to himself. "Believe me, Hannah, I don't mean to pry into your personal business, but someone out there has literally gotten away with murder at this point. My only interest is in the possibility that you might have seen or heard something that would help identify that person. Can you think of anything … anything at all, no matter how seemingly insignificant?"

Hannah fidgeted with her necklace and shifted in her seat. "But we weren't even there that day!" she said defensively. Regardless of what he had said about his lack of interest in her personal life, she wondered exactly what he knew about her and Tim.

"Were you ever there when Mr. Cooper was there?"

She hesitated and then answered weakly, "No."

The veteran teacher knew that she was lying, but it would serve no purpose to challenge her at this point. He decided to keep probing. "Did you ever see anyone or hear anyone on any of those occasions?"

Bishop's last question triggered a memory. "I used to drop my stuff off in the locker room before going to the stage. It was very early in the morning so I didn't expect anyone to be there, but I did see someone there several times."

Thinking that this might be the break he was looking for, he edged forward. "Whom did you see, Hannah?"

"Mr. Slater."

***

Was this the breakthrough evidence that he had been seeking? It was obvious that Jack disapproved of the new employee, but was that alone a motive for murder? Jack also displayed a temper of late. Could he have caused Ed to fall from the ladder without intending to kill him? It reminded Bishop of a key scene in *A Separate Peace* by John Knowles. The main character, Gene, jounces a tree limb causing his classmate, Finny, to fall. Although Finny does not die from that fall, Gene struggles to understand what made him jounce the limb. On the other hand, it was perfectly reasonable for Jack to be in the building at that early hour.

"Did you ever see anyone else?"

"No," said Hannah conclusively, "no one else."

Bishop thanked her for her time, asked her not to tell Tim of their conversation even though he knew that she was likely to do just that, and wished her well at Northwestern. As she left the room, he put the desks back in order, and closed the door so that he could make a phone call.

Fortunately, Lieutenant Hodge was in his office and was able to take the call.

"I was just about to give you a call myself," said Hodge. "We've been able to establish a few facts." Bishop listened attentively as Hodge shared what his team of investigators had learned. "We contacted Cooper's mother in Ohio and she confirmed that Amy Davis is Ed's half sister. She was disappointed but not surprised that Amy did not attend Ed's funeral which was this morning."

Bishop had a feeling that Amy had been telling the truth about her relationship with Ed and the mother. "Were you able to verify Ryan Baxter's employment?"

"Yes and no."

"How so?" asked a confused Bishop.

"He did work for UPS, but he was let go last week."

"That means that he doesn't have an alibi for his whereabouts at the time of the murder."

"That's correct," Hodge replied in a cautionary tone, "but he doesn't appear to have a motive." He added, "I'm also concerned that Amy lied about Ryan's work. She must have known that we would find out the truth sooner or later."

143

"She might have been telling the truth," offered Bishop. He went on to explain his fortuitous meeting with Lori, the girl who had been waiting in her car at Amy's place the day before. He told Hodge of the text that Lori received from Amy. "If Amy broke up with Ryan because of his 'lies', she might not have known that he had lost his job when she spoke with us."

"That's true," Hodge admitted. "Ryan may not be our man, but I definitely want to talk with him."

"Along the same lines, Jack Slater may not be our man either, but I'd like to ask him a few questions as well. Apparently, he was seen in the building earlier than normal although not on the day of the murder. I also heard that he might have been having some money problems recently although I don't know that there's a connection to Ed."

"It's worth a try," he said. "At this point, that's about all that we can do."

"Before I let you go, let me ask you one more question. Has Hollins had a chance to canvas the neighbors on Newbury Street?" Bishop's theory was that the killer might have parked his vehicle on that street, cut through the wooded lot, and entered the building through the unlocked back door. Someone might have noticed an unfamiliar car parked in that residential area. If Ryan Baxter was involved, someone might have heard his motorcycle.

"I'm afraid Hollins struck out on that one," he said with a note of disappointment. The baseball analogy resonated with Bishop. How many strikes had he decided to give himself? Ten? Hodge went on to explain that the only person who saw or heard anything that morning was a man in his nineties who claimed he saw a car with numbers on it parked in front of his house.

144

"Well, that's sounds promising. Did he get the numbers?"

"That's the problem. The guy unfortunately suffers from dementia. Every vehicle has a license plate with numbers on it. I don't think that he can help us."

"What's his name and street number?" Bishop asked, unwilling to give up on even a remote chance that the old man might know more than he realizes.

Hodge shuffled some papers. "His name is Elwin Crimins, and he lives at 224 Newbury."

After ending the call, Bishop packed up his belongings, left the mostly deserted building, and drove over to the home of Debbie Bates. There was something that she wanted to tell him, and he was more than curious to find out what it was.

***

On his way to Debbie's place, he stopped at Siracusa's Bakery where he treated himself to some rich Italian pastries on a regular basis. Grace was of Italian descent, and her Nana Ippolito had shared with her many of the family recipes. Desserts were her specialty, and Bishop easily developed a weakness for them. He could have lingered in the bakery with its aroma of freshly baked bread, but he didn't have time. Luckily, there was still a good selection from which to choose. He purchased a half dozen pasta ciotti, three filled with vanilla cream and three with chocolate. The old woman behind the counter dusted them with powdered sugar and carefully placed them in a box. She secured the box with string from a spool mounted high above the counter.

He pulled into Debbie's driveway, parked behind her Ford Bronco, and walked up to her front door with the pastry box in hand. She opened the door before he had a chance to knock. "I heard you pull into the driveway," she explained. Her dog, Max, was barking and jumping and wagging his short tail. "Max, stop that!" she shouted to no avail. She smiled at Bishop. "He'll calm down in a minute. Come on in."

Bishop handed her the box from the bakery. "These are for you. I hope that you'll like them. You should keep them in the fridge."

"Thanks, Mike. Would you like some coffee?"

"Tea, if you've got it." Bishop couldn't remember the last time that he had had a cup of coffee.

"Sure. No problem. Why don't you sit down in the living room. I'll just be a second."

Bishop sat in one of the oversized chairs, and after darting around a bit, Max decided to check on Debbie in the kitchen. The shabbiness of her furnishings saddened him, but it was evident that this was the most she could afford. She definitely could not afford to lose her job at Trinity. He started paying attention to the television. Dr. Phil was talking with a well-dressed, handsome man in his twenties. Apparently, the man in question was living a lie in refusing to accept the fact that he was an alcoholic. Dr. Phil was trying to explain to this man that he was not only hurting himself by refusing to admit the problem, he was also hurting his family and friends. By the end of the program, Bishop assumed, this man would have an epiphany in which he confronts his inner demons and agrees to get the help that he needs to put his life back together. How wonderful it would be, thought the veteran teacher, if all of our problems could be solved within the hour.

Debbie emerged from the kitchen carrying a tray with two cups and several of the pastries. Max danced around her in anticipation of getting something to eat. She placed the tray on the coffee table, picked up

146

the remote, and cut off Dr. Phil mid-sentence. "These pastries look delicious," she said as she settled in on the sofa. "What are they?"

Bishop explained as he stirred some sugar into his tea and picked up one of the pastries and a napkin. They spent the next few minutes in small talk as they savored the rich Italian dessert. Realizing that he wasn't going to be given even a crumb, Max stretched out on the carpet near Debbie's feet. She was worried about how long her Bronco was going to last. It had been giving her trouble lately, and the estimated repair costs were more than the vehicle was worth. Bishop suggested that she look for a used vehicle at Morehouse Motors. "The owner is on the Holy Trinity Board of Trustees, and he might be able to give you a break," he added. She went into the kitchen to get more coffee for herself and to get more hot water for him.

He wondered what it was that Debbie wanted to tell him. Did it have to do with her relationship with Ed? He knew that she had not been entirely truthful when they had talked on Monday. At that time, Ed's death was considered an accident. Now, everyone knew differently. Did she have some idea of who might have wanted to kill her friend? Might she be involved in some way? If she had done it herself, it was highly unlikely that that was what she wanted to tell him. He decided that it was time to get some answers.

"I was really worried about you these last few days," he said in a more serious tone as he held his second cup of hot tea in both hands.

"I guess I should have called, but I just needed some time to deal with Ed's death. And I wasn't sure that I wanted to go back there anyway after Sister Pat called Ed a loser right to my face. That woman is a monster."

Bishop could not disagree. "I'm glad that you've decided to give it another try. They were just about ready to write you off," he said as he placed the cup back on the tray.

"I was just about ready to write them off too," she said with a laugh. "After the way I was treated, I figured I'd find another job and them tell them that I quit." A look of surprise swept over Bishop's face. He had assumed that she had left town for a few days, but that wasn't the case. He waited for her to continue.

"I must have been to over a dozen places, and the only offer I got was at a convenience store. They were looking for someone for the all-night shift. It was minimum wage, and most of the time, they said that I'd be in the store alone." She reached down to pat the dog. "I didn't want any part of that, did I?" She seemed to be talking to Max at that point.

It was time to add another dose of reality for Debbie to consider. "You know, Lee mentioned that you've been late for work on more than one occasion lately and that you've appeared distracted as well. I hope you realize that I am telling you this as a friend. You really need to address those issues if you plan on keeping that job."

Debbie's speech suddenly became much more animated. "I can explain all that. That's what I wanted to tell you!"

"Go on," he said, although he had no idea what she was about to reveal.

She took a deep breath as she knew that there would be no turning back once she started. "I was in the auditorium the morning that Eddie was killed."

Chapter Sixteen

For a moment, Bishop felt frozen in place. He could not have been more flabbergasted had she said that she had been appointed as the next principal of Holy Trinity High School. His heart began to race as did his mind. What had she just said? Why had she waited until now to tell someone? She was *there*? What did that mean? Had she witnessed the murder? Had she committed the crime herself? He tried to marshal control as quickly as possible.

"I'm afraid that I don't understand," he said softly. If he had ever uttered a stronger understatement, he could not recall it.

Debbie patted the couch next to her as a signal for Max to jump up which he did effortlessly. She put her arms around the dog as he obligingly licked her face. Perhaps she had a moment of regret at having divulged her presence there that morning, but now that she had, she realized that there was no turning back. She continued to hold Max tightly as she began to explain. "I met him at the Blue Moon about a week after he got out of prison. We talked until closing time. It felt like he had not been gone at all, you know?" She added, "I told you that he had lived here for a while." Bishop nodded. He thought it best that he let her tell the story the way she saw fit.

"Anyway, when I heard that they were looking for a janitor at school, I told him about it, and he got the job." She smiled as she recalled that triumph. "I didn't think that they'd hired an ex-con, but he didn't exactly tell them, and they didn't check either." Bishop wasn't surprised to hear of Sister Ann's questionable decision-making abilities.

"Would you like some more tea?" she asked unexpectedly.

"No, thank you. Please continue." Had she offered something stronger, he might have accepted.

"Well, we were talking about getting back together, and my hours and his hours weren't exactly in sync, so he asked me to come in early so that we could talk, you know?"

Bishop thought that he did know what she meant; however, he still was confused. "I thought that Ed left work around 9 or 10 p.m.?"

"Yeah, but he missed the bus one time so he just slept on the couch down in the storage room. That gave him the idea, so he stayed a couple more times, and I came in early using the kitchen entrance. He told me about the trap door on the stage. That was so cool!"

He still was confused. "Why didn't you just meet him here?"

She looked down as if she were embarrassed. "Well, I was still seeing somebody else, and I hadn't made up my mind what to do."

Bishop decided to let that part of the story pass. "You said you were there that morning. Can you tell me exactly what happened?"

She closed her eyes briefly as she relived the moment. "When I got near the trap door, I heard voices coming from the room below, so instead of going down, I went back to the kitchen." Tears came to her eyes as she spoke. "If I hadn't been so afraid of being seen, Eddie might still be alive." She reached into her pocket, pulled out a tissue, and wiped her eyes. Sensing her distress, the dog pawed at her arm as if to remind her that he was still there. She gave him a hug. "You're a good boy, aren't you, Max?"

Bishop gave her a moment to collect her composure. Perhaps she was right. Perhaps if she had gone down there, Ed would still be alive. Yet, there was no point in thinking that way. He offered a different scenario. "You shouldn't blame yourself, Debbie. It seems to me that there's a good chance that if you went down there, you might have been killed as well." She stroked Max as she thought about what Bishop had just said. It obviously was a possibility that she hadn't considered. "I guess you're right," she said as she signaled for Max to get back on the floor.

"Do you mind if I ask a few more questions?"

"No. Go ahead." She pulled her legs beneath her on the sofa, and tucked some loose strands of hair behind her ear.

"How many voices did you hear?"

"Two. Eddie's, of course, and one other man." She seemed much more relaxed now.

"Were they talking or arguing?"

"Talking," she replied without hesitation. Had they been arguing, she might have reacted differently.

"Did Ed sound inebriated?"

"Not really. Not that I noticed."

"Did you recognize the other man's voice?" he asked even though he was reasonably certain of her answer.

"No."

"Would you recognize that voice if you heard it again?" Debbie scrunched her face as she considered how to respond to that unexpected question.

"I … guess so." She paused as she placed herself once again near the opened trap door. "Yes, I can still hear him. I'm sure that I would recognize that voice."

Even as an amateur sleuth, Bishop realized that an earwitness was not nearly as valuable as an eyewitness. Nevertheless, it was something. Although he still had a strong suspicion about Jack's involvement, Debbie's account seemed to eliminate Jack as the other man in the storage room that morning. "Do you remember what they were talking about?"

"They were talking about stocks and sales and stuff like that. Eddie really followed the market, and he talked about it all the time. I never much understood why, but he always read up on it, and he remembered everything. I guess he thought he'd be rich one day." Thinking about him made her smile. "Oh!" she said suddenly as she remembered something else. "Eddie told me that he knew someone had been stealing from the school, and I told him to tell the principal. He told me he couldn't do that because he'd get in trouble too. He told me that he'd handle it himself." She looked at her friend and asked as if it had not previously occurred to her, "Do you think that's what got him killed?"

He raised his eyebrows and shrugged his shoulders. "I don't know, Debbie. I really don't know."

***

He had only stayed at Debbie's apartment for a few more moments. He thanked her for opening up to him, and she thanked him for dropping by and for the Italian pastries.

Bishop was listening to *All Things Considered* on NPR as he drove home. The story concerned a man who left his job as a bail bondsman and became a teacher. It was always good to hear a story about the importance of education. However, it was difficult for the veteran teacher to concentrate on the story. He had his own world of things to consider. Who was the other man whose voice Debbie heard on the morning of Ed Cooper's death? Could it have been Jack? Perhaps she didn't recognize his voice as it emanated from the storage room up into the empty stage area. The two men that Debbie heard had been discussing the stock market. Bishop couldn't recall Jack ever discussing stocks, but that wouldn't necessarily eliminate Jack as a suspect.

A number of nagging questions remained. One involved Ed's comment that someone was stealing from the school. Stealing what? He knew of a series of recent thefts of cash from the girls' locker room. Charlie Mitchell's exam folder and his telephone cord were missing. Perhaps Debbie was right. Ed might have confronted the thief on his own and paid with his life. Yet, if Ed did know who was stealing, why didn't he simply report that to the principal? How could he get in trouble for doing the right thing? On the other hand, what if Ed were the thief himself? He had told Debbie that he was expecting to come into some big money. If he wasn't drunk, perhaps he intentionally had striped the parking lot the way he did as a parting shot to the school. Instead of Ed confronting a thief, maybe someone had confronted him.

As he pulled into his own driveway, one more troubling thought occurred to him. What, if anything, did the paper in Ed's wallet with *Avignon 1868* written on it have to do with Ed's death?

***

After a quick change of clothes, Bishop went into the sunroom and opened all of the windows to let in some fresh air. He watched as two hummingbirds engaged in aerial combat over the bright red feeder filled with sugar water that hung from a shepherd's hook near the house. With a recording of "Opus No. 40 Two Polonaises" by Frederic Chopin playing in the background, he called Lieutenant Hodge and filled him in on his conversations with Hannah and with Debbie. Hodge, in turn, explained that he had failed in his attempt to talk with Ryan Baxter on the telephone, and that he planned on talking with him in person tomorrow.

Having had that filling pasta ciotti in the late afternoon, he didn't want much for dinner which was just as well considering that his options were quite limited. He settled on a tuna salad sandwich and some carrot

153

sticks which he ate while watching *Jeopardy*. When he noticed that one of the categories was "Shakespeare," he played along and answered all of the questions correctly. Grace had often suggested that he audition to become a contestant on that program, but he knew that it was far easier to come up with the right answers when you were in your own home.

About an hour later, he had finished all of the work that he needed to do for his classes the next day. Having made little progress in solving the real life mystery surrounding the death of Ed Cooper, he decided to enter the fictional world of Donna Leon's Commissario Brunetti as he unraveled yet another murder in Venice, the city of masks. He read only a few pages when his cell phone rang. It was Ron Jennings. Since their afternoon conversation had been abbreviated, Bishop assumed that Ron either wanted to discuss Frank's suspension or that he was curious as to the reason for Hannah Ward's visit to his classroom. Neither assumption turned out to be correct.

Bishop filled in the assistant principal on his conversation with Debbie. Ron was pleased that she planned on returning to work, but was troubled that she had not come forward sooner with the fact that she had been in the auditorium the morning of Ed's murder and that the voice she heard was most likely that of the murderer.

"She was frightened and confused," Bishop said in her defense. "Once she realized that his death was not an accident, she began to blame herself for not saying or doing something, and nothing productive can come of that. I've already relayed that information to Lieutenant Hodge, but I don't expect that it will prove to be of any real use."

"What do you make of that business about someone stealing from the school?"

Not wanting to admit that his first thought was that Jack might be involved, he said vaguely, "I've got a couple of ideas that I want to follow up on."

Changing the subject, Ron asked, "Did you happen to talk with Terry at the end of the day?"

"No, I didn't. I spoke with Hannah Ward for a while, and then I stopped by Debbie's place." Knowing of Ron's keen interest in food, he didn't want to sidetrack the discussion by mentioning the pasta ciotti that he had purchased at Siracusa's. "Why do you ask?"

There was a moment of hesitation as Ron considered how to begin. "Just before the last period of the day, Erin Bradley was rushing to get to class, and she slipped and fell down some stairs."

"Is she all right?" asked a concerned Bishop. He had taught Erin the previous year. She was sweet girl with a winning smile. Although she was quite bright, at this point in her life, socializing with her friends took priority over her studies. He wasn't surprised that she might have been running late to class.

"Luckily, she was more than half way down the stairs when she fell. She has some bruises, and a sprained ankle. Nothing broken."

"Glad to hear that," said Bishop, "but what does that this have to do with Terry?"

"I'm getting to that," replied Ron, realizing that he wasn't doing a very good job of getting to the point. "Terry heard the commotion when Erin fell and rushed over to see if she could help. Erin was more embarrassed than hurt, but she couldn't put pressure on that ankle. Just to be on the safe side, Terry asked one of the students to get a wheelchair from the nurse's office."

From the background noises that he heard, Bishop assumed that Ron was in his kitchen fixing himself a snack. He also assumed that there had to be more to the story, so he just waited for Ron to continue.

"Sister Ann came over to investigate the situation. Maybe she was worried that Erin's parents would sue the school or something. Anyway, once Sister Ann showed up, Sister Pat was bound to follow." Ron stopped again as he took a bite of whatever he had prepared. "Instead of showing a little compassion for the girl, Pat took one look at the heel of her shoes, blamed the fall on the fact that she was wearing illegal shoes, and gave her a detention on the spot."

Bishop was disappointed, but not surprised, by the behavior of Sister Pat. However, he still didn't understand where this story was headed. "And the connection to Terry is...?"

"Sorry. I'm getting to that. Shortly after the others arrived, Terry went back to the office. A call came in for Sister Ann who was with Erin. After taking down the message, she decided to put the memo on the principal's desk. Well, you know Terry," he said as he paused to swallow what he had been munching. "Knowing that the two nuns were pre-occupied, she took the opportunity to do a little snooping. She found a list with names on it."

Bishop didn't condone Terry's tactics; nevertheless, his interest was piqued. "Was it a list of appointments for the day?"

"I can't be positive, but I think that it's a list of the teachers they plan to let go."

His anger over their ill-conceived notion that that was the way to solve the school's problems resurfaced. "I don't want to know whose names are on that list," he stated emphatically.

"Yes, you do," said Ron in a forceful voice. "Your name is at the top of the list."

Bishop took a moment to reflect. Once he had refused the principal's request to convince the faculty to accept a salary freeze, he was fairly certain that his name would be added to such a list if one existed. What Terry found merely confirmed that suspicion. The administration had been waiting for him to retire for years. They could use the school's financial difficulties to justify ridding themselves of someone they perceived as a threat to their autonomy. He was sure that the names of some of their other more vocal critics were also on that list.

"I appreciate your concern, but I wouldn't worry about it. If it happens, it happens," he said stoically. "I have a feeling that figuring out who killed Ed Cooper will solve some other problems as well."

"I hope you're right," said Ron, trying to sound as optimistic as possible as he ended the call.

Bishop had given himself ten strikes to find the killer. He wondered how many he had left.

Chapter Seventeen

Bishop woke to the sounds of windswept rain pelting against his bedroom windows. He went about his usual routine in getting ready for another school day. If Sister Ann and Sister Pat had their way, this would be one of his last teaching days at Holy Trinity. He was determined not to let that prospect affect him. Living alone in a house with no mortgage meant that his expenses were relatively low. Financially, he was well prepared for retirement; psychologically, he was not. Over the years, he had been asked to teach at Summit Community College several times. If it came to that, he was certain that he could pick up a class or two as an adjunct instructor. He would also have the time to write that mystery novel that he had put off for so long.

By the time he sat down in the sunroom with his cup of tea, the rain had begun to let up. It was impossible to see his backyard clearly as drops of water clung to the screens. It was equally impossible to know whether his attempt to identify Ed's killer would be successful. Regardless, he was determined to continue to pursue that goal. While Hodge questioned Ryan Baxter, he hoped to talk with Tim Kelleher, Jack Slater, and Elwin Crimins before the end of the day.

His opportunity to chat with Tim came sooner than expected. They both arrived at school at the same time, Tim driving a late model BMW coupe and Bishop in his old Toyota Corolla. Two other senior boys were with Tim. It had stopped raining, and small breaks in the clouds were visible. As they all converged on the main entrance, Bishop asked Tim if he had a few minutes. He explained in front of the others that he wanted to go over a few details of the project that his AP class was working on. Tim readily agreed to meet his teacher in his room after he stopped at his locker.

That gave Bishop just enough time to give Terry a thumbs up as he walked by the office, check his mailbox, and open up his classroom door and windows. By the time he had logged into his laptop, Tim was at the door.

"Come on in, Tim. Have a seat."

Tim appeared his usual relaxed and confident self. He was probably thinking about the senior prom to be held later that night at the country club. Beyond that were graduation parties and the beginning of college life at Villanova. As a high honor roll student and as student council president, Tim had demonstrated the qualities that were likely to lead to a successful career in whatever field he chose. Bishop was about to find out whether honesty was among those qualities. He hoped that Hannah had kept her promise not to discuss their conversation with Tim.

Bishop leaned forward in his chair. "Tim, I know about your use of the trap door on the stage to get to the storage area below."

The young man's confident demeanor quickly faded, replaced by a look of puzzlement and worry. "I thought you wanted to talk about our class project?" he said timidly.

"I had to make some excuse for the benefit of the other guys. This is just between you and me."

"Okay," said Tim with some hesitation.

"I'm not about to get you in trouble for going down there. I already have a pretty good idea of what's been going on, so I need you to be absolutely truthful with me." As he spoke, Tim wiped his sweaty palms on his uniform trousers. "Did you ever run into Mr. Cooper when you and Hannah were in that storage room?"

Tim did not respond right away. After weighing his options, he decided to trust his teacher. "Yes, I did."

Bishop glanced at the wall clock. "We only have a few minutes before the homeroom bell. Tell me what happened."

Tim looked at the clock as well. The minute hand seemed stuck in place. If only the bell would ring, he would have an excuse to leave. Realizing that that would only postpone the inevitable, he was, in an odd way, relieved that he could tell the story.

"The truth is that Hannah and I had been getting to school early and meeting down in that storage room beneath the stage. About a week ago, Mr. Cooper caught us in the act, so to speak." He flushed with embarrassment as he spoke; however, Bishop's outward demeanor remained unchanged as he listened to Tim's account.

"As he came down the ladder, we scrambled to get ourselves together. We didn't even know who he was until he told us. He asked us our names and threatened to report us to the principal unless we gave him some money."

"What happened next?"

"Hannah didn't have any money on her, but I had a twenty, so I gave that to him."

"Are you sure that he demanded the money for his silence, or did you offer to buy his silence? Both of you obviously had a lot to lose if he reported you." Bishop found the fact that someone had silenced Cooper permanently only days later very troubling.

"He asked us for money. I swear!" he said more forcefully.

"I believe you, Tim. Go on." Bishop knew that Hannah had not been completely truthful when he had spoken with her the day before. He also understood exactly why she would have been reluctant to say more than she did.

"He told us that if he ever caught us down there again, it would cost us a lot more than twenty bucks."

"Did you ever think of reporting him to the principal?" asked Bishop.

"For what?"

"Demanding money for his silence? That's extortion," he explained.

"How could we turn him in without getting in trouble ourselves?" Tim asked just as the bell for homeroom rang.

Bishop thanked the young man for his honesty, promised him that what he had shared with him would remain confidential, and watched him as he left the room. Was it possible that Tim feared that the twenty dollars would not be enough to prevent Cooper from reporting them anyway? Could that fear have prompted him to silence him permanently? Bishop had gotten some answers from Tim, but those answers had only led to more troubling questions. Then his thoughts turned to Cooper, the man whose murder he so desperately wanted to solve. What kind of man would extort money from those young people? What else might he have done to seal his own fate?

***

The last announcement of the morning was vintage Sister Ann. *This is a reminder to all students attending the senior prom this evening. All students will be thoroughly screened before entering the facility. Anyone found in violation of the school's substance abuse policy will be denied entrance. Your parents will be notified to take you home.* The students in his homeroom had no reaction to her comment as they were accustomed to such blunt warnings. Bishop, however, inwardly cringed regardless of the number of times he had heard similar announcements. In the carrot vs. the stick debate, the principal clearly preferred the stick as if threats alone would change their behavior. It was his view that the vast majority of students knew better than to spoil their own once-in-a-lifetime senior prom by making poor choices. He recognized that some would partake in underage drinking or other illegal activities, but this would occur at parties later that night or that weekend. The sad fact was that some parents in this permissive society not only condoned, but in some cases actually facilitated such behavior.

Just a moment after morning announcements ended, Charlie Mitchell walked in. It seemed to Bishop that Charlie had spent more time in his homeroom during the past week than he had in his own. When Charlie got to the front of the room, Bishop noticed that several of the boys were whispering to each other and trying to contain their laughter. The veteran teacher simply cleared his throat in an especially forceful manner. When the boys looked up, he gave them a look that said, "Settle down!" With message received, they opened their books.

As if to apologize for their behavior, Bishop whispered to his colleague, "Friday."

"Don't I know it! I've been working on this new exam all week, and it's finally done. Will you take a look at it?" He handed over a manila folder that looked identical to the one that was missing.

"I'd be glad to," replied the department chairman. Left unspoken was his hope that Mitchell had not decided to vent his frustration at having to write a new exam by making it impossibly difficult.

"By the way," Charlie added in a confidential tone, "my little kleptomaniac struck again."

Bishop was only mildly surprised. Charlie didn't seem to connect constantly leaving his room unattended with these thefts. "What's missing this time?"

"My nameplate," he said with some exasperation in his voice. "It wasn't on my desk when I came in this morning. I could understand pilfering that exam, but why would anyone take a nameplate for goodness sakes?"

"For the same reason that they took your phone cord," I imagine.

"Good point," replied Charlie. "When I find the culprit, there will be hell to pay."

As the homeroom period ended, Bishop wished everyone a good weekend and dismissed the group. He asked Greg Ramsey, one of the boys that he had to settle down, if he could have a word with him. Bishop waited until the others had left the room.

"Greg, would you mind telling me what was going on back there?"

"Nothing was going on," he said somewhat defensively.

"Now, Greg," said Bishop, "I believe that you are an honest person. You wouldn't want me to begin to doubt that, would you?"

"No, sir." He wondered why this old man had picked him to question and not one of the others.

"Then let me ask one more time. Does this have anything to do with Mr. Mitchell's nameplate by any chance?" Bishop had a strong feeling that the appearance of Mitchell in the room and the reaction of the boys were connected. He had a group of students waiting to come into class, so he needed to move this discussion along.

Had Bishop pulled a quarter from behind his ear, Greg could not have been more surprised. How had he known? The truth was Greg's only option. "We didn't put it there," he said.

163

"Where?" asked Bishop calmly.

"In the men's room. Someone put it on the grate in one of the urinals."

It took great power of will for Bishop to control his desire to burst out laughing. "Do you know who did that?"

"No, sir, I don't," with a tone of finality that suggested that he really did not know.

Bishop thanked Greg for his honesty, gave him a pass in case he was late for his first class, and let his own class get settled. He asked them to work quietly for a few moments. After taking attendance, he sent off a quick email to Charlie alerting him to the whereabouts of his nameplate. As he typed, he had to suppress thoughts of taking aim at "Mr. Charles Mitchell."

***

The other day, his 9th graders had expressed their anxiety regarding final exams; today, the 11th graders articulated a different concern. When Bishop began the class by asking if there were any questions, Mary Dumont's hand shot up into the air. "Why is so much of the literature we've read so depressing?" Several others indicated that they had the same question.

He always welcomed questions that gave him the opportunity to engage his students in spirited discussion. "That's an excellent question, Mary. Give me an example of what you have in mind."

Without any hesitation, she offered an example. "Well, in *A Separate Peace*, why did Finny have to die?" Students often struggled to understand the ending of that novel by John Knowles. Although they had spent time discussing it earlier in the year, this was the purpose of review. It also gave him an opportunity to address the larger question that Mary had raised.

"I know that you don't have your copies of that book with you, but that's all right. When you really own a book, you shouldn't need to look something up in order to make a point. You won't have any of your books with you when you take the exam, right?" A number of students shook their heads in agreement although every single one of them undoubtedly wished that they could do just that. "Does anyone remember what Gene himself said about Finny's death?" He waited a moment for the question to sink in.

Andrea partially raised her hand. The pained expression on her face indicated that she felt that her answer was probably wrong. In fact, she prefaced her answer by saying, "This is probably wrong." He had always tried to discourage his students from making that remark. "What is so wrong about being wrong?" he often asked. He would explain that making a mistake was a very good way to learn. In addition, Bishop knew that almost anything that a student might say was unlikely to be so far afield that he could not find something of value in it to further the discussion. After her self-deprecating preface, Mary continued. "Didn't Gene imply … sort of anyway … that it was only through his acceptance of his role in Finny's death that he was able to … you know … move on with his own life?" She needn't have worried that anyone would dismiss or ridicule her response, not that Bishop would have allowed that to happen under any circumstances. Quite the opposite was true as he noticed several students pick up their pens and jot down Mary's comment in their notebooks.

"Absolutely right, Mary! Once Gene is able to accept the evil in himself, which only occurs after Finny's death, once he makes his own 'separate peace' with that, if you will, he is able to face the world beyond the school where the events occurred."

Wanting to contribute something to the discussion, Don raised his hand to add, "The school was Devon Prep."

"That's right," said Bishop who quickly brought the focus back to Mary's original comment. "We might conclude, then, that John Knowles, puts the emphasis at the end of the novel on Gene's growth rather than on Finny's death."

"The sadness is still there," insisted Mary.

"Yes, there's sadness, but there is also a sense of hope,' added Bishop. "To get back to Mary's initial question, it seems true that many of the works that we've studied have an element of sadness. However, out of that sadness an important lesson about life emerges that could not have been delivered as effectively in any other way. And, I think that it connects the literature to real life, where, as we know, not every situation ends happily ever after."

The students took a moment to consider what he had just said. Zack was furiously flipping through his notes. When he found what he was looking for, he raised his hand. "I think I've found one story that is just plain depressing … 'The Minister's Black Veil' by Nathaniel Hawthorne." As he announced his choice, Jane quickly voiced her approval. "Oh, God!" she said. "I think I had nightmares for a week after reading that story." A few students indicated their agreement.

"There's no doubt that Hawthorne's work is on the dark side," Bishop responded, "but remember that the subtitle of the story is 'A Parable'. What does that mean, Phil?" Bishop had a habit of asking a question and then indicating the name of the student from whom he wanted an answer. It sometimes led to interesting exchanges.

When Phil heard his name called, he jumped to attention. He flushed as he realized that everyone was waiting for him to give the answer. The problem was that he didn't know what the question was and everyone else did.

"What?" asked a bewildered Phil. Other students were waving their hands in the air, hoping to get Bishop to forget Phil and get the answer from one of them.

"What 'what'?" replied his teacher.

"What was the question?" Phil said as he squirmed in his seat.

"I've already asked the question. I was hoping for an answer."

"Would you please repeat the question?"

"I'm not even sure that I remember the question at this point," Bishop was clearly teasing Phil and subtly making the point that he needed to avoid daydreaming in class. "I believe that I asked for the definition of a parable."

"Oh," said the young man, relieved that he knew the answer. "A parable is a story used to teach a moral or a lesson."

"Exactly!" Bishop not only had the answer he wanted; he also had the undivided attention of the entire class for the remainder of the period.

Mary raised her hand again. Reference to this story validated her point. "Hawthorne seems to be saying that every person lives behind a mask. Isn't that depressing?"

Bishop spent the next few moments helping the class arrive at the following summary: The story centers on the actions of a Reverend Hooper who one day appears before his congregation wearing a gossamer black veil covering his face. The townspeople are troubled by his sermon on "secret sin" and the part of ourselves that we hide from the world. Rather than a one-day gimmick, the veil becomes a permanent part of the minister. The townspeople speculate on the nature of the sin that he hides from the world. Even at the hour of his death, he refuses to lift the veil. Having established the summary, Bishop quoted from memory Hooper's dying words: "'I look around me, and, lo! on every visage a Black Veil!' What does that mean?"

Phil Perry blurted out his answer. "He's hallucinating! He's the only one wearing the veil." That evoked a few laughs from his classmates.

Mary looked directly at Phil as she explained, "He's not hallucinating. That's the way he really feels, and that's just sad if you ask me."

He looked around the room and called on someone who had not yet contributed to the discussion. "What do you think, Alex?"

Alex thought for a moment before answering. "I remember you telling us when we first read it that Hawthorne based the story on a real person. That's pretty bizarre if you ask me," he said.

"Do you mean that it's bizarre that Hawthorne based his story on a real person?" Bishop asked, knowing that that was not what he meant but hoping to make a point about the need for precise communication.

"No, the fact that someone actually lived his life that way is what's bizarre."

"Granted, none of us would go through life wearing a literal veil, but don't we all wear metaphorical veils?" As if proving his point, as he looked around the room, he noticed that few students were making direct eye contact with him. "Aren't there some aspects of *our* lives that we share with few, if any, others? You can say that Reverend Hooper's life was sad or depressing or that his behavior was bizarre; however, the point of the story, the lesson or parable, if you will, is that we are all sinners in some way. Perhaps Hawthorne's story reminds us of the need for compassion, tolerance, and understanding of others. My problem with Hooper, and with Hawthorne for that matter, is not that he makes us acknowledge the secret

168

sin in all men, but rather the fact that that is all he sees." He paused for a moment to let that idea sink in before moving on to another topic for review.

After class, Bishop found himself drawn back to Hawthorne's story. Wasn't the investigation into the death of Ed Cooper an attempt to lift the black veil from the face of the murderer? Who had committed that secret sin? Was it Jack Slater who had expressed his dislike for Ed from the start and apparently was having some financial problems? Was it Ryan Baxter who had not been working for UPS at the time of the murder as they had previously thought? Why had Ryan and Amy broken up? What about Tim Kelleher? Supposedly, he had been forced to buy Ed's silence after being caught with Hannah in the storage room. Might he have lashed out at Ed when Ed demanded more money or threatened to report his behavior? Could Debbie Bates have made up the story of hearing another man's voice in the storage room to hide her own involvement in her boyfriend's death? Who owned the car with the numbers on it that Elwin Crimins claims to have seen on Newbury Street? Had he really seen anything significant? Might the murderer be someone else who walked the halls of Holy Trinity with a look of apparent innocence? Whoever it was had been well schooled in the art of deception. Whoever it was, Bishop was determined to lift that mask and expose the truth.

Chapter Eighteen

After yesterday's brouhaha at lunch, Bishop was looking forward to
spending a few relaxing minutes with his colleagues. If the list that Terry
had seen on Sister Ann's desk was what he thought it was, this would be
one of the last days that he would have his peanut butter and jelly sandwich
in the faculty lunchroom. Of course, the list might not have anything to do
with those about to be let go. It might simply be a list of teachers that she
needed to see about a particular student. Using the approach that ninety
percent of the things people worry about never happen, he forced thoughts
of the end of his teaching career out of his mind. He had other, more
pressing concerns.

As he walked past the main office, he noticed that two girls were
in an animated conversation with Sister Pat. From what he heard, he
quickly pieced together that the girls were attempting to sign out of school
for the remainder of the day. Given the facts that it had stopped raining, it
was a Friday, and they were seniors, it wasn't surprising that they would
try to skip out. It was also the night of the senior prom, and these girls
probably had a lot to do to get ready for the biggest social event of the
year. Sister Pat was in their faces as she screamed, "You're not going
anywhere but back to class, and if I hear another word out of either of you,
you won't be going to the prom either!" With that, Sister Meany succeeded
in making both girls to cry. Bishop was about to get into the fray. What did
he have to lose? He was at the top of the list for a pink slip anyway.

Just as he was about to speak, Ron Jennings rushed over and got
between Sister Pat and the girls. A small crowd of onlookers had
assembled out of curiosity. Ron explained to his fellow assistant principal
that both girls had legal excuses written by their parents for them to leave
school. He waved the notes in the air as he spoke, signaling to the girls that

they were free to go. "There's nothing we can do when a student has the permission of a parent," he said, hoping to reason with Sister.

"Well, that stinks!" she said emphatically as she turned around and noticed some of the students still gathered nearby. "What are you busybodies standing around for? Get some place fast!" The group could not have dispersed more quickly had they seen a ghost. Bishop winked at Ron as he made his way to lunch.

He made a point of walking through the kitchen. He wanted to be sure that Debbie had returned to work. She didn't see him, but he did catch a glimpse of her stirring the contents of a large pot on the stove. The steam was swirling into her face. It was a tough job with little pay and little thanks, but until she could find something else, it was better than no job at all.

As he entered the lunchroom, he saw his old friend, Sister Annunciata, seated at a table by herself. "Well, hello there, stranger!" She stood up to greet him as he gave her a hug. "It's so good to see you!"

"Oh, Michael! It's good to see you too!" Sister Annunciata wore the simple black habit of the Sisters of the Holy Rosary. A veil covered most of her white hair, and large wooden beads hung from her belt. No one knew exactly how old any of the sisters were, but it seemed a safe assumption that she was well into her eighties. Her clear blue eyes radiated warmth when she smiled. A demanding but excellent teacher, she had obediently accepted a retirement orchestrated by the nefarious Sister Pat.

"How does it feel to be back in the classroom?"

"It's something I hadn't expected, but I'm enjoying it so far."

"I'm sure that it must be difficult to step in at the last minute."

"Not really," she said modestly. "It's not as if they've changed the Articles of Confederation," she said with a laugh.

171

They spent a few minutes catching up on old times and old friends. "When I walked in this morning, I realized that none of the students would know who I am, and I don't recognize half of the faculty either," she admitted.

"Well, you know how it is around here," he winked, knowing that she knew exactly what he meant.

"I was so saddened to hear that there had been a death here earlier this week and a fight here yesterday," she said, "and to think that teachers were involved!" She shook her head in disbelief.

He assumed that she meant teachers were involved in the fight and not the murder. As a master of understatement, he said, "It's been a difficult time for the faculty."

"Sister Ann was so upset when she called me yesterday and explained the situation." She dipped her spoon into the Styrofoam cup holding her soup.

"Everyone was quite shocked by Frank's behavior, and his suspension for the remainder of the school year was a bit of a shock as well," he said truthfully.

"To attack Dan Morehouse of all people," she said as she finished her soup and looked at the clock. "Michael, you'll have to excuse me. I better get back to my room before the kids do."

"Of course," Bishop said. "I'm just curious, though. Why did you say 'of all people' when you mentioned Dan?"

He assumed that she would refer to all of Dan's hard work on the board over the years. He was wrong.

"Because Dan is Sister Ann's nephew," she said softly as she left the room.

***

172

As he walked back to his room for his afternoon classes, he thought about what he had just learned. Why hadn't he known that Dan was related to Sister Ann? That certainly helped to explain why Dan was on the board and on the finance committee. It was more than the donation of a car to the school. If Sister Ann had somehow mismanaged the school's funds, she had her nephew in place to cover her tracks.

He saw Hannah walking towards him in the hall, but she avoided eye contact with him as she passed by. Tim had probably filled her in on his conversation with Bishop that morning. Perhaps she felt some guilt that she hadn't mentioned their confrontation with Ed Cooper. Perhaps she was embarrassed that her former teacher now knew of her intimate relationship with Tim. Yes, people were far more comfortable with their masks firmly in place.

His afternoon classes were uneventful, and for that he was grateful. It had been a long week. A sense of exhilaration was palpable in the halls as the seniors prepared for their big night, and everyone else headed out for a weekend of rest and relaxation. With finals quickly approaching, some of them would even manage to squeeze in a little time for study.

Bishop remained at his desk in the empty classroom. He picked up the folder containing Charlie Mitchell's replacement exam for Modern Novels, hoping that he wouldn't need to ask Charlie to make any changes. As he read through the exam, he was pleasantly surprised to find that the extensive section of multiple-choice questions had been replaced with some identifications that required answers of several sentences each. There was also a section of questions requiring one-paragraph answers as well as a final section requiring a full-length essay. Each section had several options so that students could choose which questions they felt most prepared to discuss. Overall, the exam was challenging but fair. It would provide the students with an opportunity to demonstrate their knowledge of the course material as well as their writing ability. The exam could easily be completed within the three hours allotted. It was a major improvement over the exam that Charlie had been recycling for years. Bishop was almost glad that the folder with the old exam had been misplaced.

Bishop walked down the hall with the folder in hand hoping that Charlie was still in the building. The lights were still on, and the door was open. His room got the afternoon sun that made for some uncomfortable conditions at this time of the year. It also made it a perfect place for plants. Along the back wall and suspended from hooks along the windows were as many plants as there were in all of the other classrooms combined. Bishop recognized a snake plant in an enormous container and some sort of a palm that was taller than Charlie. He was either talking to himself or to the plants while he watered them.

Bishop rapped on the open door to get his attention. Charlie turned to see who it was. "Come in, Michael, come in."

"I had a chance to look over the exam, and I wanted to make sure it got back to you safely."

"I appreciate that. There's no way I would write a third one. What did you think?"

"It's a good exam, Charlie. You just need to adjust the point values. What you have adds up to only ninety points."

"What a relief! That's easy enough to fix. I'll drop it off in the office on my way out. Thanks for looking it over so quickly."

"Not a problem."

Charlie started laughing to himself.

"What's so funny?" asked Bishop.

"I messed up the point values on purpose just to see if you'd catch the mistake." Bishop had no way of knowing if that was true or if Charlie was just covering for his error. Charlie shook his head as he laughed again. "I should have known better. You're still as sharp as ever."

As he walked back to his room to pack up for the weekend, he thought about what Charlie had said. If he was still so sharp, why hadn't he figured out what had happened to Ed Cooper?

***

He had wanted to talk with Tim Kelleher, Jack Slater, and Elwin Crimins at some point during the day. He had managed to catch Tim before homeroom period, and from that conversation he had learned that Ed had taken money from the young man in exchange for his silence regarding the actions of Tim and Hannah. If Tim was telling the truth, what did that say about Ed? If he was capable of blackmailing those kids, what else might he have been doing? He had told Debbie that he was coming into some big money. Twenty dollars wasn't big money by anyone's standards. Who else might have been the target of a shakedown?

He hadn't seen Jack all day. For a guy who usually spent a fair amount of time hanging around the faculty lounge trying to pick up the latest bit of gossip, he had been practically invisible for the last few days. He had even missed the pizza and wings fiasco. Something was clearly not right. Was he simply worried about his wife's health? Luigi, the pizza man, had mentioned that Jack had been spending a lot of money on lottery and scratch-off tickets, and then suddenly stopped. His changed behavior coincided with Ed's death. Hannah said that she had seen Mr. Slater in the area. Bishop and Jack needed to talk and the sooner the better.

Elwin was next on the agenda. Since he lived so close to the school, Bishop decided to walk. Instead of going up to Elm Street and then

175

down Newbury, he took the shortcut through the wooded lot. If his theory was correct, this was the path taken by Ed's killer. He had parked on Newbury Street, and Crimins was the only person who saw something. How reliable a witness was a man suffering from dementia? He was about to find out.

There was a fairly well defined path through the lot. Apparently, a number of other people besides the killer found this a convenient shortcut. Once he was off of the hot pavement at the back of the school, the air became noticeably cooler. The air was still quite damp and muggy from the morning rain. Wouldn't it be ironic if he found something like a monogrammed cufflink or packaging from a special brand of cigarettes that would lead him straight to the culprit? Other than a few cans of Bud Lite, there was nothing to be found.

When he emerged from the woods, he faced the back yards of the even-numbered houses on Newbury Street. Most of them looked as if they had been built by the same contractor. All were one-story structures with a small back porch on the right. Most had a detached garage in the back with a long narrow driveway leading to Newbury Street. A few of the yards were fenced in, but most were not. He walked into the back yard of the nearest house without a fence, down the driveway, and onto the sidewalk. The neighbors must not be overjoyed to have strangers trespassing on their property in order to take that shortcut to the school. He just added his name to the list of offenders, but at least, he hadn't used the shortcut simply because he was lazy. As far as he could see, each house had its own driveway, so there was no need for a car to park on the street, unless of course, its owner wasn't from the neighborhood.

224 was only a few houses down from where Bishop had cut through the yard. The cement walk that led to the front door needed repair.

Some of the sections had shifted over the course of many winters. Weeds left unattended had taken over in the many gaps and cracks. Although the roof looked new, the rest of the exterior gave the impression of benign neglect. As he approached the front door, he heard the sounds of a television coming through the open windows.

A middle-aged woman looked out at him before answering his knock. She was short and heavy. She was wearing a pink blouse and a pair of tan slacks that only emphasized her shape. Her short hair was mostly gray, and the wrinkles on her face indicated that she either spent a great deal of time outside or that she was a smoker.

"May I help you?" She probably assumed that he was lost.

"Yes, I hope so. My name is Michael Bishop, and I teach at Holy Trinity. I was wondering if I might speak with Elwin Crimins for a few moments." From the corner of his eye, he caught a glimpse of the old man seated in a recliner watching Judge Judy on television.

"My Dad isn't well. What's this about? My name is Shirley. Maybe I can help." Her smile revealed her nicotine-stained teeth.

"That's very kind of you. May I come in?"

"Yes, of course. Let's go in the kitchen." She pointed him in the right direction. He glanced again at the old man in the living room. He kept repeating, "You're a liar!" to someone on the program.

The kitchen was clean but badly in need of an update. There was a tray with a number of prescription medications on the counter. Shirley offered Bishop some coffee, but he declined. She sat across from him and waited for him to explain the reason for his visit.

He hadn't planned out what he wanted to say. "As you know, there was a terrible tragedy at Holy Trinity on Monday."

"Oh, yes!" she interjected before he had a chance to say any more. "To think that that happened so close by. This has always been such a quiet neighborhood. I've been keeping the doors locked." She looked at the well-dressed older man with kind eyes sitting across from her. "I only let you in cause you don't look like a murderer to me." She laughed half-heartedly as she probably hoped that her assumption was correct.

Bishop responded with a reassuring smile. "The police are doing their best to apprehend the culprit, and we're all trying to do our part. I know that Officer Hollins was here earlier in the week, and I'd like to follow up on what your father told him. It would only take a moment."

She shrugged her shoulders. "I don't know that Dad can be of any help. The last few months his dementia just seems to be getting worse."

"That must be very difficult for you," he said although he actually had very little idea of what was involved in the 24/7 care for such an individual.

"He took good care of me for a lot of years," she said as she stood up. "Let's see what he remembers, but don't expect too much." She led the way into the living room. The carpet was worn in places, and portraits of John F. Kennedy and Pope John Paul II hung on the wall behind the sofa. Elwin looked confused when he saw a man walking into the room behind his daughter. Apparently, he hadn't noticed when Bishop had come into the house. He was wearing a flannel shirt, a pair of baggy pants, and slippers. He had numerous liver spots on his hands and face. He was mostly bald except for a few wispy white hairs. "Is this the mailman?" he asked his daughter.

"No, Dad." She picked up the remote and hit the mute button. "This is Michael Bishop. He teaches at the school across the way. He

178

wants to talk to you for a minute." She stood beside her father and put her hand gently on his shoulder.

Bishop sat in a wooden rocker next to the television. "Hello, Mr. Crimins. It's nice to meet you." He gave him a reassuring smile.

"Are you the mailman?"

"No, sir. I'm a teacher."

He thought about that for a moment. "Why would a teacher be delivering the mail?"

"I'm not delivering the mail. I wanted to ask you a question. Do you remember talking to Officer Hollins earlier this week?"

"Hollins? Is he the mailman?" Shirley shook her head as if to tell Bishop what he already knew. Elwin was not going to be able to help.

Bishop answered patiently. "No, sir. Hollins is a police officer."

"Well, that's just who I need. Somebody has been stealing my mail!"

"That's not true, Dad. Some days we just don't get any mail." Bishop got the impression that they had had this conversation a number of times. He stood up to say goodbye.

"I'm sorry," Shirley said. "Some days are better than others."

"No need to apologize," said Bishop. "I was hoping that he would remember the car that he described to Hollins."

She picked up the remote and turned the sound back on. As she walked him to the door, Mr. Crimins spoke. Bishop thought that he was talking to the television again. "That car had numbers all over it. I didn't think that was the mailman."

Bishop turned back so quickly that he stumbled on the edge of the carpet. "Yes, that car. Can you tell me about that car?"

Elwin became more animated as he talked. He kept pointing to the street. "I was looking for the mailman, but that wasn't him. I think that somebody has been taking my mail." He looked to Shirley as he asked, "Is this Hollins? Is he going to find out who's been taking the mail?"

"No, Dad. This is Mr. Bishop. He's a teacher. No one has been stealing our mail. Sometimes we just don't have any mail."

Bishop knew the chances of getting any meaningful information from the old man were slim; nevertheless, he felt that he had to try one more time.

"Does the mailman park his truck in the same spot on the street every day?"

"Yes, that's right." He seemed pleased that Bishop understood him.

"Was a different car parked in that spot early Monday morning?"

"That's right. It was a different truck. It had numbers all over it."

"Did you see who was driving the truck?"

"How could I see him? There were numbers all over it." He took a sip of water from a cup on the small table next to the sofa. He then turned his attention back to the television where Judge Judy was listening to the story of one of the individuals before her court. "You're a liar!"

Bishop once again headed for the front door. He thanked Shirley for her cooperation.

"I'm sorry that he wasn't able to provide you with any information."

"There's no need to apologize. He's a very lucky man to have you as his caregiver."

Bishop took the same route to get back to the school. He thought about the old man. He wondered if he would end up like that in another

180

twenty years. Who would take care of him? He forced those fears from his mind by focusing on what Elwin was trying to tell him. Every vehicle had a license plate. Were those the numbers that he meant? If the vehicle was a truck, it might have had a company phone number displayed on the side panels. He had a feeling that Elwin Crimins had seen the murderer that day, but the identity of that person was lost in the recesses of his mind.

Chapter Nineteen

Spring weather is quite unpredictable, and this day was no exception. The driving rain of early morning had given way to a perfectly delightful afternoon. It was not as if senior prom would have been cancelled due to bad weather, but Bishop was happy for the students that the weather would cooperate.

He reflected on the ways that prom night had changed over the years. It was not uncommon for parents to spend around a thousand dollars on this one event. Girls needed to find that perfect dress that no one else had and that would probably not be worn again. That cost alone could easily run into the hundreds of dollars. Not to mention a trip to the salon to get their hair and nails done. Gentlemen had to rent a tux and buy flowers. Some of them orchestrated elaborate and expensive "promposals." Bishop wondered if that word had made it into *Merriam-Webster's Dictionary* yet. In addition to the cost of the tickets themselves, a pre-prom dinner, limousine rental, professional photography, and after-prom party added to the expense. For the indulgent parents, no cost was too great in order to ensure that the young people had "a night to remember."

Bishop tried to remember his own senior prom. He could scarcely recall that event some fifty years later. What was the name of his date? Linda. Linda something. He could still bring to mind what she looked like, but what was her name? Why was he having difficulty remembering? Linda. Linda DiDonato? No, that wasn't right. Linda DelDonna? Perhaps if he didn't try too hard to remember, it would come back to him.

He hadn't planned what to have for dinner. A quick search of his pantry served as a reminder that he needed to do some serious grocery shopping. Just as on the previous night, he settled on a can of tuna fish that he dumped into a bowl along with some chopped up celery and onion. It wasn't until that point that he checked to see if he had any mayonnaise or even bread for that matter. Fortunately, the jar of mayo was not quite empty and there was still a half a loaf of 12-grain bread. He ate the sandwich in less time that it took to make it. Shopping and making meals were tasks that he avoided as much as he could. Grace had done all the cooking during their thirty-eight years of marriage, and since her death, he chose to dine out or to pick up something prepared to take home. That combination was far from ideal, but it worked.

He had an hour or so before he had to leave for the country club where the prom was being held. He placed a CD of Domenico Scarlatti's keyboard sonatas in the player in the sunroom, and picked up the Donna Leon mystery that he had been reading. Bishop knew that in this work of fiction, the relentless yet patient pursuit of justice would eventually lead Commissario Brunetti to solving another murder in his beloved city of Venice. Would Bishop's pursuit of Cooper's killer be as successful in real life? Bishop was no Brunetti. Nevertheless, he thought of Brunetti's dealings with his officious superior, Vice-Questore Giuseppe Patta. If Brunetti had to navigate around Patta, so too did Bishop have to contend with the incompetent Sister Pat and the mercenary Sister Ann. If Brunetti often relied on the efficient but devious secretary, Signorina Elettra Zorzi, Bishop could count on the resourceful and inquisitive Terry Mortenson in the main office. There was, however, one glaring difference between the fictional detective and himself. Brunetti had Paola, his intelligent, independent wife whose wit, humor, and wisdom contributed to his success. Bishop had only his memories of Grace.

***

His reading was interrupted by a phone call from Lieutenant Hodge.

"Sorry to bother you on a Friday night, but I thought you'd want to know that I caught up with Ryan Baxter."

"What did he have to say for himself?"

"He admitted that he had lied to Amy about where he was the morning of the murder. As we established, he had already lost his job at UPS. Amy broke up with him when she found out where he really was that morning."

"At Holy Trinity?" Bishop suggested.

"I'm afraid not. He was with another woman."

"Oh, I see." After a moment's pause, he asked, "Do you believe him?"

"Mr. Bishop, in my business, it pays not to believe anyone. I checked out his story for myself. The young lady's name is Amanda Minton. She lives in Ridgefield. I talked with her myself, and she claims that he spent the night there."

"I thought you just said that you don't necessarily believe anyone."

"That's right. That's why I spent an hour talking to her neighbors who all seemed to agree that her car and his motorcycle were in the driveway that night. A few of them apparently follow Amanda's love life quite closely, and that motorcycle announces Ryan's comings and goings rather emphatically."

"I guess he did have something to hide, but it wasn't murder. If we can safely remove him from the list of suspects, I have two names that we can add." Bishop went on to tell Hodge about his conversations with Hannah Ward and Tim Kelleher. Hodge agreed that it was an angle worth pursuing. Fear of Cooper reporting them might have been enough of a motive for one or both of them to silence him.

"It raises another good question," said the lieutenant.

"What's that?"

"Who else might Cooper have tried to blackmail?"

It was, indeed, a very good question.

***

While taking a shower, Bishop mulled over what Hodge had told him. Ryan Baxter was no longer a suspect. Another strikeout. He hadn't had a chance to talk with Jack again. After that, who else?

He put on his charcoal gray suit, white shirt, maroon tie, and brown Oxfords, and checked himself in the mirror. Not bad for seventy. Although he didn't feel much differently from when he had arrived at Trinity forty-five years ago, he certainly had changed over the years. A collage of all the photos of him that had been taken for the *Trinitarian*, the school's yearbook, would capture the aging process. If Sister Ann and Sister Pat succeeded in implementing staff cuts, this year's school photo would be his last. There had to be a way to stop them. He just didn't know how he could do it.

He arrived at the country club about ten minutes early. He parked in a lot farthest from the entrance so that he could walk the extra steps. The scent of lilacs filled the air, and the scattered trails of cirrus clouds in the western sky promised a stunning sunset. As Bishop reached the door, a limo pulled up under the portico of the building, and three couples emerged to join their classmates. Parents and prom-goers were taking photos and selfies with the meticulously kept gardens as a backdrop. Bishop anticipated a few relaxing hours as the seniors enjoyed each other's company as a class for one of the last times before graduation sent them on their separate journeys. The evening, however, turned out to be far from relaxing.

He bypassed the small line that had formed awaiting inspection by one of the assistant principals before being allowed into the dance. Bishop waved his greeting to Ron who was complimenting the students on their attire while he checked them in. Sister Pat, whose scowl indicated that she was in a particularly bad mood, didn't bother to acknowledge Bishop's presence so he made a point of saying something to her.

"Good evening, Sister."

"What's so good about it?" That was a typical comment from Holy Trinity's Sister Meany. Perhaps the prom was cutting into her television time. Just then the two girls who had been harassed by Sister Pat for their early dismissal arrived with their dates.

"I see that you two made a miraculous recovery," she said sarcastically.

One of the girls flushed with embarrassment but said nothing. The other girl wasn't about to be intimidated. "We never said we were sick. We had legal excuses to leave."

Before that conversation escalated, Bishop motioned for those who had been checked in to follow him. The members of the prom committee had done a remarkable job of transforming the banquet hall into the world of a "Starry Night," the theme that the seniors had chosen. To the left were a number of round tables with white tablecloths and a floral centerpiece. At each place, there was a tall glass filled with party favors. To the right stood an enormous star with an arch-shaped opening. Clusters of tiny twinkling lights were strung along the far wall. Hundreds of stars of various sizes hung from the ceiling. Spotlights positioned from the left and right caught the glittering surfaces creating a dazzling display.

Some couples milled about on the dance floor, not quite sure what to do or how to act. Others gravitated to the trays of snacks that were

186

beautifully arranged around an enormous punch bowl. As Bishop chatted with a group of students about the weather and complimented them on their attire, he noticed Sister Ann in an animated conversation with the deejay, a tall man in his twenties wearing a Grateful Dead T-shirt and faded jeans. He wore a baseball cap backwards with the visor in the back. More than likely, she was dictating what music she did and did not want him to play. He listened respectfully as she did all of the talking, more than likely not planning to comply with any of her demands.

Bishop spotted a couple of the other chaperones over by the large star. They were talking among themselves and watching as couples posed in the archway as a professional photographer gave them instructions and snapped away. Heads turned as Sister Pat stomped across the dance floor. Like the parting of the Red Sea, students made way for her. Bishop wandered in that direction to see if he could figure out what bee had gotten in her bonnet this time.

"Did you see that Hoffman girl?" she barked at the principal. Before she had a chance to respond, she added, "That dress! It's disgraceful!"

Sister Ann put a finger to her lips in an attempt to get her good friend to lower her voice. A quick glance around the room failed to locate the offending party. "Where is she?" whispered Sister Ann.

"She's right over there!" she said loudly as she pointed in the direction of several couples queued up for their portrait. "She's wearing a scarlet gown with a split on the side that goes halfway to Kansas." A few of the seniors exchanged anxious looks as the conversation continued.

Sister Ann signaled to the deejay that he should play some music, hoping that that would neutralize Sister Pat's loud voice. "It's not that bad,

Pat. Just ignore it." She smiled at a few students who were nearby and started to walk away.

"What about that top?" the assistant principal bellowed. The music had only made her speak even louder. "She isn't leaving much to the imagination! I say we tell her to cover up, and if she refuses, we call her parents to come and pick her up." In her mind, it was a done deal, and she was looking forward to seeing it play out.

Sister Ann checked her watch. It was only a few minutes past eight o'clock, and she already had a headache and wanted to go back to the convent. She looked around the room. Few of the girls were dressed modestly. Most of the gowns the girls wore were either strapless, backless, or too tight. She knew that this was a battle not worth fighting. She remembered what had happened a few years earlier when Sister Pat had been on a similar rampage. About half of the seniors left early, and many of them demanded their ticket money back. The parents naturally sided with their kids, and it took a week or more for tempers to calm down. "We can't expect them to come in their school uniforms, can we?" Hoping to divert her friend's attention, she added, "This music is starting to give me a headache."

"You call this 'music'?" she asked as she scowled at the deejay and took aim at the table of refreshments.

***

Having finished checking everyone in, Ron Jennings wanted to introduce his date to his good friend, Michael Bishop. Over the years, Ron had been in a couple of relationships that had left their emotional scars. Bishop was pleased to see Ron smiling again as he escorted the lady to meet him. She was rather petite with short, dark, curly hair and a winning smile. Her sleeveless aqua dress, which was modestly only slightly above the knee, emphasized her physical fitness. She looked familiar. Did he know her or did she simply look like someone that he knew? He was fairly certain that she was not a former student. Why did his memory fail him now? Was she a waitress at one of the many restaurants that he frequented? No, that wasn't right. In just seconds, they would arrive. Wait! The bank! That's it!

"Mary Ellen! How nice to see you! You look lovely!" Bishop said as he shook hands with her and then with Ron.

Before either one of them could respond, a young man who approached from the opposite direction said, "Excuse me, Mr. Bishop. May I speak with you privately for a moment?"

He turned around, saw the look on Billy Sprowl's face, and told Ron and Mary Ellen that he would catch up with them in a few minutes. Billy's date was nowhere in sight. Could he have had an argument with her so soon after arriving? Billy was a star baseball player and well liked by his classmates and the staff. Bishop had been particularly impressed by a decision that Billy had made at the end of his junior year. The young man had been in honors English since his freshman year and was scheduled to take Bishop's Advanced Placement English Literature and Composition as a senior. Around this time last year, Billy had also asked to speak privately with the veteran teacher. He explained that after careful consideration of all of the challenges that he would face as a senior, he concluded that he would not be able to give one hundred percent effort to an honors English class. The majority of students in a similar situation would have been satisfied with less than one hundred percent effort and taken the class because it would enhance their transcript for college. Bishop respected this young man's maturity and integrity. After talking with him for a few moments this evening, he would have reason to change his mind.

***

"You did what?" asked a bewildered Bishop. He and Billy had decided that a walk around the well-lit grounds of the country club would afford them the ability to talk freely. Billy told his date that Mr. Bishop wanted to speak with him for a few minutes.

Like the ancient mariner in Coleridge's poem who had to admit that he had shot the albatross, Billy painfully repeated what he had done. "I took the Modern Novels final exam from Mr. Mitchell's desk." Billy's voice was shaky, and his face was pale.

So many thoughts ran through Bishop's mind. Billy was just about the last person that he would have suspected. Why did he steal that test? What would Charlie Mitchell do when he found out? How would Sister Ann and Sister Pat discipline him for such an offense? How would this affect his scholarship to Holy Cross? Why did Billy decide to tell him?

"Did you take the phone cord from Mr. Mitchell's room?"

"No."

"Did you take his nameplate?"

"No, I didn't."

"Do you know who did take those items?"

"No, sir. I don't."

Bishop was silent for a few moments as he considered a course of action. In his many years at Holy Trinity, he had dealt with situations that were far more serious than this. Billy hadn't hurt anyone except himself, and it was clear from his demeanor that the young man had already figured that out.

The sun had set, and there was a chill in the air. They had walked to the far end of the parking lot and had begun the loop back.

"Why did you do it?" Although there was no reason that could justify his action, Bishop was curious as to his motivation.

Billy shrugged his shoulders as if to say that he didn't know why. "I hadn't planned to do it. I knew it was a stupid thing to do as soon as I did it."

"Why didn't you just put it back?"

Instead of answering the question, Billy pulled out his cell phone and started tapping on the screen. It seemed to be an odd time to check his phone. "I was going to find a way to put it back on his desk until I got this." He handed the phone to Bishop.

Billyboy I know u stole that exam. If u don't give me a copy I'm telling

"Who sent this?"

"Promise you won't tell."

"I'll do no such thing!" Bishop snapped back. He stopped walking and turned to face the young man. "You're in no position to be making any demands. Now, who sent this?" He plunked the phone into Billy's hand.

After a moment's indecision, he said softly, "Clare Mooney." Clare? Squeaky-clean Clare? He thought back to the discussion of that Hawthorne story. Another veil removed? This past week had brought with it murder, lies, secrets, theft, and threats. The irony was not lost on him that all of this was taking place in a Catholic school.

"When did you receive this?"

"About an hour after I took the folder. She's texted me every day since. I got another one just before I came to talk to you. She's given me a deadline of next Monday at noon."

Bishop now understood the cause of the look of panic on Billy's face when he had approached him moments earlier. They had almost reached the main entrance of the building once again. "You have to talk to Mr. Mitchell," he said unequivocally.

"What if Clare tells him first?"

"Clare doesn't have anything to do with it. Think about it. If she were going to turn you in, she would have done it right away. Plus, she knows that you have those texts. You have to face Mr. Mitchell because of what you did."

"Yeah, I know," sounding more resigned to the inevitable. "I don't know what he's going to do to me."

"Neither do I, Billy, neither do I."

"Thanks for listening, Mr. Bishop." Billy reached out to shake his hand.

Bishop shook his hand firmly and smiled. He couldn't condone Billy's actions, but he couldn't abandon him either.

"One more thing," Bishop said as they reentered the prom.

"Yes?"

"Make sure that you save Clare's texts. Just in case."

Chapter Twenty

Bishop's internal alarm woke him at 6:00 a.m. on Saturday. After showering and dressing, he went into the sunroom for a leisurely breakfast. The morning sky was a deep blue, giving promise to a beautiful day ahead.

With a CD of Artur Rubenstein playing Chopin in the background, he sat in his favorite recliner with his tea and toast. It had been a rather tumultuous week, starting with the discovery of Ed Cooper's dead body. One minor mystery had been solved when Billy Sprowl admitted that he had taken Mitchell's exam. Many others still awaited resolution.

He had left the prom early the night before. He noticed that Billy spent most of the evening seated at one of the tables farthest from the dance floor. He probably was already dreading his meeting with Mitchell on Monday and the consequences that would follow. Clare Mooney, on the other hand, had kicked off her shoes and danced the night away, seemingly without a care in the world. Did she really believe that her threats would be successful? Bishop had considered advising Billy to give her a copy of the stolen exam, and then watch her reaction when she sat for a totally different exam and realized that she had been duped. Ultimately, Bishop had decided to inform the faculty council of the unethical behavior of both young people. After an investigation and due process, those five teachers would decide whether probation or removal from the National Honor Society was warranted.

***

With his leisurely breakfast finished, Bishop headed off to the grocery store. He didn't need a list since he knew he was out of just about everything. Two hundred and sixty-five dollars later, he was back at home putting everything away. That done, he changed into work clothes, grabbed his straw hat, and went out to mow some of the lawn. Since the area he

193

mowed was the equivalent of several football fields, he usually mowed for an hour at a time. In between, he might do some laundry, grade some papers, or catch up on his reading. Although some found mowing so onerous that they gladly paid someone to do it for them, Bishop considered the repetition relaxing. Other than in the shower, he did some of his best thinking while riding the tractor.

He was just settling into the routine when he noticed an older-model truck pull into his driveway. Thinking that someone might be in need of directions, he switched off the blades and rode the mower across the field and toward the house. A man had gotten out of the truck and waved. As he got closer, he realized that it was Jack Slater. In the eight or ten years that they had worked together, he couldn't recall that Jack had ever been to his house. They were acquaintances, but not close friends. Why was Jack here now? Had something happened to his wife? To one of their colleagues? When he reached the driveway, he turned off the mower's engine and greeted Jack. He had hoped to catch up with Jack on Monday anyway. This was actually more convenient.

He was wearing the same sort of clothes that he wore to work most days. As the only maintenance man at the moment, perhaps he had already spent some time at school this morning. "Sorry to take you away from your mowing."

"Don't be. The grass isn't going anywhere," he said with a laugh. "Come on in the house." He led the way through the garage and into the kitchen. "Sit down," he said as he gestured to a chair at the table. "Can I get you some coffee or iced tea or maybe a soda?"

"I guess I'll have a Coke."

"No Coke. Pepsi." He smiled as he said it, hoping that Jack would catch the *SNL* reference. He didn't.

"Sure. Whatever." Jack's eyes wandered as he took in the unfamiliar surroundings. Something was clearly bothering him.

Bishop filled two glasses with ice, grabbed two cans of soda, and placed them on the table. Congratulating himself for getting the shopping done early, he also put some chocolate chip cookies on a plate. Jack popped the top of the can and filled his glass. He took a long swallow and just sat there looking at the glass. It was obvious that Bishop would have to start the conversation. "What brings you out to my neck of the woods?"

"I … I just … had to talk to you," he managed to say without looking at Bishop.

That was the second time in a little more than twelve hours that someone had said something similar to him.

He gave him a reassuring smile. "Okay. What's up?"

Looking down at the plate of untouched cookies, he managed to say, "I … did it. I did it." His eyes filled with tears, and he covered his face with his calloused hands.

He did it? Did what? Was the man sitting across from him at his kitchen table a murderer? Had he just confessed to killing Ed Cooper? Bishop sought to maintain his composure as Jack struggled to regain his.

"Why don't you take your time and tell me what happened?"

He looked at Bishop. "It's just like you said."

So it was Jack after all. His first instinct had been correct. The other suspects … and there were many … were innocent. Amy Davis. Ryan Baxter. Debbie Bates. Tim Kelleher. Hannah Ward. Elwin Crimins' man with the numbers if he even existed. All innocent.

"I took the money from those girls."

What? He did what? It took Bishop a moment to process what he had just heard. Without prompting, Jack explained.

195

"One of the girls had complained that her gym locker door didn't shut right, so I went in there early one morning to take a look. There was a twenty just sitting there. I don't know what came over me." He paused for a moment as if he were still trying to understand his own behavior. "After that, I started opening other lockers and took any cash that I found. Most of these kids have more money than they know what to do with, and they are so careless with it."

Bishop wouldn't allow him to rationalize his wrongdoing. "It doesn't matter whether they have money or not."

"Yeah, I know that."

"And leaving money in a locked locker doesn't sound careless to me."

"I know. I know," he replied as he rubbed his hand across the stubble on his face. "What am I going to do? I can't afford to lose my job." Tears came to his eyes again as he expressed his worst fear. "I don't want Mabel to find out. It would kill her."

Bishop recalled seeing Mabel in the grocery store earlier in the week. He understood why Jack didn't want to burden his wife with his misdeeds as she battled a life-threatening illness. "Well, for starters, you need to make restitution."

"With what?" he asked in a tone of hopelessness. "I gambled it all away. I don't even know how much I took or who I took it from."

"When Luigi delivered the pizza and wings, he mentioned that you had been spending a lot on tickets and scratch-offs. Is that why you skipped the party? Were you afraid of what he would say if you bumped into him?"

He managed a little smile. "You don't miss much, do you?"

"And the locker room thefts stopped when you stopped gambling."

196

"Right again. When Ed got killed, I figured that if I didn't take any more money, everyone would assume that Ed had been the thief." There must have been a momentary sense of relief as he unburdened his guilty conscience, but his fears soon returned. "Do you think I'll lose my job?"

"I don't know." Jack was a bit of a busybody and temperamental at times, but he was basically a good person, a good husband, and a good worker. He had made a terrible mistake, not unlike everyone else at some point or other. Would Sister Ann and Sister Pat give him a second chance? Even though compassion was a charism of the Sisters of the Holy Rosary, retaliation and revenge were more their style. One factor working in his favor was that he was the only maintenance person on the staff at the moment. Would they abruptly dismiss him without having a suitable replacement? "Perhaps we can resolve this without informing the good sisters."

"What do you mean?" asked Jack, clearly intrigued by the possibility of keeping his job.

"I know that Ron Jennings has a list of all of the girls who reported thefts in the past few weeks and how much each of them lost." Bishop was formulating a plan as he spoke. "If you made full restitution, there would be no need for anyone to press charges."

"But I don't even know how much I took and sure as hell don't have the money to pay it back," he said dejectedly.

"I know that it's at least five hundred dollars. I'll loan you the money."

"I can't let you do that."

"Do you have a better idea?" When Jack failed to respond, Bishop continued. "I'll loan you the money on three conditions: one, you tell Ron everything you just told me; two, you agree in writing to repay the loan at

197

the rate of twenty-five dollars a week; and three, you agree to be evaluated, and treated if necessary, for a possible gambling addiction as well as to seek professional help in dealing with your wife's illness."

"I don't know what to say." He reached across the table to shake Bishop's hand. "Thank you, my friend."

Jack stood up to leave. He thanked Bishop again and promised to get in touch with Ron Jennings as soon as possible. As he watched Jack get in his truck, Bishop hoped that he had done the right thing. As he had learned over the years, knowing the "right thing" wasn't always perfectly clear. He had done what he thought was best considering all of the circumstances.

Jack started the engine and leaned out of the window. "I bet you thought I killed Ed Cooper," he said with a grin. He seemed a different man than the one who had arrived earlier.

Bishop didn't want to admit how right he was. "Well, anyone who had contact with him would have to be considered a suspect, I guess."

"I don't mind telling you I'm glad he's gone."

"Why is that?"

"He hadn't been working more than a day or two, and I caught him hitting on one of the girls. Can you believe that? I ripped into him good. Told him if I ever caught him with one of the girls, he'd be out on his ass."

"Mind telling me who the girl was?"

"Samantha Graham," he replied as he put the truck in gear, waved a goodbye, and headed down the hill.

***

Bishop grabbed his straw hat, hopped back on the mower, and resumed his mindless journey back and forth on the dandelion-filled yard.

Samantha Graham. He knew who she was. Just about everyone in the school knew her. The kids called her "Crackers." Apparently, she had the potential to be an honor roll student, but she preferred socializing to studying. Although she was only a junior, she could pass for twenty-something. Given her stunning good looks, it wasn't surprising that she had gotten the attention of Ed Cooper. He wondered whether that relationship had gone beyond the talking stage.

It seemed clear that Jack was no longer a suspect in Ed's murder. His recent behavior could be explained by his feelings of guilt surrounding the thefts in the locker room. If Jack was in the clear, his account of Ed's interest in Samantha warranted adding a few more suspects. Might Samantha have been secretly seeing Ed? Might she be responsible for his death? What about a jealous boyfriend? He made a mental note to get the name of her current boyfriend from Terry. What about her father? If he found out that his seventeen-year-old daughter was involved with an older man, might he have taken matters into his own hands?

After about an hour of mowing, he went back into the house for a break. He picked up one of the chocolate chips cookies on the kitchen table, poured a glass of milk, and checked his phone for messages. Not surprisingly, there was one from Ron. He hit the call button, and Ron picked up right away.

"I called you as soon as Jack left my house. It's been some week, hasn't it? First, Frank gets suspended for throwing some punches, and now Jack admits to stealing that money."

"Don't forget Ed's killer. That person could be one of the staff, one of the students, or someone not connected with the school at all."

"Let's hope it's the latter." Bishop heard the sound of a refrigerator door closing. Ron was probably looking for a mid-morning snack. "I know the girls will be happy to get their money back, and I'm happy that the case is closed."

"Assuming that Jack follows through on all of the conditions," Bishop added.

"Yeah, right. I think he will, don't you?"

"I certainly hope so. I just didn't want to see Sister Ann or Sister Pat destroy that man for one mistake."

"Agreed. I think that your conditions were more than fair, and Jack told me several times how much he appreciates what you are doing for him."

"Jack's situation just underscores the fact that we never really know what someone is capable of doing in any given situation." Bishop again thought of the killer in their midst.

"Switching gears, can I ask you what was Billy Sprowl's problem last night?"

"Oh, that," he said as if he had momentarily forgotten. "I'm sure that you'd hear about it on Monday anyway. Billy admitted taking Charlie Mitchell's folder containing the final exam."

"No kidding! What are you a priest or something? Seems everyone wants to confess his sins to you," he said teasing his good friend.

Bishop dismissed the comment with a forced laugh. "Everyone except the murderer, that is."

"Charlie's going to explode when he finds out."

"I hope not. Billy is not the only one involved in this."

"Really? What do you mean?" he asked as he munched on something.

"Clare Mooney knew that Billy had the exam, and she was pressuring him to give her a copy. I am going to give both names to the

200

faculty council. I am hoping that Charlie will let the council decide on their punishment."

"They could get bounced from the National Honor Society?"

"That's right. I'm disappointed in both of them. They will have to learn that poor choices have consequences."

They talked for a few more minutes, mostly about Mary Ellen. From his limited contact with her at the bank, Bishop agreed that she seemed to be a very lovely person. What he kept to himself was the knowledge that people were not always what they appeared to be.

He was about to return to his mowing when it occurred to him that he needed to transfer funds from one account to another in order to give Jack the money that he had promised him. As he sat down at his laptop to make that online transaction, he wondered how rapid advances in technology might put people like Mary Ellen out of work. He logged in, but before he could conduct any business, the bank's security system forced him to change his password. Although he knew that it was a good practice to change passwords frequently, he still found the process somewhat annoying. He had so many passwords to remember that he had begun to write them down in a small memo pad that he kept locked in the top drawer of his desk.

He followed the directions on the screen for creating a new password. He had read somewhere that the most common password was 123456. Another favorite was the word "password" itself. The bank's system would not allow for such easy-to-guess passwords by requiring that the password be between 8 and 20 characters in length. Customers also had to use at least one letter, one number, and one capital letter. As he contemplated creating his new password, it suddenly hit him. *Avignon 1868* was a password!

Chapter Twenty-One

He jumped up and started pacing the house. A password! Of course! Given the relevance of that place and date to the Sisters of the Holy Rosary, he suspected that Ed Cooper had somehow managed to obtain access to the confidential files of Holy Trinity High School. According to Debbie, Ed had discovered that someone was stealing from the school. He might very well have made that discovery using the password that he kept in his wallet. From his prison report and from Debbie's comments, he knew that Ed was a stock market whiz. Perhaps the theft had something to do with stocks, assuming that the school even owned any stocks. He had told Debbie that he was going to take care of the problem on his own. That might have been his fatal error in judgment.

How could he test his theory? He sat back down at the computer and logged out of the banking site. He would take care of that little item of business later. As a teacher, Bishop had access to places on the Trinity website that were denied to the public. He could, for example, access attendance records and grade reports. He could also add, change, or delete items in those files. If his assumption was correct, he now had the password to gain access to all of the school's records. But who was the user associated with that password? He knew that the system would lock him out after three failed attempts. He also knew that faculty usernames consisted of the first initial of the first name followed by the last name. His user name was *mbishop*.

He pulled up the school's login page. His fingers became moist as he typed in *acowie* and the password.

Username or password incorrect appeared in red on the screen. Had he remembered to start the password with a capital letter? Perhaps his theory was wrong and *Avignon 1868* wasn't the password at all. Had he typed a space between the city and the date without thinking? He knew that he had only two more chances to get this right. After three failed attempts, the system locked the user out until the network administrator could be contacted to reset the password. In Trinity's case, one of the network administrators was Sister Pat. She had nagged the principal to be given that role even though she was always annoyed when anyone needed her assistance. Most of the actual work was done by Jim Stevens in technology. Bishop knew that he couldn't ask anyone for help now.

He had to try again. This time he decided to try the name of the assistant principal as the user. He stared at the blank space on the screen as if doing that might cause the correct letters to appear. He slowly typed in *pmeehan* for the username. Then, he very carefully typed in *Avignon1868* making sure that he started with a capital letter and that he didn't leave a space between the *n* and the *1*.

Username or password incorrect appeared again in red on the screen. What now? He got up from his desk to consider the possibilities. He had only one more chance to do this correctly. He felt strongly that the password was correct. The problem was the username. Certainly, one or both of them had to have complete access to the website. Why didn't either name work? He was considering getting on the riding mower to clear his mind when he remembered something. He rushed back to his desk and pulled up a directory of faculty email addresses. That was it! How could he have forgotten? All of the sisters at the school used *sr* before their first initial. His memory lapse had almost cost him a chance to continue his investigation.

One problem still remained. Which sister's name should he use? Which one was more likely to have unknowingly compromised her password? The answer was as obvious as the thick moustache on his face –

203

Sister Pat. He exhaled deeply as he began to type *srpmeehan* in the space for username and *Avignon1868* in the space for password. He prepared himself for a reappearance of the error message. Instead, a menu of all of the school's databases appeared on the screen. His low estimation of Sister Pat's abilities had once again been proven correct.

Everything that one could possibly want to know about Holy Trinity was now mere clicks away. He selected the *Governance* tab and located a *Board of Trustees* folder. Within that folder were various subfolders including one marked *Minutes*. Upon opening that folder, he found links to monthly minutes of the board dating back to 2009. Over the years, Bishop had requested that the minutes of board meetings be made available to the faculty and staff. They are major stakeholders in the school, and it seemed to him a reasonable request. His requests had been summarily dismissed.

He paused before he opened the file containing the minutes of the last meeting. Was it proper for him to read those minutes? He hadn't done anything illegal in obtaining access. It had been a fortuitous hunch that led to these documents. The school's refusal to share information with the faculty except on an "as needed" basis had all the hallmarks of a totalitarian dictatorship. The school was in some sort of a financial crisis. As a result, teachers were about to be let go. Furthermore, it was probable that someone was stealing from the school, and Ed Cooper's murder was possibly linked to his discovery of that wrongdoing. To Bishop, it seemed not only proper, but also necessary, that he break through the administration's shroud of secrecy.

The minutes consisted of a series of reports from various subcommittees, most of which were rather boring. Admissions indicated that enrollment for the next academic year was stable and in line with expectations. Reports regarding academics, student affairs, curriculum, buildings and grounds, and marketing didn't yield any surprises. He expected the finance report to be more interesting, and it was. The chair proudly announced that the current fiscal year ending on June 30th was projected to conclude with a surplus of about $25,000. Surplus? Why were they eliminating staff positions if there was a surplus? What about the $1.2 million deficit? Sister Ann and Dan Morehouse had definitely used that figure as the amount of the gap that required such draconian measures as reductions in personnel, a wage freeze, and even the end of free lunches for the staff.

Bishop didn't stop for lunch even though he actually had some food in the house. His reading fed a desire for answers that was more urgent. The principal's report provided the key. Among the many items in her report, Sister Ann mentioned that the school's endowment fund balance was approximately $85,000 compared to $1.3 million at the same time last year. There it was! There was the $1.2 million gap. Instead of explaining what had caused such a large decline, Sister simply moved on to offer suggestions for closing that gap including staff cuts and an increase in tuition. Motions were made and passed without any questions or discussion, at least according to the minutes. No questions? No discussion? How could that be true?

***

He closed the folder containing the minutes of past meetings and began searching the site for access to the endowment fund. He navigated to the appropriate folder quite easily. Whoever had created this site was at least well organized. The problem was that only a few select individuals were given the rights to read its content.

The vibrating of his cell phone startled him. He picked up the phone, saw that the caller was Debbie, and decided to let her leave a message. Why would she be calling him on a Saturday? Perhaps she just wanted to thank him for helping her keep her job. His shoulders and neck ached from spending so much time hunched over his laptop, but he quickly got back to the task at hand.

As he opened various folders and files, he confronted columns of numbers whose significance eluded him. He was an English teacher, not an accountant. He opened a portfolio folder and found that the school had positions in a number of stocks. He was reminded of the title of a Robert Heinlein science fiction novel, *Stranger in a Strange Land.* What little he knew about the stock market could fit on one side of an index card. Grace had dabbled in stocks. In fact, she had been quite successful at it. As a realtor, she sometimes received bonus money for achieving a certain dollar amount of sales. She paid attention to trends, and when she found a stock that she liked, she used her bonus to buy in early. By the time other investors piled in and pushed the stock price up, she usually liquidated her position, making a tidy profit. Her strategy didn't always work, but it did more often than not. Win or lose, she always had been a bit of a gambler. In fact, she was at the casinos in Las Vegas when she died.

It hadn't occurred to him that the school would be invested in the stock market. That would appear to be too risky a place for Holy Trinity to invest its funds. He realized that the school hadn't actually purchased the stocks that they held. Rather, they had been donated by various benefactors, some living and some deceased. He remembered that his wife often complained about the capital gains taxes that she had to pay on the profits of her stock transactions. One way of avoiding such taxes was by donating the stocks to a non-profit. This benefitted not only the recipient, but also the donors who could lower their taxes by taking the value of the gift as a charitable deduction.

The question remained: How did the school lose $1.2 million at a time when the market was rising? Then it occurred to him that Ed Cooper had probably looked at these same files. He had written the password on a piece of paper he kept in his wallet, and he had made a hobby of studying the stock market. What discovery had he made while looking at these pages? Whatever it was most likely had led to his death. Bishop could only hope that a similar fate did not await him.

Two hours later, he was just about ready to give up. The words from Alfred, Lord Tennyson's poem, "Ulysses," came to mind - "To strive, to seek, to find, and not to yield." That was when he noticed something unusual. He compared the current list of holdings to a list from the previous year. Something wasn't right. The number of shares of certain stocks had declined in a strange pattern. The school currently held 154 shares of Google compared to the 1,154 shares listed in an earlier report. Exactly one thousand shares had been sold. Bishop quickly checked yesterday's closing price for that stock. $612. A thousand shares of Google were worth more than $600,000. Trinity's position in some other stocks had been liquidated in similar fashion. Doing some quick math in his head, he realized that these stock sales would have yielded approximately $1.2 million. Once the stocks had been sold, the cash equivalent should have been credited to the account. The problem was that the stocks were gone as well as the cash. Someone had stolen that money, sending the school into a financial crisis. Why hadn't anyone on the board realized what had happened? Who could have done this? Whoever it was had probably killed Ed Cooper.

***

After printing out copies of all pages that he thought might be relevant, he logged out of the school's website. He got up from his desk and went out to get the mail from the box at the end of the driveway. The smell of freshly cut grass reminded him of the task that he had left unfinished.

Back inside, he made himself a grilled cheese and tomato sandwich. He added some chips and some baby carrots to his paper plate, grabbed a cold soda from the fridge, and went into the sunroom to have a late lunch. He ate quickly, cleaned up, and went out to finish mowing. He had a lot to think about.

The sun was now much stronger as he continued his methodical movement across the field. He had accessed sections of the school's records without authorization. Had he committed a crime? He assumed that if Sister Ann became aware of his activity, she would not hesitate to dismiss him. If the list of names that Terry had seen on her desk was any indication, she planned on letting him go anyway. His action would only make it easier just as Frank Wilson's physical assault on Dan Morehouse assured that his days at the school were at an end.

On the other hand, he hadn't accessed the files in order to change, damage or delete them. His intention had been simply to follow a hunch that the murder of Ed Cooper was in some way connected to his possession of that password. Ed had, after all, told Debbie that he knew someone was stealing from the school and that he was going to take care of it. He also told her that he would be coming into some big money. If accessing those files led to solving the mystery of Ed's death, Bishop's ethically questionable incursion into the school's data would have been both necessary and worthwhile.

It seemed highly unlikely that his examination of the files would be detected. He hadn't hacked into the system; he had used a password that

Sister Pat had clearly not sufficiently protected. For the moment, he decided not to discuss his use of that password with anyone, including Lieutenant Hodge. It was possible that he had discovered nothing more than a clerical error in the listing of the school's portfolio of stocks. It was also possible that he had uncovered the motive for Ed's murder.

The mower's engine suddenly sputtered and quit. It had run out of gas. As he made his way to the garage to get more fuel, he wondered whether the pursuit of Ed's killer had similarly run out of gas. Many of the original suspects seemed to have been cleared. Amy Davis with whom Ed had been living turned out to be his half sister, not a spurned lover. Ryan Baxter, Amy's boyfriend, hadn't been working at UPS at the time of Ed's death, but he apparently had been with another woman at that time. Debbie Bates had helped Ed get the custodian's job, and took his death especially hard as they were planning to get back together. Jack Slater, who didn't hide his dislike for Ed, had just admitted to a crime, but it was stealing money from the girls' lockers, not murder. Of course, there was also the man in the car or truck with the numbers that Elwin Crimins claims to have seen near the school grounds on the morning of the murder. How reliable was that information?

A couple of new angles had emerged. Ed had caught seniors Tim Kelleher and Hannah Ward in the storage area beneath the stage and forced them to pay for his silence. Fear of Ed's hold over them might have been enough of a motive for either one or both of them to commit murder. In addition, Samantha Graham's name had come up. Ed had taken an interest in this attractive but flighty girl. Had she done something that she regretted and wanted to cover up? Had her boyfriend or her father found out and sought revenge against Ed?

The mowing finished, he realized that he wasn't any closer to understanding why Ed had been killed or who had done it. After a quick shower, he decided to touch base with the lieutenant. Jack no longer appeared to be a suspect; Samantha Graham or someone close to her, might be. He told him that he had spent much of the afternoon mowing the lawn which was true. What he failed to tell him was that he had also spent hours on his computer. It wasn't a lie; it just wasn't the whole truth.

After that short call, Bishop settled on the sofa and started watching the Mets. Bartolo Colon, one of the oldest players in the majors, had eight strikeouts in only four innings. As Bishop watched the hapless batters swing and miss, he wondered whether another old man could use his guile to catch a killer. He soon fell asleep, having completely forgotten that Debbie had called and that he meant to call her back.

Chapter Twenty-Two

As is often the case, the weekend slipped by all too quickly, and Bishop found himself sitting at his desk waiting for his homeroom students to arrive. As usual, Sister Pat had been holding up the wall near the main entrance. What was unusual was the obviously good mood that she was in. She practically beamed at him as he greeted her and walked by. "Enjoy your day!" she smirked. Something was definitely in the works; he just didn't know what.

He had considered confronting Sister Ann regarding the school's diminished stock portfolio. However, the only way that he could do that was to admit that he had accessed the confidential database, and he wasn't about to do that at this point. Who else might know what was going on? He assumed that the board members would know, but he didn't have a close relationship with any of them. In fact, he didn't even know the names of all of the members of the board until he had looked at the minutes of their last meeting which listed those who were in attendance and those who were absent or excused. Dan Morehouse was the most visible member of the board in the school, although after being attacked by Frank Wilson, he might think twice about dropping by the faculty lunchroom. Dan might be able to explain the school's financial difficulties off the record.

Students began trickling into homeroom. He greeted each one as they surveyed the scene, deciding whether they really wanted to sit down and get some work done or just drop their books on their desk and head back out into the halls where the action was. The few students who had taken their places were speculating as to why Billy Sprowl was in Mr. Mitchell's homeroom with the door closed. Bishop knew exactly why. The first step in the process of forgiveness was admitting the mistake. Bishop hoped that Charlie's response would be measured. He had already sent an email to Diane Ramos, moderator of the National Honor Society, with the particulars of the actions of both Billy and Clare Mooney. He had requested that Diane convene the faculty council to review the matter at their earliest convenience. Would that be sufficient to placate Charlie?

Bishop was mildly surprised that Charlie did not make an appearance in his room before the homeroom period ended. He didn't know whether to take that as a good sign or not. Was he simply waiting for a more opportune time to unleash his fury against Billy?

During the year, Bishop kept a folder of every paper written by each of his students. From short reading quizzes, to spelling and vocabulary quizzes, to tests, essays, major papers and other projects – all were collected in the folder. It was, in a sense, a written record of their achievements in his class. With finals only a week away, he gave the students time to review their portfolios. Their task was to revisit each paper and decide what papers to save as representative of their progress during the year. He had a dual purpose in mind. In looking through their papers, he wanted his students to remind themselves of all that they had accomplished as a class. He also wanted them to make observations about their individual strengths and weaknesses.

"At the end of this week, you will leave this class for the last time," he said. Several of them smiled at the thought of a summer without schoolwork. "What I'm interested in are the skills and insights that you take with you when you leave." The smiles faded as they understood the significance of what he said. What followed was a furious shuffling of papers as each student took seriously the task of evaluating an impressive stack of papers.

When the class period ended, each folder had been reorganized with the papers that they felt best represented their work grouped together at the top of the stack. As they left, many were sharing their reactions to what they had just done. On the last class day, he would ask them to record their reflections on paper, not for a grade, but for a sense of completeness to the ten months that they had spent together.

***

After class, he went down to the main office to talk with Terry. The windows were wide open, but there was no breeze. She looked a bit frazzled as she tried to get some relief from the heavy, muggy air with the small fan on her desk.

"How's it going today?"

"Don't ask," she replied, as she made sure that the fan was at its highest setting.

"Why don't you turn on the air conditioner?"

She glanced around to see if anyone was in listening distance. "I'll tell you why. It was quite hot last Friday afternoon, and I closed the office doors and turned the A/C on for the first time this season. Within fifteen minutes, Sister Pat came in, left the door open, walked right up to the window, shut the unit down, and headed back to her office without saying a single word.

"Didn't you ask her why she did that?"

"I sure did, and I got my head handed to me. Honestly, that woman …" Although Terry didn't finish that sentence, Bishop had a fairly good idea of what she was thinking. Even though he had a lot to accomplish during this free period, he couldn't resist asking Terry for further details.

"How did she explain herself?"

"According to her," Terry said mockingly, "it's unprofessional to close the doors to the main office, and it's a waste of electricity to run the air conditioner with the doors open."

"Well, why did they install a unit in that window in the first place if you aren't allowed to use it?"

"Good question, Mike. She also informed me that she was going to have Jack remove it as soon as he had a chance."

"Unbelievable!" He shook his head and laughed at the absurdity of the situation. "And she's sitting in her air-conditioned office with the door close doing whatever it is that she does."

"You got it!" said Terry, feeling no cooler but pleased that she could vent to her friend.

"Listen, Terry, I've got a quick question for you."

"Okay, shoot."

"Samantha Graham."

"Graham Crackers?" she responded with a laugh. "What about her?"

"Boyfriend?"

"Several. Why do you ask?"

"I heard that Ed Cooper had expressed some interest in her, and I wondered if there was anything more to it."

Terry raised her eyebrows as if to suggest that she had something to share. The phone rang which seemed to annoy Terry, but she answered in her typically perky voice. After listening for a moment, she efficiently dispensed with the caller by punching in an extension and announcing, "There's a Mr. Martin for you on Line 3."

As soon as she put the receiver down, the phone rang again. Her frustration building, she exhaled deeply before answering. Bishop considered catching up with her later, but before he could decide, she was free again.

She glanced around again and motioned him closer so that she wouldn't be overheard. "A few of the girls told Sarah all about it. Apparently, Ed had his eye on her during her gym class. Started chatting her up as the kids went back to their lockers. When she caught up with the other girls, she told them that this creep had hit on her. She thought it was funny that this guy that came to work on a bus and cleaned toilets for a living was trying to make a date with her." Bishop nodded his understanding. He had once again benefitted from the gossip pipeline between Sarah in guidance and Terry.

A very pale student came up to Terry's desk and announced that she felt sick. As Terry bounced up and escorted the girl to the nurse's office, Bishop headed over to Ron's office.

He could hear Charlie Mitchell before he saw him. "I want that scoundrel expelled!" Bishop knew exactly who that "scoundrel" was. He peeked in through the open door, pretending that he didn't know who was in the office with Ron.

"Sorry for interrupting. I'll stop back later," he said as he turned to leave.

"Wait!" Ron called out. He looked to Charlie to see if he would object. "Come in. You're in on this anyway."

Charlie was seated at one of the straight-backed wooden chairs facing Ron's desk. Bishop sat at the other. Charlie's face was flushed, and there was a slight tremor in his hands. "I spent hours and hours writing a new exam all because of that kid."

"Charlie, I can understand why you're so upset. I would be just as outraged if a student had stolen one of my exams. From talking with him on Friday night, I think it's safe to say that he is genuinely sorry for what he did, and he is willing to accept his punishment."

"Well, he should be," Charlie said decisively.

"The question is," as Bishop looked from Charlie to Ron, "what punishment is most appropriate? Do we really want to expel a senior just days before graduation? Do we really want to derail his college plans for the fall?"

"Yes and yes!" answered Charlie.

"What about the National Honor Society?" asked Ron, knowing that Bishop had already mentioned this as a possible avenue to pursue.

"I think that the NHS is the proper path here."

"They'll just slap him on the wrist," countered Charlie. He deserves a harsher punishment than that. If not expulsion, at least a suspension."

"Then Clare Mooney should receive the same."

Charlie looked puzzled. "What does Clare Mooney have to do with this?"

It was Bishop's turn to look puzzled. "Didn't Billy mention Clare?"

"No, he did not. What did she do?"

"Apparently, she knew that Billy had taken the test…"

Charlie interrupted to say, "Stolen the test."

"Okay, stolen. However, instead of reporting that to you or to Ron, she pressured Billy to give her a copy of the test."

"Are you kidding me?"

"No, Charlie. Billy showed me the texts in which she threatened him if he didn't comply. Billy's theft of the exam was an impulsive act that he regretted almost immediately. Clare's behavior was premeditated and just as wrong if not more so. If Billy is suspended, Clare should be suspended also." He sat back in his chair having made his position clear.

216

It took a moment for Charlie to process this new information. Bishop knew that Clare's father was one of Charlie's closest golfing buddies. If Charlie's response resulted in a suspension for Clare, how would that play out when he met her father on the links?

Ron turned to Bishop who sensed that Charlie's outrage had cooled considerably once Clare's name was brought into the discussion. "What did you say about the NHS?"

"I think both students should be brought before the faculty council. In fact, I've already contacted Diane about putting that process in motion." He turned to Charlie. "Let's let the council decide what punishment is most appropriate for these two young people."

Charlie was noticeably calmer as he shook hands with both Bishop and Ron. "I hope the council takes this case seriously," he said as he got up to leave.

"You know Diane as well as I do, Charlie. She'll conduct a thorough investigation."

After Charlie left, Ron breathed a deep sigh of relief. "Man, he came in here on fire. I'm glad you stopped in when you did. You must have known that mentioning Clare's name would tip the scales."

Bishop just smiled.

***

"I've got to get to the bank during this period. Do you want to come along for the ride?"

Ron jumped at the chance to get out of the office, grabbed his keys, and announced, "I'm driving." Bishop had a fairly good guess as to why. As they walked by the main office, Ron told Terry that he would be back in fifteen minutes.

As they buckled in, Ron asked, "Where to?"

"Groveland Savings. I had planned on switching some funds online over the weekend, but I was distracted, and then I forgot all about it." The fact that he had completely forgotten irritated Bishop. He wondered if his memory issues were normal for his age. Perhaps he should discuss it with his doctor during his next appointment. He thought of Elwin Crimins. He certainly hoped that he wasn't going to end up like him. He also had the nagging feeling that he had forgotten something else.

The bank was located only a couple of miles from the school, but before they reached that destination, Ron pulled into the drive-thru lane of a fast food establishment. Bishop's hunch about why Ron offered to drive had been confirmed.

"Want anything?"

"No, thanks."

"Sure?"

"Very sure."

Ron ordered an egg and sausage sandwich and a vanilla shake. By the time he arrived at the pick-up window, his order was ready.

As soon as he squeezed his Nissan into a parking space between two SUVs, he grabbed the bag containing his sandwich and popped a straw into his shake. Bishop carefully opened the door so as not to hit the vehicle next to him and got out. He closed the door and leaned in through the open window.

"Do you think $600 is enough to cover what the girls lost?"

Ron had taken a big bite of his sandwich and simply nodded his agreement.

Bishop made the withdrawal and returned to the car within a couple of minutes. All that was left of Ron's snack was the crumpled bag that it had come in. Ron was humming along to Willie Nelson's "On the Road Again" when Bishop handed him a thick envelope.

"I got small bills because I thought it would make it easier to distribute."

Ron turned the radio off and looked at his friend. "You know, you really don't have to do this."

"I know that."

"Well, I sure hope that Jack appreciates what you've done for him."

"I'm sure that he does."

"Mike, the way you've dealt with Billy and Jack in the last couple of days, and Charlie just now, I wish you were on the administrative team instead of on …" He stopped before completing the thought so Bishop did it for him.

"…on the chopping block."

Somewhat embarrassed that he had brought the topic up, Ron said sheepishly, "…on that list. Can you imagine how Sister Pat would have handled those situations?"

"I'd rather not."

As the car approached the school's driveway, Bishop said, "Listen, Ron. I appreciate the sentiment, but I never would have traded the classroom for administration." He paused for a moment, and then continued. "If I am out at the end of the year, I'll have only one regret."

Ron looked at his friend. "What's that?"

"That I wasn't able to figure out who killed Ed Cooper."

"You've still got a few days left," Ron remarked as both men laughed and reentered the building.

***

He rushed upstairs without checking his mailbox. The students were crowded around the door waiting for him. He apologized for his tardiness and quickly launched into the day's work.

At lunchtime, he picked up his lunch bag and headed down to the faculty lounge. As he walked by the kitchen, he thought of Debbie. It suddenly occurred to him that she had called him on Saturday but hadn't left a message. Perhaps she had called his number by mistake. He had intended on returning her call. Distracted by his unexpected luck in gaining access to the school's files, he had completely forgotten. He assumed that her call couldn't have been that important, or she would have called again. That assumption turned out to be very wrong.

Chapter Twenty-Three

He walked through the kitchen area but did not see Debbie. He asked Lee Davidson where Debbie was. She simply shrugged and turned her attention to a large tray of tater tots that she had just pulled out of the oven. He didn't know how to interpret her shrug, but she clearly didn't want to be bothered. He hoped that Debbie wasn't slipping back into the bad habits that had almost gotten her fired last week. He decided that he would leave lunch a few minutes early so that he could check on her then.

He sat across from Sister Annunciata at lunch. Bishop thought that suspending Frank Wilson for the rest of the school year was too harsh a punishment. It did, however, result in the return of his old friend.

She greeted him with a warm smile. "Michael, how was your weekend?"

"Too short," he replied with a grin. He couldn't very well tell her about Billy's admission of guilt at the senior prom or about Jack's admission of guilt on Saturday morning or about his accessing the school's confidential databases. "I did some grocery shopping, and I mowed the lawn. Nothing too exciting. How about you?"

She pushed some tater tots back and forth on her tray. "These seem a bit undercooked," she said quietly.

"Lee was just pulling a fresh batch out of the oven. Do you want me to get you some?"

She dismissed the idea with a wave of her hand. "Thanks anyway. I'm fine." She took a sip of coffee and glanced around the room before she spoke again. "You know, I'm staying at the convent while I'm subbing, and I heard them talking about letting some teachers go."

"It's awfully late in the school year for that." He couldn't hide his frustration when he thought of those impending cuts.

"I think that they're planning to wait until Friday, the last day of classes before exams."

"Well, that gives me five days to figure out how to change their…"

Before he could finish that thought, there was a loud uproar from the students in the cafeteria. Bishop jumped up as did a few other teachers. "The natives seem a bit restless. I better see what's going on." He left his half-eaten lunch on the table as he rushed across the hall. The noise was exponentially louder as he opened the door.

Some of the students had discovered that the undercooked tater tots made excellent projectiles. One table of seniors and one table of juniors were engaged in an old-fashioned food fight. With exams only days away, the possibility of something like this occurring was rather high. Ron Jennings had followed Bishop into the cafeteria and pushed his way through some onlookers to put a halt to the battle between the classes.

Bishop looked around to see which teacher had cafeteria duty for that period. Other than a couple of teachers who came in to see what was going on, the teacher assigned was nowhere to be found. That explained why the students had chosen that moment for their antics. There really was no harm done. There were dozens of tater tots on the floor, but those could easily be cleaned up. Unfortunately, many of the taters that were launched were covered in ketchup. That added to the mess as there were streaks of red on the floor, on the walls, and on the uniforms of a number of the combatants. Most of the other students were on their feet laughing and cheering until Ron arrived and took control. That might have been the end of it had Sister Pat not entered the cafeteria from the far side. When the commotion began, she must have rushed to her office to grab her megaphone.

"Attention! Attention!" she barked. "No one leaves until I find out who started this!"

Ron had succeeded in getting everything under control until the appearance of Sister Meany with her megaphone and her threats of punishment. Some students laughed, others booed, and a few took out their cell phones to capture Sister at her worst. Ron signaled to her that everything was under control, but she ignored him and continued screaming through the megaphone.

Suddenly, she dropped the megaphone, grabbed at a nearby table, and slumped down. The cafeteria became eerily quiet as the students watched her collapse. Bishop rushed over to her. She was quite pale, breathing hard, and sweating. He instructed one of the students to call 911 and asked another to get the nurse. Sister Pat was so heavy that Bishop knew he wouldn't be able to move her, but he did his best to see that she didn't fall to the floor.

She looked at him with panicked eyes. "I think I'm having a heart attack!"

"Just try to relax. Help is on the way."

Margaret Foster, the school's nurse rushed in, followed closely by Sister Ann. While they tended to her, Ron and Bishop asked all of the students to leave the area. The aftermath of the food fight had been quickly cleaned up, and Ron had the names of the instigators. He would deal with them later.

An ambulance arrived within minutes, and two EMTs wheeled in a stretcher. They checked her vital signs and asked a few questions. Sister Pat had not lost consciousness which was an encouraging sign. It took the two responders with an assist from the nurse and the principal to move the overweight victim onto the stretcher. Interspersed with her cries of pain were a few rude comments directed at the very people who were trying to save her life.

Sister Ann told Ron that she was going to ride in the ambulance with Sister Pat.

"Let me know as soon as you get any information," Ron said. "Good luck!" he added as they wheeled the stretcher out of the cafeteria.

***

Not surprisingly, the mood in the building was quite subdued. The students seemed more worried about the ramifications of the food fight. Teachers who passed one another in the halls asked if there was any news from the hospital. Without a doubt, most of the faculty wanted Sister Pat out of the building, but no one wanted it to happen this way.

It wasn't until nearly dismissal time that Sister Ann called Terry in the main office. Sister Pat hadn't suffered a heart attack at all. She had had a severe gall bladder attack that required immediate surgery. When Bishop heard the news, he realized that she certainly fit the profile. She was a middle-aged, overweight woman who liked to eat rich foods. If the doctors decided on laparoscopic surgery, she would be back to normal in a couple of weeks. She would have to avoid some of her favorite foods, and that was bound to sour her mood more than normal.

Sister Ann told Terry to have a large bouquet of flowers sent to Sister Pat at the hospital and to place a get-well card in the main office. Apparently, she ended the conversation by adding, "Make sure that everyone signs it." When Bishop heard this, he thought that it might be fun to have a shadow card available for the faculty to write what they really wanted to say to Sister Pat along with the card for the usual chorus of well wishes. It could be fun and therapeutic … as long as Terry was careful to deliver the right card. He decided not to share his idea with the others.

When he saw Terry later in the day, she stopped him to ask a question. She had a devilish grin on her face. "Guess what I did right after they wheeled Sister Pat out of here."

"I give up."

"I turned on that damn air conditioner … full blast!"

***

With all of the commotion occurring at lunchtime, Bishop breathed a sigh of relief as the dismissal bell rang. From the noise in the halls, he concluded that things were returning to normal. Spring sports were over, but kids had busses to catch, afterschool jobs to get to, or finals to study for. A few of them were undoubtedly nervously waiting outside of the office of Mr. Jennings to tell their version of the food fight. He found himself just gazing out the window trying to dispel the uncomfortable feeling that he had forgotten something important.

Just then, there was a knock on his opened door. He turned around expecting to see one of his students with a last-minute question. He was more than mildly surprised to see Samantha Graham standing there.

"Mr. Bishop, do you have a minute?"

"Of course, of course. Come in and sit down." He pointed to one of the student desks as he sat down at his own desk. Samantha was wearing the school uniform with her skirt falling about one inch above the knee in keeping with the Trinity dress code. Because it was such a warm afternoon, she had tied her sweater around her waist. She had a large handbag looped over her left shoulder, but no backpack full of books.

Before she sat down, she asked if she should close the door. Bishop told her that he didn't think that would be necessary. One of the golden rules for a male teacher was to keep the door open when there was only one student in the room. It was obvious that she was a stunningly

225

beautiful young woman. She had wavy blonde hair and big blue eyes. He thought that she used a bit too much makeup around the eyes. He could understand why people said that she turned heads when she walked by. Once they were both settled, he asked, "What can I do for you, Samantha?"

"Well, I heard from a friend of mine that you were asking about me and Ed Cooper."

Bishop hadn't expected that. How could she have known about the conversation he had with Terry? He doubted that Terry would have said anything to her. She might, however, have mentioned it to Sarah who then might have said something to one of the girls. Sometimes the gossip pipeline worked in his favor; this time it obviously had not.

"Who told you that?'

"Just a friend," she answered. She seemed intent on keeping her source confidential.

"I've been working with Lieutenant Hodge on the Ed Cooper case, and I happened to hear that Mr. Cooper was seen talking with you. I was just trying to follow up on that."

"Who told you about me and Ed?"

"Just a friend," he said with a smile. Two could play that game. He thought it interesting that she referred to the victim as "Ed" and not as "Mr. Cooper."

She smiled as well. If you wanted to know anything, why didn't you just ask me?"

It was a very good question. He would have talked with her directly had he thought that she could be helpful in the investigation. "You're quite right, of course. I should have come to you directly, and for not doing that, I apologize."

226

"No problem," she responded. "It happens all the time around here. People prefer talking behind your back rather than talking directly to the person in question." The cell phone in her bag began vibrating, but she ignored it.

The word he had gotten was that this girl was flighty. There didn't seem to be anything flighty about her. By confronting him with her concerns, she demonstrated a maturity that he had not anticipated.

"Okay, then. Let me just ask you directly. Was there anything going on between you and Mr. Cooper?"

Without any hesitation, she said, "We were friends."

"In school or out?"

"Both."

This conversation was headed in a direction that he hadn't anticipated. Both? She had met him outside of school? Was it possible that she had information that would lead him to the killer? Could she be the killer herself? If she had killed Ed, he doubted that she would have come to him of her own accord, unless she was much more clever than anyone imagined.

"Tell me about you and Ed." He sat back, not knowing what she would say.

"I first met him at the Blue Moon. That was before he started working here."

To Bishop, this was a moment of *déjà vu*. Debbie Bates had also met Ed at the Blue Moon. She was the one who told him about the job opening at Trinity. Of course, Debbie had known Ed previously. Samantha had not.

The Blue Moon was a bar in one of the seedier neighborhoods on the other side of town. It didn't seem to him the type of establishment that

227

Debbie would frequent. It was even less likely that a seventeen-year-old would do so.

"The Blue Moon?" he asked as if he hadn't heard correctly.

"Yeah,' she explained matter-of-factly. "Lots of Trinity kids go there, especially on weekends. They have live music."

"Don't you get carded?"

"Sure, but there's this one bartender, Phil. If you slip him an extra five-dollar bill, he'll take care of you, you know?"

It didn't surprise Bishop that underage students would find a way to get alcohol or whatever else they wanted. It made him realize how difficult it must be for parents of this generation. Those were issues for another day. He wanted to get back to Ed.

"So you met Ed at the Blue Moon. Go on."

She started twirling the ends of her hair through her fingers. She seemed suddenly less confident. Perhaps she was still dealing with the fact that this man that she had met only weeks earlier was dead.

"He wasn't like most other guys, you know? He didn't try to impress me. He didn't talk about himself all that much. He was really interested in me. Besides, he was funny and good-looking. He made me feel … good, that's all." She let go of her hair and started fidgeting with a silver bracelet on her left wrist.

"Did he buy you that bracelet?" It was a shot in the dark, but what did he have to lose?

"This? No way."

Another swing and miss for Bishop.

"He didn't even have a car. I gave him a ride home a few times. I didn't mind picking up the tab. He didn't really have much money at all even after he started working at school. I guess they don't pay their help very well."

Bishop thought of Debbie Bates whose hopes for a raise of ten cents an hour were dashed by the salary freeze. He wondered if Samantha knew about Debbie.

"Why did you tell your friends that Ed was a creep?"

Samantha gave him an annoyed look. "That was after Mr. Slater yelled at Ed for talking to me. I didn't want my friends to know about Ed and me. They wouldn't have understood."

She was probably right about that. They might have pointed out that this guy was about ten years older than she was. He had conned her into buying him a few drinks. Who knows what he might have done next?

"Do you know of any reason why someone would have wanted to hurt Ed?"

"No," she said as she remembered that day. "I was sick that day and stayed home. Someone from your AP class texted me that they had found his body under the stage. Nobody thought it was murder at that point. I was totally shocked. He was a nice guy."

There was no point in trying to dispel her of that notion. He thanked for her for stopping by and promised that anything that she had just told him would go no further.

***

Debbie Bates! He had completely forgotten that he had intended to check in with Debbie after lunch. Between the food fight and Sister Pat's health scare, he forgot to stop by the kitchen to ask Debbie why she had called on Saturday. Since she would certainly have left the building by now, he decided to give her a call before he had a chance to forget again.

"Debbie? This is Michael Bishop. How are you?"

"Good," she answered unenthusiastically. "How was your day?"

"Other than a food fight in the cafeteria and Sister Pat collapsing and being taken to the hospital, not bad," he answered with a laugh.

"I left before they had any word on her condition. How is she?"

"It wasn't a heart attack. It's her gall bladder. She'll be back to normal in a few weeks."

"Oh, that's too bad."

"Excuse me?"

"Considering what her normal is, being back to normal isn't such a great prospect."

"I hear you."

"I'm glad you called, Mike. I was going to give you a call later this afternoon."

He decided not to tell her that he knew that she had called on Saturday and that he had forgotten to call earlier. "What's up?"

"I've been thinking about this for a few days. I don't know if it's my imagination or what."

Bishop had no idea what she was talking about so he just listened.

"Remember I told you that my car was about ready to conk out?"

"Yes."

"Well, I took your advice and called Dan Morehouse on Saturday to see if he had anything that might be in my price range."

"Good." He assumed that Dan would offer her some sort of a deal since she was a part of the Holy Trinity family.

"Not really."

"What makes you say that?"

"He was very nice on the phone. He told me that he had several vehicles with decent mileage that I might like. He even offered to work out a loan payment plan that wouldn't break the bank."

Bishop was trying to figure out what the problem might be. "Have you gone over there to look at the cars?"

"No."

"Would you like me to go with you when you go for a test drive?"

"No. That's not it." She sounded increasingly upset. "I'm not going for a test drive. I don't want to go near that place."

"I don't understand."

"It's his voice."

It was as if she were speaking a foreign language. He just didn't understand why she was so upset. He let her continue.

"After I hung up, I realized something."

"What?"

"Remember I told you that I heard Ed talking with another man the morning he was killed?"

"Yes." He felt a sudden chill course through his body as he realized what Debbie was about to say.

"I think Dan Morehouse killed Ed."

***

Could this be it? Could Debbie's memory of that voice lead to an identification of the killer? He had known students whose voices were quite similar. Could Debbie be mistaken? Could hearing his voice over the phone have altered her perception? Why would Dan have been in that storage room? Why would Dan kill Ed? Debbie had previously told him that Ed and the other man had been talking about the stock market. As a businessman and as the board's finance chairman, he would most likely be quite knowledgeable on the topic. If Dan were the killer and if he knew that Debbie could place him at the scene of the crime, Debbie's life might be in danger.

"I'm going to call Lieutenant Hodge and tell him what you've just told me."

"I can't be sure that I'm right," she admitted.

"I understand that, but it's the best lead we've had thus far. Just sit tight and don't tell anyone of your suspicion." He didn't want to alarm her, but he was concerned for her safety.

After ending that call, he tried to contact Hodge without success. He had left the station for the day, and he wasn't picking up on his cell. Bishop left a short message relaying what Debbie had just told him and suggesting that Debbie might be in danger if Morehouse realized what she knew.

He checked the clock on the classroom wall. The dealership would still be open. He quickly packed up his briefcase, closed the windows, turned off the lights, and headed out to the parking lot.

He wanted to confront Dan.

Chapter Twenty-Four

As he opened his car door, a blast of hot air hit him. He was reminded of a line in Shakespeare's *Sonnet 18*, "Sometimes too hot the eye of heaven shines." He lowered all of the windows and made the short drive to Morehouse Motors, hoping that Dan would be there.

What possible connection could there have been between Dan and Ed Cooper? They didn't exactly move in the same social circles. Dan might not even have known that Trinity had hired a new custodian. Ed was talking to someone about the stock market. Lots of people followed the market. The more he thought about it, the more uncertain he was that Debbie's belief that the man talking with Ed in the storage room that morning was Dan.

He had passed by the place hundreds of times without paying much attention. This dealership looked like most dealerships throughout the country. There was a showroom with the latest models on display, and there were hundreds of shiny cars and trucks parked in neat rows. Some vehicles were parked close to the street. The intention was to attract prospective buyers to stop in by focusing on a few loss leaders.

Then it hit him. He recalled a grammar school teacher from many years ago. Whenever a student who had been particularly obtuse on a topic, suddenly understood it, she would announce to the class, *Light dawns over marble head!* Most people from the Bay State were familiar with the reference to Marblehead, a town on the coast of Massachusetts. Why didn't he think of this sooner? The windshields of these cars and trucks had numbers and letters written all over them. "2013 … 4 x 4 … $19,995 … Special 1.9% for 60 mos." Elwin Crimins had seen one of these vehicles parked on the street in front of his house that morning.

Even though it was quite warm, as he got out of his car, he grabbed his sport coat and put it on. A young man wearing a white long-sleeved shirt and dark gray pants almost tripped as he rapidly prepared to greet a potential commission. "Beautiful day, isn't it?" he asked as he reached out to shake Bishop's hand. "My name is Greg. How can I help you today?"

"I'm here to see Mr. Morehouse."

His hopes for a sale before closing time dashed, Greg's big smile and enthusiasm vanished. "Through the showroom. Second door on the right." With that, he turned and walked slowly back in the direction from which he had come. Such was the life of a car salesman. Ten percent using every gimmick in the books to close a deal. Ninety percent boredom.

Bishop walked through the showroom without looking at any of the cars on display. He passed a row of empty cubicles where salesmen could meet with customers in semi-privacy while waiting for the manager to approve their "best offer." The second door on the right was open. As soon as Morehouse saw Bishop, he jumped up to greet him in a manner similar to that of Greg. He still sported the shiner that Frank had delivered in the faculty lunchroom.

"Michael Bishop! Nice to see you! Come on in. Sit down. Can I get you something to drink?"

"No thank you," said Bishop as he sat in a comfortable leather chair. He reached into his jacket pocket and pulled out a mint.

"So, you've finally decided to trade in that old Corolla. Smart move. Are you interested in new or used?"

"Neither," replied Bishop. "I'm afraid you've misunderstood the purpose of my visit." Bishop saw the same dramatic change in manner that Greg had displayed.

"Look, if you're hear to discuss the salary freeze or the staff cuts, I'm afraid you're wasting your time." He picked up a stack of papers on his desk as if to suggest to Bishop that he had a lot of important work to do.

When Debbie told Bishop that she thought that the voice she heard that morning was Dan's, he had made up his mind to confront him, but he hadn't had much time to think through exactly how he should do that. Seeing the display cars with the numbers on the windshields as Elwin had described also supported his theory. In addition, Ed had told Debbie that someone was stealing from the school. With the irregularities that Bishop found in the school's financial records, it all started to make sense. Perhaps he should have discussed this with Lieutenant Hodge first, but he hadn't been able to contact him. Besides, he thought he might get more out of Dan if Hodge wasn't there. He decided to use the approach that he had used so often with students who had done something wrong. Make them think that you know more than you actually do and let them incriminate themselves.

He looked directly at Dan and spoke in an authoritative voice. "Dan, I'm not here to discuss board decisions." He paused to let that sink in. "There are two witnesses who can place you at Trinity on the morning of Ed Cooper's death." He paused again as shock registered on Dan's face. When Dan jumped out of his seat, Bishop didn't flinch although the possibility that Dan would attack him crossed his mind. Dan closed his office door and sat behind his desk once again. He glanced at the monitors that gave him different views of what was happening in various areas of the dealership.

"Mike, I don't know what you're talking about," he said without making eye contact. He poured himself a glass of ice water from a pitcher on a small table near his desk and tried to regain his composure. "Who are these witnesses? They're lying."

"I'm not going to put their lives in danger by giving you their names." Bishop's primary worry was for Debbie. If Dan knew that Debbie could identify the voice of the killer, she would be a target. It didn't occur to Bishop that he was also putting himself in danger of retaliation.

"I think those witnesses are telling the truth, Dan, and I think you know that as well." He then proceeded to recount what he felt must have happened. "You went to meet Ed because he figured out that you were stealing from the school. You drove one of your display vehicles to the school early that morning, parked on Newbury Street, and cut through the wooded lot. You used the back entrance to enter the building. You got into an argument with Ed Cooper, and you caused him to fall to his death." Dan kept shaking his head as Bishop described what happened next. "Then, you broke a few of the steps of the ladder to make it look like an accident."

Dan rubbed his face with both hands as if he could remove the guilt that he felt. "All right," he said with resignation. Bishop's heart began to pound. Had he extracted a confession? Would it hold up in court? Dan spoke softly. "All right. I was there that morning," he said as he looked directly at his accuser, "but I didn't kill him."

***

Bishop did not have to prompt him to continue. Once that initial barrier had been breached, it seemed clear that Morehouse wanted to unburden himself of his guilt.

"Somehow Cooper had managed to hack into the school's records and discovered evidence of stock manipulation. He asked around and found out that I was chairman of the finance committee. He threatened to expose me if I didn't give him five thousand dollars." He picked up a pencil and began doodling on a pad of paper on his desk.

Extortion. That was consistent with Tim Kelleher's claim that Cooper had demanded money for his silence. Both Debbie and Amy remembered Ed bragging about coming into some big money. Dan's five thousand dollars was the big money.

"Go on."

"He told me where and when to meet him. He was a little drunk when I got there. I guess he was already celebrating his good fortune. He kept telling me how he was a genius when it came to the stock market and how easy it had been for him to detect the fraud. I wanted to kill him, believe me, but I swear I didn't."

"What made you think that he wouldn't contact you again demanding more money?"

Dan shrugged his shoulders. "Wishful thinking, I guess. I figured if he really did make some money in the market, he'd leave me alone."

The veteran teacher didn't want to reveal to Morehouse that he had followed a path similar to that of Cooper in discovering some abnormalities in the school's stock portfolio. "I still don't understand how you did it."

"That was easy." He became more animated as he explained the process. "Over the years, a number of people have donated stock to the school in order to avoid paying taxes on their gains. Let's say the school has 585 shares of Microsoft on the books. When the next report comes out, there are 85 shares on the books. That's a difference of about fifteen grand. Do that enough and you're talking some serious money."

Bishop recalled finding a similar error in the number of shares of Google stock.

"Wouldn't someone on the board realize what was going on?"

"No one looks at that stuff that closely. If anyone did notice, we could just say that they were clerical errors. No one would know until there was an outside audit, and by then, the errors would have been corrected."

"I'm still confused," admitted Bishop. "If these were just paper losses, why do it in the first place?"

He gave Bishop a sheepish look. "It was her idea."

"Her?"

"My aunt," he said as he glanced again at the monitors.

"Sister Ann?" How blind had he been? He should have known that she would be involved in this in some way.

"It was her idea to show some significant paper losses."

It was all starting to make sense. Sister Ann needed to demonstrate the school's financial difficulties so that she could justify making staff cuts, one of which was himself, the thorn in her side. This was to be her finest hour. He had to get Dan to confirm his suspicions. "Why would she want losses?"

"I don't know if you've noticed, but Sister Pat has a huge influence on my aunt. I think they decided that the only way they could push through some changes was to convince people that the school was in trouble financially."

"I've noticed," Bishop responded, "but if this stock business is all a ruse, why would you submit to Cooper's attempt at extortion?"

He started doodling on the pad of paper again. "Because once I got the idea in my head, I decided to do it."

"Meaning?"

"Meaning that they weren't just paper losses. I transferred the money to my business account."

Bishop looked at him in disbelief. "You stole $1.2 million?"

"Well," he said hurriedly, "I planned on putting it back. This business has become very competitive, and I needed an infusion of cash to pay off some debt."

"And the twenty-five thousand that you so generously donated to the school to help bridge the gap?"

He shook his head up and down. "Stolen."

"Does your aunt know about this?"

"God, no!" he exclaimed. "That's why I had to pay Cooper off. I couldn't take a chance that he'd tell her. If this gets out, I'll be ruined! She'll be ruined!"

Bishop pounced at the opening. "Is that why you killed him?"

"No, I didn't. I swear. I already told you what happened."

"How did Cooper figure out what you had done?"

"I wondered about that myself. He told me that when he was hired, Sister Pat brought him into her office to enter his name into the system. As she slowly typed in her password, she said every letter and number to herself, but it was loud enough for him to hear. He had quite a good memory, and he wrote down her password as soon as he left her office. When he realized that the school had a portfolio of stocks, he started looking more closely, and that's when he noticed some discrepancies."

"How did he know that you were responsible?"

"Because I was the one who approved the transactions," he said remorsefully. Bishop believed him. He also believed him when he said that this would ruin both him and his aunt. The problem was that such a scandal might also result in the school's closure. That was the one result that Bishop wanted to avoid.

There had to be another way. "Can you raise the cash before the school is audited?"

239

"I'd probably have to let one of my competitors buy in. Why? What are you going to do?"

Bishop stood up to leave. "If I were twenty years younger, I'd finish what Frank Wilson started." Morehouse instinctively raised his hand to his bruised eye.

As he walked back to his car, he popped another mint into his mouth, then took off his jacket. He noticed that Greg looked up from his phone, saw who it was, and quickly turned his attention back to the screen in his hand.

He needed some time to think this through. He also had to grapple with two nagging questions: If Dan didn't kill Cooper, who did? And what happened to the five thousand dollars hush money?

Chapter Twenty-Five

Bishop was again unsuccessful in his attempt to discuss the rapidly changing situation with Lieutenant Hodge. He didn't bother to leave another message. He listened to a CD of *The Well-Tempered Clavier* by Johann Sebastian Bach as he considered the possibilities. Assuming that Dan was telling the truth, he was a fraud and a phony but not a murderer. Assuming that Jack was telling the truth, he was a petty thief but no more than that. Amy Davis, Ed Cooper's half sister, and her ex-boyfriend, Ryan Baxter, had been eliminated as suspects earlier, and there was no reason to question those decisions. Who else had a motive and the opportunity? Debbie was certainly telling the truth about hearing Dan's voice that morning, and she was in some sort of a relationship with Ed. Tim Kelleher and Hannah Ward both had reputations to protect. As with Dan but on a smaller scale, Tim had succumbed to Ed's extortion. What about Samantha Graham? She had gone out of her way to explain the nature of her relationship with Ed. Might she have done that in an attempt to prevent Bishop from digging any deeper?

He pulled his Corolla in the driveway behind the black Ford Bronco. As he got out of the car, he put his jacket on again. With the sound of his car door closing, Max, the Jack Russell terrier, started barking. By the time he got to the front door, Debbie had already opened it. She was wearing a sleeveless pink blouse and tan shorts.

"Mike! This is a surprise. Please come in." The dog was a blur of movement as he greeted their visitor. Debbie swooped Max up in her arms and said, "Be a good boy or I'll have to put you in the basement." Bishop had heard her use that line without success before.

Debbie invited him into the living room, and they both sat in the same places as they did about a week earlier, she on the sofa, and he on the old oversized chair near the television. The old set with the rabbit ears had been replaced by a large flat screen model that seemed too big for the small room.

"Can I get you something to drink? I've got tea and soda. Maybe you'd prefer a cold beer?"

"No, thanks. I'm fine." He reached into his jacket pocket and pulled out a mint. "Care for one?" he asked. Max dashed over thinking that there might be something for him. Debbie waved off the mint and called Max back to the sofa.

Bishop wasn't quite sure how to begin. He decided to use the approach that had worked for him in the past. "I just left Morehouse Motors."

"You did?" She just about jumped from the couch. "Did you tell Dan that I recognized his voice?" she asked excitedly.

"No, of course not. That might have put your life in danger."

"Oh, I'm not afraid of him now. He's going to be arrested, isn't he?"

"I thought you said that you weren't sure?"

"Well, I wasn't but then I was. I mean … I think it's him. It has to be him!" She stamped her feet on the floor in frustration, startling Max, who had settled down under the coffee table. She grabbed the remote to her new television, slumped back on the sofa, put her bare feet up on the coffee table, and began playing with the buttons. She kept her eyes on it as she spoke. "This remote has so many buttons," she said with a little laugh. "I don't even know what all of them do." Bishop said nothing. He felt a sudden chill as she sounded like a little child trying not to be afraid of the dark. She talked softly as she stared at the remote. "Morehouse is a bad

242

man. He stole money … and he killed my Eddie." Bishop noticed the tears welling up in her eyes.

"That's half of the truth, isn't it, Debbie?" he asked gently.

She glared at him. "What do you mean by that?"

He was too close to back away now. "I mean that he is a bad man for stealing money, but you and I both know that he didn't kill Eddie."

"He didn't?" she responded in a childlike voice as she turned her attention back to the remote.

"No, he didn't. Eddie was still alive when Morehouse left. You were there, Debbie, near the trap door. You told me so. That was the truth, wasn't it?"

"Yes."

"After he left, you climbed down the ladder to see Eddie. You'd done that before, but this time …"

She stopped him mid-sentence. The tears and the childlike voice were gone. She practically spit out the angry words. "He lied to me! Again! He told me that he loved me, but I knew he was lying. I'd seen him leaving the Blue Moon with that slut, Samantha."

Bishop sat quietly, feeling a mixture of sorrow and relief.

"He tried to hush me up. He said we'd both get in trouble if they heard us. Then he tried to grab me, but I knocked his arm away from me. The envelope fell to the floor, and I grabbed it and started to run up the ladder." She paused as she relived the horrifying moment. "I didn't mean to hurt him," she shouted, "but he started coming after me. And he'd been drinking. I didn't know what he'd do!" Tears were streaming down her face as she rocked back and forth on the edge of the sofa.

"I understand," Bishop said, assuming that the most painful part of this was over.

243

"No you don't! How could you understand?" she screamed as she threw the remote at him with as much force as she could muster. She had held onto it for a fraction of a second too long, and it missed its target and struck the television instead, leaving a crack from top to bottom.

What happened next stunned Bishop. The dog ran over to the remote lying on the floor, pawed at it, and tried to pick it up. Debbie screamed at Max as she jumped off of the sofa. "Bad boy! Bad boy! You're going in the basement!" She grabbed the remote and hit him in the snout with it. As the dog yelped, she began kicking at him with her bare feet. A similar outburst had ended Ed Cooper's life.

"Debbie, stop that!" Bishop yelled as he picked up the frightened animal. Debbie slumped to the floor, and sat cross-legged in front of the broken screen. She crossed her arms tightly around herself as she rocked back and forth. In that childlike voice, she said over and over again, "I didn't mean to hurt him."

***

Max was still trembling as Bishop put him on the floor. Instead of going over to Debbie, he ran up to a man standing inside the unlocked front door. It was Lieutenant Hodge.

"What's going on here?"

Debbie seemed unaware of Hodge's presence as Bishop gave him a quick summary of what happened.

When Bishop called her name, Debbie got to her feet and wiped her eyes. He introduced her to the lieutenant. She placed the remote back on the coffee table and sat back down on the sofa. She acted as if the last few minutes hadn't occurred. She had returned from that dark place inside her and seemed to be her normal self. Hodge stood next to her as he placed her under arrest and read her her rights.

She looked at Max who was lying down at Bishop's side. "What about Max? Who'll take care of him?"

"I'll take care of him for a few days if you want me to," offered Bishop. He knew that it would be a long time before Debbie would return. She needed a psychiatric evaluation. Those results might mitigate the charges against her, but she was likely to face years of incarceration for her actions.

When she went to her bedroom to gather a few things together, Bishop had a question for Hodge. "How did you happen to be here at just the right moment?"

"I got your message that she might be in danger if Morehouse knew that she could identify him. I just swung by on my way home to see that she was okay."

"I'm certainly glad you did. I'll fill you in on my conversation with Morehouse later. His hands are not exactly clean."

Debbie emerged from her room ready to leave with Hodge. The dog cowered as she bent over to pat him. "I think he likes you," she said to Bishop. "Take good care of him."

"I will."

"And tell those nuns that I won't be going in to work tomorrow."

"I will." To one nun in particular, he would have much more than that to say.

***

Just as Bishop was about to let Max jump into the front seat of his car, Debbie shouted, "Wait!" and ran back into the house. He had no idea as to what was going on. He and Hodge exchanged worried looks as Hodge quickly trailed her. A moment later both emerged. She was carrying a collar and leash, and Hodge had a small box.

"You're gonna need this stuff," she said as she leaned in to give Max a kiss on the head. "Sorry, Max." Bishop didn't know if she was apologizing for having to let someone else take care of him, or if she was apologizing for the times that she had mistreated him. He thanked her for the bag of dry dog food, two bowls, and a few chew toys that she had placed in the box and promised that he'd take good care of Max.

As soon as the car started moving, Max settled down on the seat. Whenever the car stopped, he would bounce up to look out of the window. He didn't seem to mind the classical music coming from the car's stereo system. That, in itself, was a sign that this just might work. He hadn't had a dog in the house since Skipper, a West Highland White Terrier died just six months after Grace had passed away. Skipper had been so attached to Grace that Bishop was convinced that the dog had died of a broken heart. He had considered adopting a dog from the local shelter but was never fully convinced that it was a good idea. Now, he would have a chance to find out.

Before he brought Max into the house for the first time, he put the collar on him and attached the leash. They went for a long walk around the yard. Max must have been used to the leash since he was able to heel fairly well, although he stopped frequently to mark his new territory.

Once inside, Bishop set the box that Debbie had given him on the counter. Max paid very close attention as he heard the familiar sound of his bag of food being opened. He put a few handfuls of food in one of the bowls and filled the other with water. He set both down on the kitchen floor. Since he doubted that he would remember what to buy when he was at the supermarket, he wrote down the brand name on a slip of paper and placed it in his wallet. By the time he had done that, Max had devoured the last of the nuggets and was looking for more. A quick check of the guidelines on the package assured Bishop that Max had been adequately fed. He found a little bag of cookies in the box and gave him one for dessert.

Bishop went into his bedroom to change, and Max scampered in to investigate. When Bishop closed the bathroom door, Max waited patiently in the hallway. The poor dog must have been confused and uncertain about the sudden change in environment as he followed Bishop wherever he went.

After having a three-egg omelet with diced peppers, onions, and tomato for dinner, he took Max for another long walk. He realized that Max's first night in his new surroundings might be difficult, so he wanted to tire him out as much as possible. After the walk, he grabbed one of the chew toys from the box for which Max immediately started jumping. Bishop tossed the floppy chipmunk, and Max pounced on it, shook it violently, and brought it back for Bishop to toss again and again. Eventually, Max tuckered out, drank from his bowl of water in the kitchen, and settled down in the sunroom as Bishop did some online research about Jack Russell terriers.

Focusing on Max had been a welcome distraction for Bishop. Now, as he listened to a recording of violinist Nadja Salerno-Sonnenberg playing concertos by Mendelssohn, he had a chance to reflect on the day's events. Ironically, it had begun with Sister Pat's suspiciously good mood and her "Enjoy your day" greeting. He considered the possibility that her good mood might have been the result of her knowledge that certain teachers, himself included, were to receive their letters of termination. It remained to be seen whether her gallbladder attack had simply delayed the inevitable or whether it had provided an opportunity to reverse course.

He had given Jack the chance to reverse course by providing the money to reimburse the girls from whom he had stolen. He had convinced Charlie Mitchell to reverse course in accepting the decision of the faculty council regarding the poor choices of Billy Sprowl and Clare Mooney. He had begun the day considering Samantha Graham as a possible suspect in Ed Cooper's murder until her unexpected visit to his classroom forced him to reverse course in his speculation. He had gone to Morehouse Motors with the intent of confronting the killer until Dan's admission of guilt in lesser crimes forced him to again reverse course. Finally, he had gone to the home of Debbie Bates, one of the first suspects that he had considered but dismissed. For her, there would be no opportunity to reverse course, to undue that outburst of anger, jealousy, and hurt. It had been a day that Bishop would not soon forget. And tomorrow, he realized, would be the day when he would learn whether or not his career at Holy Trinity was over.

Before getting ready for bed, he took Max out to what was quickly becoming his favorite spot near the lilac bushes, hoping that the dog wouldn't need to be taken out again until morning. He found an old blanket in the linen closet for Max to sleep on until he had a chance to buy a dog bed. The number of short white hairs that the dog had shed since his arrival convinced Bishop that the furniture would have to be off limits. Using a firm voice and rewarding the desired behavior with a piece of kibble, it took less than ten minutes for Bishop to train Max not to jump on the bed.

The next morning, Bishop found Max patiently waiting for him on the living room sofa. He realized that he couldn't teach an old dog new tricks, at least not in ten minutes.

248

Chapter Twenty-Six

Taking care of Max took more time than he had anticipated. He arrived at school only minutes before the first bell. Fortunately, Sister Pat was not there to make some snide remark.

Despite her absence, she managed to dominate the conversation in the faculty mailroom. Sister Ann had place a get-well card in the mailbox of each homeroom   teacher. Had they known of the arrest of Debbie for the murder of Ed Cooper, the card would not have received the attention that it did.

Bishop asked if anyone had heard the latest on Sister Pat's condition.

"According to Sister Ann, she probably will be released from the hospital today," said Kim Anderson.

Bishop surmised that the principal would leave school right after morning announcements in order to be with Sister Pat at the hospital. He had had a long conversation with Lieutenant Hodge the previous night not only about Debbie but also about Dan Morehouse. When he told him what he hoped to do, Hodge reminded him that he wasn't a lawyer and couldn't offer a legal opinion. Bishop took that as implicit approval to proceed as planned. He grabbed a blank piece of copy paper, scribbled a note, sealed it in an envelope, and placed the envelope in Sister Ann's mailbox. The reaction to the get-well cards continued.

"It was bad enough that I had to sign that card yesterday. I couldn't write what I really felt so I just signed my name. I don't see why we should make the kids sign a card for her since I'd bet that most of them can't stand her." Roger Willis was poised to toss the card in the trash.

"I hear what you're saying, Rog," said Kim, "but you gotta believe she'll be making a list of those who signed and those who didn't."

249

"Damn! Double damn!" Charlie blurted out as he pretended to hit his head against the wall.

"What's the matter?" asked Kim.

"I forgot to sign that stupid card yesterday! I was so focused on dealing with that little thief, Billy Sprowl, that it completely slipped my mind."

Bishop noticed that Charlie left the name of Clare Mooney out of the story of his missing exam. He also suspected that Charlie had forgotten to sign the card from the faculty intentionally. That way he could send his own card filled with sentimental slop that he would not want other teachers to read. He'd probably send along a box of chocolates as well without realizing that she wouldn't be able to eat them after surgery. He laughed to himself as he considered the possibility that Charlie would make a quick visit to the hospital during his prep period.

Given the intensity of resentment displayed by the faculty, Bishop expected no less from the students. However, when he explained the purpose of the card and handed it to the person in the first seat in the first row, there was no word of protest. They might have just heard the words "hospital" and "surgery" and assumed that she was at death's door. Then he realized what was probably closer to the truth. Wishing someone well who has fallen ill, no matter your personal feelings toward that person, was the right thing to do. The students were simply reflecting the values of Holy Family High School. It wasn't the first time that the faculty might learn a lesson from the students.

***

When the last student had left the room, he quickly scanned the card. Regardless of the willingness to sign without protest, he was just being prudent in making sure that no inappropriate comments had been included.

During his first class, he received a call from the office. He answered without giving the interruption much thought. Terry probably was looking for a student.

"Michael?"

"Yes."

"This is Sister Ann." After all these years, Bishop knew very well who it was by the sound of her voice. The tone of her voice also told him that she had found his note in her mailbox and was not too happy about it.

"I found your note in my mailbox, and I was hoping to run over to the hospital this morning. Could we meet some other day?" She probably had her appointment book open ready to pencil him in later in the week.

"I'm afraid not."

That answer was met with silence. She clearly was not pleased.

"Can you explain to me exactly what is so important?"

He spoke as softly as he could. "Sister, I have a room full of students with me. I can come down right after this class."

"Very well," she said as she abruptly ended the call.

When he returned to the front of the room, everyone waited patiently for him to say something. It was a bad time to have one of those memory lapses.

"Now, where were we?"

Tiffany raised her hand.

Although he had taught this young lady all year long, he suddenly could not recall her name. To avoid the risk of guessing, he simply looked at her and said, "Yes."

"If you need to go down to the office, we can study quietly." The class erupted in approval. In that moment of laughter, her name came to him.

251

"I appreciate the offer, Tiffany, but that won't be necessary." He also managed to recall the specific point that they had been discussing.

"We were reviewing how brilliantly Chaucer captures character in the "Prologue" of *The Canterbury Tales*. We've already mentioned the knight for whom Chaucer has nothing but praise. Very few of the other pilgrims are presented as favorably. In most of the other portraits, he exposes their flaws even when he appears to be complimenting them." He looked around the room. Chad looked a bit disengaged as he chewed at the top of his pen. "Can you give us an example, Chad?"

Quickly removing the pen from his mouth, he straightened up in his chair. "What about the nun?" Some students were flipping pages in their text to find that section.

"Excellent! What does Chaucer say about her?"

Without looking at his book or his notes, he offered some examples. "Well, he says that she is a very caring person because she would cry if she saw a mouse caught in a trap, and that she fed her dogs the finest foods."

Jerry already had his hand in the air, but Bishop wanted to complete the point before he took another question. "Okay, there's the compliment, but how does he turn that into a criticism, Jerry?"

"I was going to say something else," he announced.

"That's all right, but answer my question first. How does Chaucer turn those details from a positive to a negative?"

"He's suggesting that perhaps she is more concerned about her dogs than she is about her fellow man."

"Right. Now, what did you want to say?"

Jerry seemed puzzled for a moment. He had forgotten what he wanted to say. Bishop realized that some memory issues weren't confined

252

to the older generation. Just as Bishop was about to call on someone else, Jerry's thought came back to him. "I was going to mention the Latin inscription on the gold brooch that the nun is wearing."

"What are the words and what do they mean?"

"*Amor vincit omnia*," and it means, "Love conquers all."

"Tiffany, what does that inscription tell us about the nun?"

She cleared her throat before answering the question. "I think that on the surface it's a compliment. I mean ... it's a good thing if it refers to her love of God as more important than anything else. But Chaucer shows her as more concerned with herself and with her dogs than she is with other people."

Jerry added, "And that brooch is gold which makes you wonder how seriously she takes her vow of poverty."

The class went on to review some of the other pilgrims from Chaucer's work. At the end of the period, it was the portrait of the nun that lingered in Bishop's mind. This woman, who went by the name of Madame Eglantine, was not evil, but she certainly was a poor example of what a nun should be.

As he made his way down to the principal's office, he wondered what Chaucer would have thought of Sister Ann.

***

When he got there, her office door was closed, but he could see through the door's window that she was on the telephone. When he knocked, she looked up, quickly ended her call, and signaled for him to come in.

As he opened the door, a blast of cool air hit him. He shut the door and approached her desk. She folded her hands and placed them at the edge of her desk. She looked at the clock on the wall near the door. It was clear that she was annoyed that he had kept her in the building when she wanted to be with Sister Pat at the hospital. She didn't bother to ask him to sit down.

He sat in the straight-backed wooden chair on the other side of her desk. "How is Sister Pat?" he asked, although he had heard that she was doing just fine and was to be released from the hospital sometime today.

"As if you care," she snarled.

"I do care, as a matter of fact. I wouldn't wish ill on anyone." He refrained from adding that that even included someone who had plotted his forced retirement.

"Well, let's not waste time on chitchat. I want to know what is so damned important that it couldn't wait a day or two." Her phone buzzed once. She grabbed the receiver, listened for a few seconds, and said sharply, "No! And hold all my calls!" She slammed the receiver down and waited for Bishop to begin.

Bishop kept reminding himself to remain calm. "First of all, I wanted to tell you that Ed Cooper's killer is in custody."

From the puzzled look on her face, it appeared that that issue had taken a back seat in her thinking. "Oh … well … that's good. Are you going to tell me who was arrested?"

"I'm sorry to say that it's Debbie Bates."

"Debbie? She's the one who recommended Cooper to me in the first place."

"Yes, I know. I don't believe that she intended to do what she did. She's a very troubled young woman."

"Obviously," she said sarcastically. She glanced at the clock again and began to get up. "Well, if that's all, I really must be going."

He gestured for her to wait. "That's not all, Sister. In fact, that wasn't the main reason why I needed to see you this morning."

254

Sister sat back down in her leather chair, clearly annoyed and confused. "What are you talking about?"

"I had an interesting visit with your nephew yesterday." Sister's face was expressionless as she waited for Bishop to continue. Perhaps she knew what was coming. "It seems that he rigged the school's financial records to show a $1.2 million loss."

"That's ridiculous!" she snapped. "Why would he do such a thing?"

Bishop reached into his jacket pocket, but not for a mint. He pulled out a small object about the size of a pack of cigarettes and placed it on her desk.

"Don't tell me that you've been recording this conversation," she shouted angrily.

"No … not this conversation. This one." He hit the play button.

It was her idea to show some significant paper losses.

Why would she want losses?

I don't know if you've noticed, but Sister Pat has a huge influence on my aunt. I think they decided that the only way they could push through some changes was to convince people that the school was in trouble financially.

As she listened, her surprise turned to anger. "That stupid, stupid man! All he had to do was keep quiet for a few more days." By then, she would have succeeded in ridding herself of several teachers who made her life difficult, chief among them none other than Bishop. Before the audit, the "mistakes" would have been corrected, and all would be well.

255

She was trying to figure a way to extricate herself from this awkward situation without the benefit of consulting with Sister Pat. "That's not the worst of it," he said matter-of-factly.

"What do you mean?" she asked.

"Your idea sounded so good that he decided to go that extra step from deceitful to criminal."

"I don't understand."

"Those weren't just mistakes on paper. Your nephew actually transferred that money to his own business account."

Sister Ann always looked a bit pale, but now her face lost all color as she sat there in disbelief. "Jesus, Mary and Joseph!" After a moment's thought, she concluded, "Well, he'll just have to put the money back."

"I'm afraid that it's not that simple."

"Why not?"

"He used the money, most of it anyway, to cover some debt."

"How much of it does he have left?"

"I'm not sure, really. I know that he gave $25,000 to the school as encouragement for other large donors to help Trinity through its supposed financial crisis."

She looked up to the ceiling as if she were hoping for some sign that this was all just a cruel joke. "You mean that that was the school's money he was donating?"

"Exactly. And that's not all."

She seemed afraid to ask but also afraid not to ask. "What else?" she groaned.

"Apparently, Ed Cooper figured out that Dan had stolen the school's money, and he threatened to expose him if he didn't give him $5,000."

"Oh, my word! How awful!"

If Sister Ann thought that Cooper's extortion of $5,000 was awful, Bishop wondered how she might characterize her nephew's embezzlement of $1.2 million. After taking a moment to think through all that she had been told, she asked, "How did Cooper know what Dan had done?"

Bishop was intentionally vague. "I guess he knew a lot about computers."

Sister glanced at the clock again. She undoubtedly wanted to share this unfortunate turn of events with Sister Pat. Her plans were coming undone. "Will Dan be arrested?" she wondered.

"That depends."

"Depends on what?"

"Someone would have to file charges against him."

"I certainly won't do that," she said dismissively. ""It would ruin him and damage the school as well."

"Someone on the board could bring charges."

"Who on the board knows about this?"

"No one … yet."

"What do you mean by that?"

"Let me be very clear, Sister. If I went to the board with the information on this tape, Dan would likely be headed to jail, and you more than likely would lose your job." He picked up the recording device and placed it back in his pocket.

Her eyes narrowed as she gave him a steely look. "Go on."

"Here's one scenario: Dan allows one of his competitors to buy into his business so that he can make full restitution to the school within thirty days. Dan resigns from the board citing personal reasons. You meet with the board and convince them to restore all of the teaching positions that were to be eliminated. Shortly thereafter, you announce that the school's financial picture has improved and sign new contracts giving teachers a three percent increase and staff an increase of one dollar an hour."

"This is blackmail!" she shouted angrily.

"No, it isn't," he responded calmly. "It's a resolution to a problem of your own making that is beneficial to everyone involved."

She slumped back in his chair. "I'll have to think about it." That was her typical response when put on the spot.

"I'm afraid there's no time for that." He pulled some papers from the inside pocket of his jacket. "I've typed up the conditions that I just outlined to you." He handed her the papers. "If you would please read this, sign and date one copy for me, and keep the other for yourself."

She snatched the papers from him and slapped them on the desk. When she had finished reading, she picked up her pen and signed one copy. Then, she shoved it in his direction.

He quickly checked for her signature, a perfect example of the Palmer method of penmanship, before folding the paper and returning it to his inner jacket pocket. That done, he got up to leave.

"Wait! What guarantee do I have that you'll keep your end of the agreement?"

He smiled. "Sister, I've been at Trinity for forty-five years. I don't think you have to worry about that." As he opened the door, he looked back at her. "By the way, when Sister Pat gets home, make sure that she changes her Trinity password."

Bishop wished that he could have pulled out his cell phone to capture the look on her face.

Chapter Twenty-Seven

Graduation took place without incident. Both Billy Sprowl and Clare Mooney had waived their right to a hearing before the faculty council made its decision. They were not allowed to wear the medallions that indicated their membership in the National Honor Society. That distinction was also removed from future copies of their official school transcript. Both young people seemed ready to put their mistakes behind them.

Sister Pat felt well enough to attend the ceremony. She appeared to have lost a bit of weight although she still had a difficult time squeezing into one of the auditorium seats. Bishop was delighted that the theme of the valedictory speech was *Carpe Diem*. That was sure to confound the assistant principal.

After the event, as the seniors gathered outside the auditorium to receive congratulations from friends and family and to pose for photos, he found himself face to face with Sister Ann and Sister Pat.

"Good evening, Sisters."

"What's so good about it?" Sister Pat snapped back. "That speech was awful. I didn't even get half of the references, and it was way too long!"

Sister Ann quickly glanced around, hoping that no one was close enough to hear what her friend was saying.

Sister Pat pointed her index finger at Bishop. "And you! You're a disgrace!" Sister Ann tugged on Sister Pat's arm in a futile attempt to move her away from the source of her anger. "Forcing the principal to accept all of your conditions! You better believe that if I wasn't on my sick bed, I wouldn't have let her give in to your demands."

"The Lord works in mysterious ways," said Bishop.

"What do you mean by that?"

Before he had a chance to respond, Charlie Mitchell managed to get Sister Pat's attention by telling her how happy he was to see her up and about. If she only knew half of what Charlie said about her behind her back, she wouldn't have smiled at his flattering remarks. Bishop took advantage of the distraction to slip away. When he considered the duplicitous behavior of Sister Ann and her nephew, he felt that his own actions, taken in the best interests of the school, were more than justified. He knew that both administrators would be looking for ways to settle the score with him when a new school year began in September. He also knew that he would be ready for them.

***

After graduation, some of the faculty and staff met at Christy's for pizza and beer. Bishop drove over but didn't intend on staying very long. He knew that Max would be waiting patiently for him to get home.

The place was packed when he got there. Ron Jennings jumped up when he saw him enter and waved him over to his table. While he was greeting everyone, Ron poured him a glass of beer from one of the pitchers on the table.

"Thanks, Ron, but I think I'll just have a Pepsi."

"Sure thing." He got the attention of one of the workers behind the counter, ordered the soft drink for his friend, and continued with the story that he had started to tell.

"So, I'm a hundred miles from here, right, and I stop at this place called Tomaselli's. I order a large pizza with a few toppings, and when I taste it, I tell the guy 'This sauce tastes just like Christy's in Groveland.' The guy looks at me like I'm nuts, but he goes and tells the owner. Next thing I know, the owner, Tomaselli, comes out and I tell him the same thing. He starts laughing and reaches out to shake my hand. He looks

260

around the place and says, 'This man knows his pies!'" Everyone at the table started laughing, including Bishop, even though he had heard the story many times before. Clearly, Ron was enjoying himself as he announced, "I was right! Turns out Tomaselli is Luigi's cousin, and when he opened his place, Luigi gave him the recipe for the sauce."

Mary Ellen seemed to fit right in with the Holy Trinity crowd. It was much too early to predict where this relationship would go, but if anyone deserved a bit of good fortune in that department, it was Ron.

Frank Wilson came over and tapped Bishop on the shoulder. When he realized who it was, he got up, and shook hands heartily. "Good to see you, Frank! I'm glad that you were able to attend the graduation." It was the first time that Frank had been seen since his suspension.

"It's good to be back. From what I've heard, I have you to thank for that. I don't know exactly how you managed it, but I'm very grateful. I really am."

Bishop shrugged. "You know better than to believe everything you hear." He quickly changed the topic. "Sister Annunciata told me that your students did very well on their exams. She was very impressed with the way you had prepared them."

He beamed proudly. "Thanks … for everything."

As Bishop turned his attention back to his table of friends, he realized that the topic of conversation had come around to Debbie Bates. He sipped on his drink and listened for a few moments. The consensus of the group seemed to be one of shock that a person that they thought they knew fairly well could have committed such a horrible crime.

He didn't want to sound as if he were lecturing a group of students, but he felt that he needed to make a point. "One theme that dominates much of the literature I've read is that appearances are deceiving, and

261

there's a good reason for that. Literature is a reflection of the human condition." He thought of his recent discussion of Hawthorne's short story, "The Minister's Black Veil." Everyone has some secret sin, some darkness within.

"How often do we find ourselves hiding behind a mask? How hard is it to know if someone is truthful or skillfully hiding the truth?" The mood at the table had turned quite somber as each person considered his words. He again thought of Iago in Shakespeare's *Othello*. He was constantly referred to as "honest Iago" although he was far from honest in his dealings with others. As a result of his experiences of the last couple of weeks, he thought especially of Jack Slater, Tim Kelleher, Hannah Ward, Billy Sprowl, Clare Mooney, Samantha Graham, Dan Morehouse, Sister Ann. In that group, he included himself, of course. Ironically, only Sister Pat had apparently mastered the ability to brazenly present to the world her true nature. Sister Meany didn't bother with a mask.

Ron broke the silence at the table. "I know that this is difficult for you. But let me ask one more question I know that we are all interested in. "How did you figure out that she had done it?"

He was reluctant to take any credit for his role in this sad affair. "I wasn't really sure that I had figured it out until she admitted what she had done." He thought back to that afternoon in her apartment as Debbie sat on the floor in front of the cracked screen of her television, rocking back and forth, crying. After she was arraigned on murder charges, she was sent to a psychiatric hospital for evaluation.

"I feel sorry for that young woman. I think that she is dealing with a lot of issues about which we know very little. Hopefully, she can get the treatment she needs." He still wasn't sure that Debbie's action had been the result of a jealous rage over Ed's interest in Samantha. Lieutenant Hodge had told him that his men found an envelope stuffed with hundred dollar bills taped to the bottom of the lid of the toilet in her apartment. Most of the $5,000 that Dan had given Ed was in it minus the money that she had used to buy her new television. Perhaps they had argued over money. It wouldn't have been the first time that greed had led to death.

He finished his Pepsi and got up to leave. "Listen, this should be a time to celebrate, not to dwell on the past. I've got to get home. Keep in touch over the summer. I'm already looking forward to next school year."

***

A week later, Bishop took Max to the vet. He had called several veterinarians before he found the one that Debbie had used for her dog. The vet turned out to be one of Bishop's former students, George Gibbons. Gibb, as his friends called him, had graduated in the early '70s, and Bishop hadn't seen him since. He didn't remember him all that well other than that he was a very good wrestler but not much of a student.

When he brought Max into the office, the receptionist, a tall woman with long red hair, asked him to fill out some forms. Apparently, Debbie hadn't taken Max for a visit in the last few years despite reminders to do so. Since there was no one else in the waiting room, she came around to give Max a little attention.

After giving Max a good pat and a little treat, she introduced herself to Bishop.

"Mr. Bishop, my name is Heather. Nice to meet you," she said as she reached out to shake his hand. "Are you Max's new owner?"

"I'm taking care of Max for now while Debbie is away." Bishop assumed that Heather had read about Debbie in the papers, but he wasn't about to get into any of that now.

263

"I noticed that Debbie has an outstanding balance of $89 on her account," Heather announced delicately.

"Please add that to my bill," said Bishop as he sat down in one of the hard plastic chairs in the waiting area. Max settled down next to Bishop until the door to the examining room opened at which point he ran up to the vet with his leash sliding behind him on the tile floor.

Dr. Gibbons bent down to greet his patient and then stood up to greet the owner. "Mr. Bishop! What a surprise!" He shook hands with his former teacher. "You haven't changed much at all. Are you still at Trinity?"

"Yes, I am. Forty-five years and counting."

"That's remarkable. Good for you."

Bishop appreciated the compliment about looking the same although he knew that Gibb was being more polite than truthful. On the other hand, Gibb had changed so much that he might not have known who he was if he had met him on the street. Of course, he wasn't eighteen any longer. He must have been in his mid-forties now. The well-conditioned body that had made him a success on the mats had become much thicker especially around the middle. His neatly trimmed goatee, which was mostly gray, was the only hair on his shaved head.

He removed Max's leash, gently picked him up, and placed him on the examining table. A folder with the dog's medical history was open on the doctor's desk. He talked to Max in a reassuring voice as he conducted his examination. Bishop stood by quietly. He had been pleasantly surprised to learn that Gibb had become a veterinarian. If memory served, and he realized that that was more in question these days, Gibb had been a rather mediocre student. That he had gone on to obtain not only a college degree but also his license to practice veterinary medicine merely illustrated that some students matured later than others.

While he examined Max, he said to Bishop, "You know, I have you to thank for becoming a veterinarian."

Bishop gave him a puzzled look. "Why do you say that?"

"I remember half way through my senior year, you took me aside and told me that if I didn't start getting serious about my studies, I'd look back someday and regret the opportunities that I'd missed. You said that it would be a shame if I wasted my potential."

Bishop had no recollection of that conversation whatsoever.

Gibb continued, "I was steamed at you at the time for saying something like that to me, but then I realized that you were right. I really started working hard, and never let myself become complacent again."

"Well, I probably didn't have very much to do with your success, but I appreciate your saying that."

After completing his exam, he put Max on the floor, and reached for the folder on his desk.

"How does everything look, Doc?"

"He appears to be in good shape for a dog his age."

"How old is he?"

"It's difficult to know for certain since the previous owner didn't get the dog as a pup, but my guess is that Max is at least ten."

"Really?"

"Yup." He glanced again at some papers in the folder. "There are a couple of areas of concern."

"Go on."

"He exhibited some slight discomfort when I pressed into his stomach. I'd like to take some x-rays and have some blood work done. It's probably nothing to worry about, but I'd rather not take chances. To my knowledge, he hasn't been seen by a vet in several years, and he's overdue for some booster shots."

"Okay. What do you want to do first?"

"We can do the x-rays, the blood work, and the rabies and distemper shots today. Bring him back in a few weeks, and we can take care of the other shots. I'd also like you to schedule a teeth cleaning for Max. He does have one tooth that should be pulled, and we can take care of that then."

"Anything else?"

"I don't see any fleas or ticks. Be sure you keep up with his treatments."

Bishop shook his head. "I just took over care of Max a few weeks ago. I'm afraid I need a refresher about those treatments."

"No problem. I'll have Heather show you what you need and how to use it. While you're doing that, I'll get started on Max."

"Thanks for everything, Gibb," said Bishop as he shook hands and headed back out to the receptionist's desk.

"My pleasure. Great to see you again."

***

A couple of weeks later, Bishop was driving home. Max was curled up on the passenger's front seat, still recovering from his dental procedure. X-rays did not reveal any abnormalities with his stomach, but Gibb did have some disturbing news. At some point in the past, Max had suffered from three broken ribs that had healed on their own. Bishop didn't speculate on how the dog might have suffered those injuries and neither did the vet.

As he drove by, he noticed that the huge sign for Morehouse Motors had been replaced with one for Cahill Motors. Rumor had it that to

266

avoid bankruptcy, Dan was forced to take a lowball offer from Cahill who already owned several other dealerships locally. Dan was now working as a salesman at Cahill Motors.

Ron informed Bishop that the board of trustees accepted Dan's letter of resignation. Bishop doubted that anyone on the board other than Sister Ann knew the reason for his resignation. It didn't really matter. What was important was that the board voted to rescind the draconian measures that they had put in place when they thought that the school was on the brink of financial collapse.

Ron also mentioned that Sister Ann and Sister Pat, who had fully recovered from her gallbladder attack, were in San Diego attending a weeklong conference. They were staying at the luxurious Hotel del Coronado, which suggested to Bishop that they would probably spend an hour or so each day at the conference and the majority of their time relaxing in the sun, shopping, and eating at expensive restaurants. The principal, whose devious and unethical behavior should have resulted in her dismissal, had managed to hold onto her position for another year. So had Bishop.

It had been a difficult year in many ways, starting with the discovery of Al Zappala's body in September. At that time, he could not have imagined that he would find himself in the middle of another murder investigation before the end of the school year. Despite all of that, his classroom experiences continued to be a source of comfort and renewal. He was already counting the days until classes resumed in September.

***

As the car pulled into the driveway, Max perked up. Bishop attached the leash to his collar, and they walked down to pick up the mail. Among the envelopes was one from Jack Slater that Bishop knew would contain a check for $25. It would take several more months, but there was no question that Jack would repay the loan.

Once inside, he made sure that Max had plenty of water in his bowl. After running around for a moment, Max was tuckered again and settled into his bed for another nap. It was too nice a day for Bishop to stay inside. The sky was a deep blue, and the sun was strong, but a northerly breeze made it feel comfortable. He went to do some weeding in the rose garden. The Mister Lincoln roses with their deep red color and rich fragrance were Grace's favorite. He decided that he and Max would bring a bouquet of Mister Lincolns to the cemetery after lunch. There was a lot that he wanted to tell her.

Made in the USA
Las Vegas, NV
16 December 2020